D1102634

"A gripping page turner with prose lik[...] straight, true and hitting the mark. *Fa*[...] ing debut. *The Storm* shows it was no [...]

THE
STORM

NEIL
BROADFOOT

CONTRABAND

Contraband is an imprint of Saraband

Published by Saraband
Suite 202, 98 Woodlands Road,
Glasgow, G3 6HB, Scotland

www.saraband.net

ISBN: 9781908643872
ebook: 9781908643896

Printed in the UK by CPI on sustainably sourced paper.

Publication of this book has been supported by Creative Scotland.

ALBA | CHRUTHACHAIL

*All characters appearing in this novel are fictitious.
Any resemblance to real persons, living or dead,
is purely coincidental.*

1   3   5   7   9   10   8   6   4   2

For Fiona
and the Everything she brings –
every single day.

1

Overhead, the sky is numb static with a low haar hanging over the city, heavy with the threat of rain. Watery daylight seeps between the clouds, throwing a crazy-paving pattern of shadows onto the buildings and streets. The wind is little more than a shimmer in the grass I've made my nest in, sharp enough to make my breath a mist to mingle with the haar. I can feel moisture bleeding in through the cracks in my waterproofs, making my joints moan with the promise of pain to be delivered later for putting them through this.

I flex my hands, pins and needles shooting like daggers into my fingers as circulation rushes back in and the tendons stretch out. I should be wearing gloves, but I can't risk it. I need accuracy.

Precision. Control.

I run a final check, but there's no real need, everything is ready. It has been for months, years. Waiting for this moment. I always knew it would come. It was inevitable.

The smell of gun oil is strong, bitter and somehow reassuring, scalding my nostrils. I chamber the bullet, enjoying the harsh click-clack as it locks into place. There is a slight tremor in my hands. I close my eyes, take a long, deep breath and concentrate, force them to be still. Then I snuggle down deeper into my nest and hug the stock close to my cheek like an old friend. Peer down the sight, waiting for my eye to adjust to the fish-eye effect of the telescopic lens. Force my breathing to slow as my heart begins to hammer in my chest, an excited thrum I can feel dancing in my trigger finger as I start to squeeze against the metal, readying myself for the perfect moment.

2

Twelve minutes before his life fell apart, Doug McGregor was flicking through the morning papers, scrawling notes on the stories in them between rushed glances at the clock on his PC.

10.52am. Shit.

He threw the last of the papers aside, turned to his computer and started hammering on the keyboard, adding what little he had found in the papers to the morning news schedule for the *Capital Tribune*. The schedule was basically a long list of the stories of the day, culled from the papers, news agencies and what reporters had managed to find. At 11am, he would walk into the editor's office, sit down and go through the list, regurgitating everything he had crammed into his brain in the previous two hours, all the time praying a question he didn't have the answer for wasn't asked.

Doug had started working on the newsdesk about a month ago. His boss Walter, the news editor, had practically begged him to do it. After the last round of redundancies there were hardly enough journalists left in the place to put together a weekly freesheet, let alone the *Tribune* – "the new voice and conscience of Scotland" as the ad men had branded it in a desperate attempt to cash in on the referendum and its aftermath. Given the sales figures Doug had seen, they'd lost the bet.

"Look, Doug, I need someone I can trust," Walter had said one afternoon in the canteen, massive shoulders hunched over the table, skull glinting in the overhead lights from beneath the five o'clock stubble of his hair. "Someone who knows a story when he sees it, won't get us fuckin' sued to hell and back, and doesnae brick it every time Greig asks them an awkward question at conference. So, how 'bout it? Couple o' days a week oan the desk?"

In a moment of stupidity, Doug had agreed. And now it was 10.55am, his head filled with stories and lines, his mouth bitter with the aftertaste of bad coffee and adrenalin. Outside, the rain finally made good on its threat, drumming on the window like impatient fingers.

At least there was one benefit of being stressed out of his mind – he didn't have time to worry about the message he'd left on Susie's phone half an hour ago.

Well, not too much.

He forced himself to concentrate on the schedule, ignore the sudden burning in his cheeks. Looked up from his computer, down the newsroom to the reporters' desks. It was a depressing sight. As part of the redundancies and "corporate restructuring" – which, as far as Doug could tell, was bean-counters' code for cutting costs – the *Tribune*'s standalone printing presses and office block on the outskirts of town had been sold off, the land halfway to being houses by now. The *Tribune* staff who had survived the cuts had been moved into an office just up the road from the Scottish Parliament, which had once served as a city-centre base for the ad men and the political and legal reporters. The chiefs sold the idea to shareholders and staff as moving the paper "closer to the heartbeat of the capital city and Scotland's political pulse". Doug had his own translation.

He remembered morning edition when he first started at the *Tribune*, when there was a team of fifteen reporters, all working stories or speaking quietly into phones. The chatter of keyboards used to be like a soundtrack to the newsroom, a pulse. Now the room was quiet, like a house after a rowdy party. And there were four reporters working.

Eight minutes. Eight minutes to hell.

"If you've got any lines, I need them now, please," Doug shouted. The reporters stirred into life and, a moment later, he got a couple

3

of emails with a headline and a brief paragraph of background explaining what they thought the story was. Not a lot, but better than nothing. He skimmed them quickly. As usual, Barry Evans' were shit, the same old mix of gossip and tabloid crap that would make a nice piece in *Hello!* or *OK!*, but nothing he could use. He thought about bollocking him, realised he didn't have time. James Marten, the political reporter, sent over three good stories – two, predictably, were election-related, plus a tale about an MSP and his expenses claim linked to a casino. Donna Brent, the general reporter, sent over her list. Mostly it was the usual stuff – dull, worthy, back-of-the book filler at best – but there was a line that caught Doug's eye, about a kid being found in a back alley in the West End and rushed to hospital in the early hours with a suspected overdose. It was the latest in a series of overdoses that had been reported over the last month. The culprit seemed to be some new drug that bore more than a passing resemblance to methadone – "Jade Junk", they were calling it. Promising.

He cut and pasted the headlines into the main schedule, printed out the last of the briefings and notes he had collected. Turned back to the schedule and skimmed over it again. Re-ordered a few stories, checked his notes. Glanced at the clock. 10.58am. He made a final check, counted the number of stories he had – twenty-three in total. Not bad. There were twenty-six pages of news planned for tomorrow's paper. Three stories short. He'd had worse. And something always happened during the day to fill the gaps.

Doug printed the schedule, asking for ten copies. Scooped up his notes and put them in order. Stood up and headed for the editor's office. Showtime.

11am.

Four minutes to go.

• • •

Jonathan Greig sat barricaded behind his desk, Arthur's Seat framed behind him like a watercolour in the floor-to-ceiling

4

windows that made up the back wall of his office. As usual, he looked more like a banker than a journalist, jacket hanging from a coat-rack in the corner, tailored waistcoat buttoned over a shirt with creases so sharp and precise you could cut yourself on them. He looked up as Doug crowded into the room with Mike King, the sports editor, Alice Ericson, the business editor, and Don Moore, the foreign editor. A curt nod from Greig, slicked-back hair glinting in the light, and they took their seats at the conference table in the middle of the room, waiting for him to join them and run through the schedules.

Conference was meant to be a routine affair – tell the boss what you thought the best stories of the day were, answer relevant questions, agree the top line and where things were going to appear in the paper. Problem was, Greig didn't see it that way. Conference was his time to be The Editor, master of the *Capital Tribune* and "the new conscience of Scotland" as the nation navigated its way in the post-referendum, post-election world. Doug had heard the horror stories from Alice, Mike and Don when they had dared to pitch a story that wasn't in keeping with Greig's thinking. Shouting-downs weren't uncommon, and on more than one occasion staff had left the editor's office with "something in their eye". In most other industries it would have been called bullying or harassment – in journalism it was just another day at the office.

Doug glanced at his list again, hoping Greig was in a good enough mood to let any slips go unpunished.

Seeming to read his thoughts, Greig pushed away from his desk and stood up, theatrically straightening his waistcoat and smoothing his tie. He was a thin, wiry man, with angular features and high cheekbones that gave him a vaguely funereal look. Doug made a mental note to squeeze Walter for some time off when he came in for the afternoon shift. It was the least he was owed.

"Good morning," Greig said as he sat at the head of the conference table directly opposite Doug and scooped up copies of the schedules in front of him. "So, Mike, let's get started."

Mike cleared his throat, adjusted his glasses and started talking. "Pretty busy schedule, boss. Three Premier games tonight and a track event at Meadowbank. We've also got the usual fun and games at I…"

A sharp, high crack cut Mike off, the room suddenly filling with yelps of shock and fear. Behind Greig, the floor-to-ceiling window shattered into an elaborate network of silvery spiders' webs, frozen in place by the safety wiring running through the glass. Doug jerked back and away from the table, heart pounding against his ribs, legs leaden with adrenalin, ears filled with the crack and a dull, heavy thud from the wall behind him. It felt as if the air had become heavy, thick – a physical force pressing on him, making it difficult to breathe in.

"What the hell is…?" Greig began as he stood out of his chair, turning away from Doug to look at the shattered window.

Alice screamed as he spun back round violently, as if wrenched by some immense, irresistible force. His upper body twisted at an almost impossible angle, blood spraying from his throat in a widening arc. His hands flailed for his neck, frozen into palsied talons clawing at the wound as he gasped and hacked for breath. He staggered forward, eyes wide and frantic, gaze locking with Doug's for one horrendous second. The facade stripped away, nothing there but terror and fear and confusion. *What's happening to me?* his eyes begged. *I can't breathe. Choking, choking…*

He let out another gagging cough, blood seeping between bone-white fingers like oil.

And then his chest exploded.

Blood and viscera erupted onto the table in front of him with a horrible wet slap and glistened there, horribly dark and textured with shreds of ruined organs standing out against the white of the forgotten pages of the schedules. Greig's back arched as though he had been electrocuted, arms dropping to his sides. He hung there for an instant, frozen, before his knees buckled and he collapsed forward, head bouncing off the table with a sickening crack that echoed around the room and drowned out the shouts of panic and cries of despair.

Mike scrambled away from the table, his face a wax-white sneer of disbelief and disgust, grabbing Alice by the shoulders and dragging her to the door.

"Come on, for fuck's sake, MOVE!" he screamed, voice rough with terror and tears. "Get the fuck out of here, move NOW! Doug, Don, for fuck's sake, GO!"

Doug couldn't move. Pinned to the spot by shock and terror and the memory of Greig's eyes. The terror. The confusion.

He heard the hammering of feet from the other side of the door as the reporters ran for the office. Caught vague snatches of words, urgent cries to "Call the police, get a fucking ambulance, it's the boss. Oh fucking CHRIST..."

Don at his side now. Arms on his shoulders. "Come on, Doug," he whispered urgently. "Let's get the fuck out of here. It's not safe, we need..."

Doug shrugged him off violently, staggered forward. He felt disconnected, alien, as though he were an office block and the lights were being switched off one floor at a time.

He shuffled forward on numb legs until he was standing over Greig. Looked down almost casually, wanting, needing, to look into those eyes again. He was dimly aware of a burnt smell in the air, the sour waft of shit and the bitter tang of iron.

Blood and shit and murder – the perfect story, he thought, ice creeping down his back as he felt himself smile and fought back a chuckle that caught in his throat.

Greig's head was twisted back, ear touching his shoulder, blood oozing slowly from his mouth. A huge gash ran over his temple like the torn lip of an open envelope, exposing a blood-smeared sliver of skull underneath. Eyes dead and empty, the same look of shock and confusion Doug had seen seared into his features by the horror of what had happened.

Doug closed his eyes and fell to his knees. He toppled forward onto his hands and heaved, bile and coffee burning his mouth as he vomited. He was dimly aware that his hand was in a widening pool of Jonathan Greig's blood. He found he didn't care. At that moment, it was the only warmth that he felt.

3

Detective Sergeant Susie Drummond stared at the message on her phone: one missed call from Doug, one voicemail. She chewed her lip for a moment. Debating. Listen or not?

With a sigh, she pocketed the phone then went back to trying to get comfortable. She was sitting on a low wooden bench in the marble-filled main corridor outside court two in the High Court building on the Royal Mile, waiting to be called to give evidence in the attempted murder case she had worked on earlier in the year.

She snorted despite herself, drawing an arched look from a red-faced, jowly man in an expensive suit, who was waddling past her clutching an untidy pile of papers. The whole trial was a waste of time, and wee Kevin Malcolm should be sitting in a cell in Saughton and shitting himself about shower time now. And he would have been too, except that "Charming" Charlie Montgomery QC had other plans.

Kevin was known around Edinburgh as a small-time thief with a big-time temper. He was five-foot-seven of bad attitude, greasy hair, cheap tattoos and skin bleached grey by too much booze, dope and fried food. For years he had been linked to some of the nastier break-ins and assaults in Edinburgh, including, infamously, the kneecapping of a security guard too stupid not to stop Kevin when he was making a bolt for the front doors of the St James Shopping Centre after smashing in the front window of a jewellery shop.

The guard – Jamie Miller, a dad barely out of his teens and a keen five-a-side football player – had sprinted for Kevin, taken him down with a flying tackle and waited for the police to arrive. They dragged him from the floor, held him back when he lunged for Jamie. And then Kevin had hawked back and spat a wad of blood-flecked phlegm at Jamie. "Yer a fast wee cunt," he hissed. "Better hope ye stay like that."

Jamie shrugged and went back to his life, unaware that he had just lit the fuse on Niddrie's nastiest ned. His run-in with Kevin got him in the papers twice: firstly, as the local hero who stopped a "dramatic daylight smash-and-grab raid in Edinburgh's busiest shopping centre"; and then a few weeks later as the local hero who had been viciously beaten and hospitalised.

About a week after he'd floored Kevin, Jamie was grabbed as he came out of the Pitz – a five-a-side football centre just on the outskirts of Musselburgh. Dragged down a side street and beaten senseless by someone with a taste for cheap sovereign rings and the sound of breaking bones. His hands had been stamped on, his ribs broken and his knees shattered. The doctor Susie spoke to couldn't say for sure, but it was her guess that whoever had done this to Jamie had beaten him unconscious then jumped on his knees until they had snapped.

"I hope he didn't like getting anywhere fast," she had muttered to Susie, eyes hidden by the reflection from the X-rays of the ruined bones shining from the wall.

It didn't take much to connect the dots back to Kevin. He opened the door to his flat in Niddrie – in a block of new-build housing association homes that somehow managed to look dilapidated and smell of cat piss despite being only six months old – and glared sullenly at Susie, one eye glinting in the cushion of a badly bruised socket. At least Jamie had managed to get one hit in.

He admitted nothing, but hardly needed to – they found blood-spattered clothes in his bedroom and a copy of the *Tribune* open on the coffee table, Jamie's face smiling nervously out of the centre spread, the paragraphs about his love of football and the local league games at the Pitz carefully underlined. It was an open-and-shut case – until Charming Charlie Montgomery had got involved.

Susie could hear him now: the cultured, Stirlingshire lilt with a confidence just this side of arrogance. *How could it be attempted murder when no weapon had been used? Were the police there at the time? Did they know the psychological trauma Mr Malcolm had been through – driven to a stupid theft by crippling debts and a young child to feed, then ridiculed while on bail by his friends who saw the story in the newspaper? Was it any surprise that Mr Malcolm, fuelled by his addiction to alcohol, had sought revenge on Mr Miller? Surely the members of the jury could see his client was not in his right mind at the time, but had merely lashed out? Surely he was deserving of some leniency and recognition of his diminished responsibility? Surely...*

Susie's phone beeped in her pocket again – a reminder of the missed call and message from Doug.

Listen or ignore?

She clamped it to her ear, turned toward the wall to hide the fact she was using it right under a sign that read, *No mobile phones in the court buildings*, and listened to the message. Smiled as he fumbled his way through "had fun last night", felt a flush of awkward guilt.

They hadn't started out on the best of terms. About three years ago, Doug got in touch out of the blue, to matter-of-factly tell Susie he had found out about her drunken one-night stand with a married Chief Super who had then gone for a press gagging order about the whole affair (excuse the pun, she thought), before the phrase "super-injunction" had even been whispered by the tabloids.

He really had been a little prick all round, Susie thought sourly. Emphasis on the little.

But then Doug surprised her. Instead of pressuring her for access or information, he told her he was killing the story because he wasn't "a gutter-mining shit". All he wanted to do was introduce himself as a face she could trust. He shared contacts where he could, got her information that people wouldn't always give to the police, and all he asked in return was a heads-up when a story was about to break, or perhaps an advance quote to get him half a step ahead of his rivals. He could be a pushy little shit, and she'd been bollocked by her DI, Jason "Third Degree" Burns, and her other bosses more than once for "being too close to certain sections of the press", but the arrangement worked for both of them. He got stories, she got information she needed and the chance to paint the police in a positive light now and again.

But lately, something had changed. They were spending more time together, focusing less on work. It seemed to start after the Buchan incident last year, but was that it? Was the trauma of almost being killed together bringing them closer to each other, or was it something else?

He was a contact, but he was also a friend: the guy who would listen to her rant about a shit day at work without judging – or running the stories she told him; the guy who fixed her car, went for pizza and a pint after a hard day.

But then there was what happened a couple of weeks ago, the "fun" last night and now…

…now…

"Detective Sergeant Susan Drummond?"

Susie looked up, startled. A court usher was leaning out of the doors to courtroom two, calling her to give evidence.

Susie switched her phone to silent and pocketed it, heading for the courtroom. As she walked through the door, the phone started its insistent buzz in her pocket. She cursed quietly under her breath, hoped the judge and jury wouldn't hear it as she entered the witness stand. Work knew she was in court all morning so it was unlikely to be them. And Doug? Well, Doug could wait. It couldn't be that urgent, could it?

4

I sit quietly in the corner of the room, listening to the soft, relentless beep of the heart monitor, stifling the urge to scream. My body has delivered on the promise it made earlier – my joints are filled with sand, my bones petrified, jutting twigs that grind against each other every time I move. Cold agony crawls up my spine and across my shoulders with every breath, making it impossible for me to fill my lungs. Not that it would take much to do that. Not these days.

I rock forward, using the momentum to propel myself out of the seat and get moving. I'm rewarded by hot pokers of pain shooting up my legs. My hand scrabbles instinctively to my pocket, searching for the comforting cool wrap of tinfoil that's tucked neatly in the corner. It would be so easy just to take some now, one little hit. Just enough to take the edge off the pain, blunt its fangs, and turn the stabbing, tearing bites into a dull gnawing.

But no. No. He deserves better than that. I've let him down enough in his life. This needs precision. Discipline.

Control.

I walk over to the bed, picking up a superhero comic from the bedside table as I move. He loves these comics, the bright colours and the larger-than-life characters. When we first started reading the comics together, I thought they'd be good for him – help him associate words with actions and, crucially, help him associate me with fun and security, perhaps even help build a bridge between us after all the lost years.

Too late for that now.

I sit down in the chair beside the bed, grunting slightly as I do.

Again, my mind flashes to the wrap in my pocket and the promise of peace and relief.

But not yet. Not yet.

I flick through the well-thumbed pages, finding where we left off after my last visit. I start reading to him, quietly, softly, as if I'm in a church. When he was a baby, the few precious times I saw him, he loved it when I made the voices of the characters – and I made sure he never saw how much changing my voice, or crying out in mock surprise or triumph, hurt me. Making my voice high and squeaky was like gargling glass; lowering it for the booming baritone of Batman or Superman was like swallowing the glass a shard at a time.

But he never saw it. Not once.

They tell me he can't hear me now, but I know they're wrong. I know that, even now, he's in there somewhere.

I just wish to God he wasn't.

I finish the story – Spider-Man swinging off into a sunset so warm and inviting it could only exist in the pages of a fantasy – then set the comic gently aside. I clear my throat, mash my hands angrily against my eyes, then start to tell him another story. A very special story I've been preparing for a long, long time.

I tell him about a monster who lied, who hid in plain sight with other monsters and pretended he was something he wasn't. I tell him about the noble hero and the life destroyed by this monster's cowardice and lies. About the hero travelling to a land far, far from home, where the unforgiving, glaring sun blistered his back as the sand tore at his flesh, borne on a hot, biting wind that burned the hero every time he took a breath.

I tell him about the hero's quest to come home to his family and the trials he endured. The sneering and disbelief, the names he was called. And I tell him that, as all this happened, the monster looked on, laughing. Smug and secure and comfortable in the life of lies he had created.

I blink back the tears in my eyes – scalding with sorrow and shame and loss. For a moment, a horribly tempting moment, I think about taking the whole wrap and just ending it now, the beep of the heart monitor a metronome counting down to the end of my life.

But no. No. I must be strong. Disciplined.

Controlled.

I heave in a breath – ragged, hitching, agonising – and go on. I tell him about justice, about how the hero destroyed the monster, tracking him down and taking his voice, leaving him clawing for breath before making his heart explode from his chest, making sure he suffered as badly as the hero had.

I promise him that it's not over; that the quest is far from finished and the hero will not rest until all the monsters are dead and everyone who did this – every one – is dead. I take his hand and squeeze as hard as I can. I close my eyes and swear that the hero will get them all.

Then I lurch forward and kiss his forehead gently, caressing the stubble on top of his head, all that's left of the unruly mop of blonde hair that used to sit there.

"Mummy's hair," I used to tell him. "You've got Mummy's hair."

I take a moment to look at him. A young man with his future stolen from him by one grotesque moment that took what he loved the most in his simple world and twisted it into his killer. I make sure he's comfortable, take his head gently in my hand and prop him forward, sliding a pillow out. I fluff it up, make sure it's soft and full.

Ignore the stabbing pains in my arms as I press the pillow down on his face, clamp my mouth shut against the scream that's only partly due to the pain. Shake my head angrily against the tears I can't fight, can't destroy, can't ignore. Beneath me, he bucks once, weak, almost imperceptible and, despite myself, I smile.

I knew it. I knew he was still there. My boy. My son. The fighter to the end.

I make sounds as soothing as I can and the movement subsides, the heart monitor starting to beep urgent warnings. I reach over and click it to "Silent" – I've seen enough nurses, been in enough hospitals, to know how. I give it another minute then slowly ease the pillow from his face. He looks peaceful. As though he's finally in a restful sleep instead of a drug-induced coma.

I feel for a pulse, just to be sure. Fight back a cough that's halfway between a cry and a scream when I find none. Gently lift his head and replace the pillow. I spend one more second on a goodbye, then I turn and shuffle for the door, trying to convince myself I'm not a worse monster than those I've promised to destroy.

5

Sitting on the southern border of Edinburgh heading into Midlothian, the Edinburgh Royal Infirmary is a sprawling network of buildings sitting at the foot of a hill, the ruins of Edinburgh's other castle, Craigmillar, looming over it. It was built to replace the old Royal, a Victorian building that loomed over the Meadows in Edinburgh like a gothic nightmare. It was shops and flats now, the dark, glowering wards replaced with walls of glass and penthouse apartments with price tags so high they would give most people nosebleeds. Ah, progress.

Susie drove in the entrance closest to A&E, took one look at the over-rammed car park and bumped up on the pavement of what she hoped was a side-road that led round the back of the hospital. The last thing she wanted was to block an ambulance from getting in or out, especially today. She propped a *Police on call* card on the dashboard then headed for the casualty department, wishing she was wearing her trainers instead of heels and a business suit.

Early afternoon and the reception area was quiet. Gone were the scenes she was used to from night and weekend shifts – the stunned faces of those forced to sober up too quickly after a night out went suddenly wrong, or those ripped from their beds by a loved one clutching at their chest and gasping for air. Instead, she found a couple of harassed parents on either side of a young boy with a towel wrapped around his arm and a bruise the size of an orange on his head.

"But Muuuum," he whined, "it doesnae even hurt now. I dinnae need tae see the doctor."

Susie watched as the mother, a thin woman with greasy black-grey hair and eyes filled with disappointed resignation, shot a quick glance over the boy's head to what looked liked a man-shaped mountain of lard packed into a ragged Snoopy T-shirt and a pair of tracksuit bottoms that had obviously mastered the trick of defying gravity.

"Now listen, Zac," the man said, his voice surprisingly soft for such a massive frame, "that was a hell of a spill you took, son, better to get it checked out. It won't hurt, promise." He leaned forward to reassure his son, the cheap plastic chair beneath him squealing softy.

Susie walked on, leaving the sound of the boy's mewling pleas behind her. A quick flash of her warrant card at the reception desk and she was pointed towards the triage centre for assessing patients who had just arrived. She found Doug in a curtained bay, perched on the edge of the bed and hunched over his phone, fingers darting across the screen. He was wearing a set of pale blue hospital scrubs, which looked less wrinkled than the suits he usually wore, and it struck her that his clothes would be sitting in a police lab somewhere, packed into neat evidence bags, waiting to be studied. She wasn't sure how to feel about that. His brown hair, which Susie once described as "fashionably tousled", stood up in crazy whorls and spikes – raked into an expression of his mood by his hands.

He glanced up, the movement almost a spasm, and Susie saw shock and exhaustion etched across his face, making his normally high cheekbones, thin lips and slightly crooked nose look brittle, one good shake away from cracking. The impression wasn't helped by the faint glistening of sweat on his forehead, and the hectic smudges of colour on his usually pale cheeks.

He studied her for a moment, his green-brown irises framed in bloodshot eyes as they darted across her, like he was looking for something – which, Susie realised, he usually was.

Finally, his eyes locked with hers. She felt a momentary flash of discomfort, forced herself not to look away or move forward. She felt as though she was under a microscope as he stood there, breathing calmly, as though that cold, even gaze could tell her everything he couldn't find the words for.

He nodded once, almost to himself, then dropped his head to his chest. Looked back up with a small smile that didn't reach his eyes and spoke, his voice a cheap imitation of his usual calm, soft tones.

"I didn't do it, detective. I know I had motive, God knows the nasty bastard had it coming, but it wasn't me. I've got witnesses. And a reporter's salary doesn't exactly stretch to a hitman."

Susie snorted back a laugh despite herself, glad the tension was broken. She stepped forward, fought back the sudden, stupid urge to reach out to him by crossing her hands behind her back.

"Well, if you're looking for a character witness, don't think about asking me, I've tasted your cooking. Now that was murder."

Doug flashed another smile, nothing more than a brief twitch of the muscles, then went back to concentrating on his phone.

"What you working on?" Susie asked.

"First-person piece on Greig's, ah… you know, the shooting. Spoke to Walter earlier, says he can't let me do the story as I'm involved, prick, but I talked him into at least running this."

Susie sighed and took another step forward, noticing for the first time how bloodied and raw Doug's hands were.

"Doug, you weren't…?"

He looked up at her, then back down at where she was looking. "What, this? No. Just took a hell of a lot of scrubbing to get Greig's blood off my hands, is all."

She nodded, thoughts of showers and baths after crime scenes – of scrubbing and scrubbing to try and slough off the smell of death and blood – flashed through her mind. Shook off the thoughts then blurted out the question she wanted to ask since she heard the news.

"Doug. You okay?"

He stopped typing, scanned the screen in front of him as if it held the answer. Somewhere far off, she heard the beep of a heart monitor, as steady as the ticks of a clock, marking time.

"I… I don't know, Susie," he said. "I mean, I've seen this stuff before, written about it – hell, remember the Buchan story last year? But this… this is different, this is… real, you know?"

She nodded. She knew all too well. All the crime scenes she had visited, the bodies she had seen, there was one constant. Hiding behind the blood and the chaos and the other signs of violence masked by the business of a crime scene – the cacophony of lab technicians taking photographs and officers talking to witnesses, the squawk of radios and calls being made – there was always another presence. Pushing down like an invisible weight, crushing, insistent.

The finality of death – and the realisation that it was waiting for us all in the end.

"So, what you doing here? Burns send you to check they didn't miss anything in my statement?"

Susie bit back a sarcastic response, ignored the sudden, sour tickle of anger she felt. "No, just wanted to check on you. Got the call from Burns when I came out of the court – he wanted me to hear it from him rather than over the radio."

Doug nodded, returning his gaze to her face. "And," he said slowly, "he wanted to tell you that you couldn't be part of the investigating team because of…" He swept a finger back and forth in the space between them.

Susie nodded, remembering Burns's words. *Look, Drummond, there's no way in hell you can be anywhere near this one, okay? Bad enough that you know that little shit McGregor, but I'm definitely not having that relationship exposed in court, no way I'm having it used to taint the investigation. Understood?*

"Shit," Doug whispered. "Sorry, Susie."

She shrugged, forced herself to stay casual. It was a big case, national big, and it wouldn't have done her slightly dented career any harm to be associated with it – or the coverage.

"Don't worry about it, I've got more than enough on my plate trying not to let Charlie Montgomery trip me up. Besides, you'd be a shit witness."

He grunted a laugh, glanced at his phone for a moment then put it aside. It looked as though it were a struggle. "Look, Susie, I should get out of here once the docs say I'm good to go. Do you... maybe... want to get a movie or something tonight?"

It was an unwritten ritual with them, which started just after the end of the Katherine Buchan affair. When one or both had a bad day, they would watch old movies, perhaps drink and talk. About the film, politics, football, the weather – anything but what had led them there in the first place. She had tried to distract him with other, healthier diversions, including her own passion, running, but inevitably, they had reverted to the couch and the chat. Counselling without the bullshit, Doug had labelled it.

"What about Rebecca?" Susie replied. "Shouldn't you...?"

"I'm not asking Rebecca, am I?" Doug snapped, his voice as sharp as the lingering antiseptic smell that hung in the triage room. He sighed, raised a hand. It was shaking slightly. "Sorry. I've spoken to Rebecca, it's fine. And besides, she knows the score. After all..."

Susie nodded. *After all.*

"Okay," she said, suddenly restless and more aware than ever that she was wearing a business suit and heels. "Give me a call when you're out of here, I'll meet you then."

"Thanks," Doug said, a kaleidoscope of emotions playing across his face before eventually settling on weary relief. "And Susie, would you mind if we went to your place? Last thing I need is my folks turning up at the door when they hear about this."

"You haven't told them yet?" she asked, disbelieving.

He pulled a face at her. "Course I have. Made sure I told them I was okay as soon as I could, or there would be hell to pay. But you know what my folks are like. And, besides, why would I want to spoil the full inside story" – he waggled the phone in front of her – "for them?"

Susie shook her head as she turned away. Always the reporter. "See you tonight, Doug," she said. "And for being such a shit of a son, the first bottle's on you."

If she didn't know him better, she would have almost said it was genuine laughter she heard as she walked out the room.

6

The stone skimmed across the water, dabbing delicate silvery ripples across its grey, mirrored surface as it bounced along – one, two, three – before plopping below a small wave.

He bent down and rummaged for another stone to throw, hating the way he grunted as he stooped. It didn't take long to find what he was looking for – the shoreline was only fit to be called a beach in marketing brochures and travel articles. In truth, it was a bowed strip of stony ground that joined the two points of the bay together in a shallow arc.

"Subs, please check," he said to the emptiness with a smile as he stood up. He paused for a moment, taking in the view. On the horizon, a yacht from one of the hotels further up the coast bobbed along like a special effect, seeming to drag a curtain of rain across the hills that jutted into the blue-grey sky beyond.

He had come here the moment he saw the story. He had been scanning the morning news – old habits die hard, after all – and saw it on the BBC site. *Fatal shooting at newspaper offices*, the headline read, a bland statement that did nothing to convey the enormity of what had happened. Clicking on the link, it told him nothing more than the bare facts: Jonathan Greig, editor of the *Capital Tribune*, had been fatally shot at the paper's offices in central Edinburgh. Four other members of staff had been hospitalised, but none were thought to be seriously injured. Police were investigating.

He had closed the computer, grabbed his walking cane and headed out.

And now, here he was, admiring the view that never failed to deliver something new, soaking in the silence he had worked for all his life.

And it was over.

The shadows grew deeper, as if the sun was little more than a guttering candle in the breeze, and he watched as the curtain of rain began to pepper the surface of the water.

He dug into his pocket and pulled out his mobile phone and a small, battered black notebook held together with an elastic band and a pen clipped over the front cover. Esther had told him he could store all his contacts in his phone; that he didn't have to write them all down in the notebook any more. He smiled and told her he would look into it. What he didn't tell her was that he didn't need the notebook or the phone to remember things – he memorised the important numbers, always had. The book was merely a reminder of another time, another life. And a useful distraction if needed.

He dialled the number, silently mouthing the digits as he did, and rehearsed his first line as he listened to the phone ring.

After all these years, the storm was coming. Now he needed to know how close to shore it was.

7

After another barrage of tests, most of which involved his reflexes, trying to blind him with a pencil light, taking blood and measuring his blood pressure with a machine that seemed to be designed to deliver a Chinese burn while making the sound of a cheap garage tyre inflator, Doug was signed out of the hospital.

Despite everything, he almost laughed when the nurse told him they would schedule a follow-up appointment to discuss the results of the tests to see if he'd been infected by exposure to Greig's blood. The thought of Greig doing anything so distasteful or strenuous that it would involve anything more extreme than loosening his tie, let alone his trousers, was, to Doug, like saying the royal family was value for money.

But he had done something distasteful to someone, hadn't he? Something someone had found extremely distasteful indeed. But what?

Doug closed his eyes in the back of the cab he had called to take him home, seeing again that frozen look of horror in Greig's eyes. The incomprehension. The terror. The fear.

What? What's happening? Why? Why?

His eyes snapped open as he fought against the sudden lurch in his stomach and forced his lungs to fill and empty. As he tried to convince them he wasn't drowning, he fumbled for his phone as a distraction. Flipped open the email and saw a new message from Walter, a reply to the story he'd sent over.

Doug, good copy. We'll run in the late edition – should be around 6pm now that we've managed to set up in the advertising department. They've sealed off Greig's office and the editorial floor, but we'll get a paper out. I'll call later, see how you're doing. But consider yourself on leave as of now. Take some time, Doug, sort this out. I've told Mike, Alice and Don to do the same, but I know you'll take more convincing. I don't want you near this, or any other story, Doug. Go see your folks, take a holiday, but don't even think of going near this one. Let the police look into it. Speak later, Walter.

Doug grunted in disgust, fought the urge to throw the phone on the floor. Fidgeted for a moment, trying not to think of the blood or the screams or the sounds…

…the sounds…

The shrill crack of the window shattering. The dull *thwump* of a bullet burrowing into the wall next to him. Greig's hacking bark. The…

Doug swallowed back bile.

…The heavy, liquid slap as Greig's guts and entrails exploded from his torso and hit the table in front of him.

Four sounds. Three shots. Two hits.

He mashed his knuckles into his eyes, crushing back the heat as he felt the prickle of tears. His phone cried for attention. One text message from Rebecca. He stopped, torn. Bit his lip. Fuck it. Opened the message.

Stuck on shift, taking a hell of a lot of calls from journos, big story. Heard you were discharged. Understand you need time, but I'm here, ok? Hope tonight is what you need. Rx

She was already at the hospital when his ambulance arrived, fighting to keep a professional, detached face as he was wheeled in. They had stolen a moment between doctors and assessments, long enough to solidify the lie that he was fine.

He hadn't told Susie about her visit, though. Why? She had asked him about her, he could have said then. But he hadn't. No reason not to, after all…

After all.

He lunged forward, as if he could leave the thoughts in the seat.

Rapped on the plastic screen dividing him from the taxi driver with a hand that wasn't steady.

"Hey, mate. There's an offie at the bottom of my street, drop me there, will you?"

"Nae bother, pal," the taxi driver said, not bothering to turn around. "No offence, you look like you've earned a drink."

Doug nodded and sunk back into the seat. He wasn't going to argue.

8

Denise Fry knew the young man in room four was dead the moment she clicked the door shut behind her. She paused, felt the heavy stillness seep into her bones and prickle down the back of her neck as it had every time she'd walked into a room with a dead body.

She remembered the first time she felt it, twenty years ago when she was just a student nurse starting out on her career and getting her first taste of the A&E department. It had been a mid-July day, a particularly warm one, and a man had been brought in to the emergency room after suffering a brain haemorrhage at work. She had been overwhelmed by the explosion of febrile activity – the frantic calls for blood and tests and readouts when he was wheeled in from the ambulance; but the frenzy soon petered away, until the inevitable moment that the lead doctor declared nothing more could be done and pronounced the time of death. And, in that moment of vacuum, she felt it for the first time – soaking up the dissipated energy, adrenalin and frustration. Something beyond silence and emptiness: a complete absence of life.

Death.

She shook off the memory, gathered herself and stepped further into the room, suddenly desperate to draw back the curtain and open the windows, let some light in and clear the oppressive, sour smell that hung in the air. She moved to the bed to make a final check, straightening the boy's head, which was propped at a strange angle on crumpled pillows, and gently pressed her fingers against skin already taking on a bluish tinge and growing cold, feeling for the pulse she knew she wouldn't find. It was a shame, she thought, looking down, he would have been a good-looking man – she could see the echoes of a strong jawline and a handsome face peeking out from behind the sunken sockets, drawn-in cheeks and roughly shaven head, across which a puckered, purpling scar was scrawled like an angry act of vandalism. His death wasn't a surprise – she hated to admit that she had been expecting this moment since they brought him in here a week ago.

As expected, nothing. No pulse. She reached for the chart at the end of the bed, about to make the necessary entry before informing the ward nurse. Clicked her pen, loud and harsh in the silence, then stopped suddenly.

The silence. No gentle sound of breathing, no squeaking of rubber heels on the harshly polished floor of the ward.

No heart monitor squealing a warning.

She lunged forward, grunting as she collided with the corner of the bed in her haste, a crawl of revulsion twisting in her stomach as she saw the body judder lifelessly. It didn't take her long to confirm what she didn't want to know, what terrified her more than sharing a room with a cooling corpse.

The heart monitor had been switched off. Which meant there had been no warning of cardiac arrest, no alarm tripped at the nurses' station. Nothing to bring anyone to the room and disturb the boy and…

…and who?

Her eyes darted to the pillows, her imagination filling in gaps she didn't want filled.

Denise backed towards the door, fighting back a scream that tickled the back of her throat and the urge to sprint as fast as she could.

You're jumping to conclusions, she told herself. Too much coffee, too many night shifts and too many episodes of *CSI*.

But she wasn't. She knew she wasn't.

The heart monitor was off. The pillows were rumpled.

The boy in room four was dead.

And the cause was not natural.

9

After leaving Doug, Susie's afternoon descended into the type of bureaucratic nightmare that made her question why she wanted to be a police officer in the first place. After all, why investigate crime and stop the bad guys when there was filing to be done, overtime claims to submit and personnel details to update?

It was partly the hangover from the amalgamation of the eight police forces around Scotland into one force, Police Scotland. Although it had taken place a couple of years ago now, there were still the inevitable problems as different forces, each with their own procedures, adapted to being part of one big, standardised family. And, thanks to being on court duty and categorically not allowed to look into the Jonathan Greig murder, DI Burns saw it as the perfect opportunity to give Susie the chance to catch up on the reports she had to write.

She initially thought that it was punishment for pissing him off about something, but when she glanced out of the window and saw the TV camera vans parking up outside, satellite dishes swivelling like oversized bowls into position – *Please sir, can we have some more story?* – she understood. This was a national story now, and Burns was doing everything to keep her away from it. And, more importantly, he was being seen by the brass upstairs to be keeping her away from it.

After the Buchan case last year, and the fall-out when the former Chief Super got dragged in to allegations of collusion and cover-up, Susie knew she was being watched very closely by her superiors. Burns himself had told her as much one night not long after the case had wrapped up. He had called her into his office, settled into his chair and smoothed his tie over the rapidly expanding beer gut that spilled over his trousers. From the wall behind him, a family portrait stared at Susie as if in judgement. Burns, his wife and their three children – a baby held tight against the woman's ample chest and two small boys, carbon copies of Burns with their heavy brows, thick-set bodies and flame-red hair – grinning down at her as she shifted uncomfortably in her seat.

"Look, Drummond," Burns said, the reassuring tone he was aiming for butchered by his blunt delivery and the cold, impassive glare that had earned him the nickname "Third Degree" in the first place. "You did good work on the Buchan case, bloody good work, and it's got you noticed. But them upstairs…" He paused, nose wrinkling at some unpleasant smell only he could detect. "…don't like it. With the shitstorm this has brought down on the Super thanks to your pal McGregor and that smarmy PR shit the Tories used, they're watching you. So tread careful, okay? Especially around that wee reporter shite."

She had assured Burns she would, and quietly vowed to ignore him. But had she? Certainly she spoke less to Doug about stories than before, partly because he was working on the newsdesk more regularly and focusing less on digging up exclusives, and then there was the Rebecca situation. Had she been acting as a friend, or had she engineered it as a diversionary tactic?

And, if so, a diversion from what?

She shook her head and hit the keyboard harder than she needed to start the log-off sequence. Got up and grabbed the gym bag under her desk, suddenly desperate to get to the gym for a workout. A simple run wasn't going to do it tonight. After a day in court, and being sidelined from the Greig case, she needed to work against something. She needed the burn of weights, the focus that came from the moment when her muscles screamed at her to stop and she forced herself to do another rep. She needed the focus. The discipline. The control.

The gym was at the top of Leith Walk, a Virgin Active in the Omni Centre, which was a collection of restaurants and pubs clustered around a multi-screen cinema. It was post-work busy, with the usual blend of guys who looked like they'd walked out of fitness magazines and office workers sweating their way through workouts they thought would help them look like the would-be models. More often than not using the weights and machines totally the wrong way, promising themselves a takeaway as a reward and wondering why they never got any slimmer.

She got changed and headed to the main floor of the gym, checking her phone to see if Doug had called yet, angry at herself when he hadn't.

She worked her way around the weights, alternating between upper and lower body moves, pouring the tension and stress of the day into the workout until her muscles burned and her lungs were a furnace. Checked her phone again after she had finished, still nothing, and headed for the running machines to cool down.

Susie was just heading for the showers, gasping for breath after the cool-down turned into a sprint finish, when her phone buzzed. A text from Doug. *All done, officially on holiday – so at least Greig was good for something ;-) See you at your place, 8ish? I've got the wine and I'll spring for takeaway. D*

She glanced at her watch, just after 7pm. Just enough time to have a shower, get home and make sure she hadn't left anything lying around that she didn't want him to see. She pinged him an answer and headed for the changing room, turning up the music on her iPod as she walked to drown out Burns's words: *Tread careful, especially around that wee reporter shite.*

10

The wind shimmered in the nearby trees and bushes, a somehow comforting sound that carried away the drone of Princes Street below. From here, Paul could see the entire stretch of the street all the way to the West End, the first of the car lights coming on as street lights began to glow softly. He could see people moving along the crowded pavements, heading home, to the shops, or for a post-work drink.

He wished he could do the same. But no. As they were heading home, closing their doors against the cold and the dark, he was just waking up, another day of sunlight lost to him in a stupor of drink and whatever he could cram up his nose. He was on an addiction counselling programme now, one of the hoops he had to jump through every week to get a benefits payment that barely covered a pint of milk and the electric bill. It was meant to be helping.

If only.

He tucked his hands deeper in his pockets, fingers searching instinctively in the corners for something to take away the steadily rising ache in his muscles and bones. Soon the ache would become sharper, stabbing, an open sore of raw hunger as his body started to protest that his latest hit was overdue.

He would have to see Frankie before that. Frankie would help. Frankie would take the hunger away.

Paul turned his back on Princes Street, eyes scanning the near-deserted car park in front of him. He saw movement in the bushes to the left; a small, squat-looking man in a long jacket moving slowly into the foliage, casting long glances back to him over his shoulder.

He patted the bulge in his jeans pocket – the condoms were still there. He tried to think of Frankie as he followed the man into the bushes, glad that the growing heat in his groin was blotting out the bitter hunger in his veins.

11

Susie glanced up at the clock on the wall as the buzzer echoed through the flat, startling her out of the Zen-like state she'd lulled herself into whilst tidying up. 7.55pm. Doug was early. Definitely not himself – for a man who spent his life chasing deadlines and hitting them, Doug's personal timekeeping was as haphazard as his hair.

She cast a quick glance around the living room, one final check to make sure there was nothing left out that Doug shouldn't see. It was one of the least pleasant parts of spending time with Doug – she liked his company, found him easy to talk to, but the copper/reporter issue was always just there, like a fresh bruise still sore to the touch. And with Doug being as observant and quick as he was, she didn't want him knowing more about what she was working on than she wanted him to know. So the case reports she was drafting were packed away in the bedroom, along with the brochures for cheap holidays she'd picked up on a whim and the latest self-improvement book she'd bought a couple of days earlier. Another little reminder of the Buchan case, she thought. She'd been forced to sit through a series of counselling sessions after the case – for some reason, her bosses were funny about letting her back on the job after she'd had a gun shoved in her face and been taken hostage by a maniac – and while most of it was tedious nonsense, some of what she had learned about using traumatic memories and taking the pain from them had stuck with her, led her to read more on the subject.

She walked into the hall, lifted the handset and pressed the buzzer. The small screen flared into life, slowly resolving into a grainy, black and grey image of Broughton Road with Doug standing just off centre.

She hit the buzzer again, heard the door unlock. "Come on up, Doug," she said into the handset. He smiled into the camera a little too widely, nodded and pulled open the door. Susie took a breath then opened her front door, listened as Doug climbed the four flights of stairs to her flat.

He arrived on the landing a moment later, the colour in his cheeks only partly due to the exertion of climbing the stairs. He lifted a plastic bag to eye level. "Hey, Susie. Wine as promised, and takeaway menus. Anything in mind?"

She shrugged. "Chinese, maybe?"

"You surprise me," he said, flashing another one of those false smiles she had seen at the hospital.

They went into the flat, Susie taking his coat at the door, catching a subtle whiff of whisky below the peppermint tang of mouthwash as she did. When he walked into the living room, he followed the same ritual as always – head for the bay window which overlooked the industrial estate behind the flats, glance out then do a slow turn back into the room, eyes darting everywhere at once.

"Take a seat," she said, "I'll get a corkscrew for the wine."

He nodded and flopped down into one of the two sofas that were crammed into the room, both at right angles to the TV that dominated the space. It was Susie's one vice, and one of the first things she discovered she had in common with Doug – a passion for movies. But while Doug was content to watch them on whatever he could find, Susie demanded the best. Blu-ray DVD player, surround sound speakers – which Doug had helped her fit – and, of course, the monster TV.

She came back into the room with a corkscrew and two glasses, found Doug had placed the wine, and a bottle of Jameson's, on the table in front of him like a mission statement. His gaze was fixed on them, but Susie knew they weren't what he was seeing. She had picked up a copy of the *Tribune* on the way home and read his article on Greig's murder. It was typical Doug – well written, thorough, concise. No time wasted on cheap plays for sympathy, no attempts to shock or titillate the reader with overly graphic detail, which made it all the more harrowing. Reading it, Susie could almost feel Doug radiating off the page – his frustration, his revulsion, his impotence as a man he knew was slaughtered in front of him for no clear reason.

She placed the glasses on the table, took the wine and poured. Decided against diving straight in.

"So, you finally call your folks back?" she asked as she sat on the other couch, her legs already starting to complain about the workout earlier.

"Hmm? Oh, yeah, yeah," he said, reaching for the glass in a reflex motion. "Promised I was fine, said I'd go see them tomorrow maybe. Also fended off the offer of a drink and a chat from Rab MacFarlane."

Susie grimaced slightly. Rab MacFarlane was a big name in the security and events industry in Edinburgh. He had doormen at just about every pub and club in town, all watched over and deployed with military precision by his wife, Janet. Susie knew that Rab had helped Doug out with contacts from time to time. She also knew about his less-than-savoury reputation in some areas of Police Scotland, and a small group of detectives taking a very close interest in his business affairs.

But that was a topic for another night.

"So, what you going to do with all this time off you've got?" she asked, trying to keep the conversation light, at least until she'd had a couple more glasses of wine.

Doug shook his head. "Later," he said, fishing in the discarded bag and producing a pile of menus. "First, we eat." An image of Greig flashed into his mind. Blood, almost black, like oil. That look in his eyes.

"If we can," he muttered.

12

Paul swilled the whisky around his mouth, trying to kill the stale, rancid taste. It didn't work, and he shuddered slightly as he swallowed. Normally he would have insisted on a condom, but the trick on Calton Hill – "Marcus, you must call me Marcus" – had offered an extra £20 if he would suck him off bareback. So he took the money. After all, he needed it.

But he needed something more than a small warm dick and a grubby £20 note now. His skin prickled with cold sweat, waves of hunger rolling through his body in oily cramps. Even sitting in the pub – a small, dimly lit dive just off Leith Walk, five minutes from Calton Hill – with his jacket on and huddled next to a radiator, he felt cold.

Where the fuck was Frankie? Paul glanced across at his mobile sitting on the table beside his whisky. No messages. He swore under his breath, picked up the phone with a hand that wasn't quite steady and hit *Redial*, clamped it to his ear as he listened to it ring.

Come on come on come on come...

A standard pre-recorded message filled his ears, asking him to speak after the tone.

"SHIT!" The phone skittered across the table, clattered to the floor. Behind the bar an old man, with grey hair cut so short that his scalp shone through, looked up from pulling a pint of bitter, a *don't-start-any-shit* look etching a deep scowl into his forehead and pulling his lips into a tight sneer.

Paul downed the last of his whisky, picked up the phone and

headed for the door – the barman's eyes sliding across the room with him.

Fine, fuck it, Paul thought. Frankie wasn't the only source in town. Didn't matter if Frankie had the best stuff, someone else always had what he needed. Maybe that wee fuckwit, Matty.

Paul wrapped himself tight against the wind, crossing his arms over his chest and clamping down on the clenching, gnawing pain as much as he could. He walked with his head down, concentrating on putting one foot in front of the other.

Matty would help him out. Matty would take the hunger away.

13

The takeaway cartons lay strewn across the coffee table like rubble, along with scrunched-up napkins and discarded chopsticks. Susie surveyed the wreckage, noting ruefully that most of Doug's meal – sweet and sour chicken – was barely touched, while she had demolished her Szechuan beef. So much for healthy eating.

With a sigh to disguise a burp, she got up and started clearing, which Doug took as a cue to top up the wine glasses.

"Easy," she said, feeling a little light-headed as she moved. "I'm back in court tomorrow, don't want a hangover."

"Noted," he replied, nodding the wine bottle to her gently then sloshing what was left into his own glass.

She rolled her eyes and took the containers to the kitchen, where she dumped them into the bin before flicking on the kettle. She only felt a hint of guilt as she glanced at the unused Tupperware containers she had bought to arrange the recycling in.

Back in the living room, Doug was hunched over his phone, staring intently.

"Thought you were here because you didn't want to be contacted," she said, putting a coffee down in front of him and hoping he took the hint.

"Research," he said, handing the phone to her, his gaze only slightly blurred by the wine. The web browser app was open, a Google search for Jonathan Greig displaying a screen full of results.

Despite herself, and the warnings from Burns, Susie smiled. Same old Doug. No matter what happened, the story came first.

And, after the hollowed-out shell she had found at the hospital, it was good to see him more like himself, even if he was riding a wave of booze to do it.

"Anything interesting?" she asked as she settled back into her sofa.

"Not really," he said, the edge of frustration obvious in his voice. "Just what I already know. Jonathan Greig, award-winning journalist and father of three. Started his career on the local press in Stirling then landed a job at the *Tribune* as a general reporter in 1981. Worked his way up to news editor, deputy editor then editor in 2007. Few links to some of his articles, some not bad stuff there. Lot of headlines around his testimony to the Commons on press regulation around the hacking scandal and his run-in with the Committee chair – you remember, when he compared him to Big Brother and suggested they set up a Ministry of Truth? Other than that, not much. Definitely nothing to explain what happened today."

"Whatever the explanation, I'd love to hear it," Susie said. "Must be a hell of a story to justify a professional hit like that."

A shudder twisted up Doug's spine. A professional hit. Four sounds, three shots, two hits. The look of terror frozen in Greig's eyes.

For an instant, something caught in the back of his mind. Like the after-image of a dream that fades the harder you try to remember it. Something. Like rocks just below the tide.

What? Four sounds. Three shots. Something about that.

Exact. Clinical. Professional.

He shook himself from his thoughts, vaguely aware Susie had been speaking to him.

"Sorry, what?"

"I was just reminding you not to get too involved in this. I hate to admit it, but your boss is right. You can't look into this, Doug. You're a witness. Give your statement and walk away, let us handle it."

"But you're not, are you?" he said, anger clearing the wine-induced blur in his eyes. "And that's my fault, isn't it? You're sidelined on a national case because of me. And we both know you'd do a better job than Burns, King or the rest of those fuckwits."

The reply was out of Susie's mouth before she could stop it. "You have the same opinion of Rebecca? Or is she excluded because she doesn't carry a warrant card?"

Doug stared at her, wine glass halfway to his lips, an expression she couldn't read flitting across his face like a fast-moving weather front.

"Susie, I…"

"No, Doug. Just fucking leave it, okay?" she snapped, surprised by the anger that flashed through her; sudden, blinding, like metal catching dazzling sunlight. "Yes, you're right, I'm off the case. And yes, I could do with being on it. And yes, I'm being watched a little too closely by Burns and all the wankers upstairs, mostly because of the shitstorm you stirred up with Richard Buchan last year."

She threw back the rest of her wine in a jerking motion then clattered the glass back onto the table, hoping it would cool the rage bubbling in the back of her throat. It didn't.

"But you know what really fucks me off, Doug? After everything, you think I'm just another one of them, just another copper blundering through their job, waiting for the brilliant Doug McGregor to ask the questions they were too stupid to think of. Well I don't fucking need it, okay Doug? You want someone to swoon at your genius, go talk to Rebecca."

Doug stared at her in confusion. He opened his mouth, closed it, and the sudden silence rushed in on them. He reached forward, took the whisky, and sloshed a shot into her wine glass before pouring one into his own. Raised his glass, tipped it towards her slightly. When he spoke, his voice was colder than the rain pitter-pattering on the windows.

"I don't want to talk to Rebecca just now, Susie. I've had a shit, shit day, and all I wanted was to talk to my friend. If that's overstepping the mark, especially now, I'm sorry. But I just thought that…"

His phone started to chatter on the table's glass surface. He reached for it, ready to switch it off, then paused. And for the second time in a matter of minutes, a wave of expressions Susie couldn't understand flitted across his face, until one settled on his features that she did understand.

Relief.

He glanced an apology to Susie and she waved him away almost angrily, biting back whatever it was that was clawing up her throat and stinging her eyes.

When he spoke, his voice was nervous, tentative, the coldness from only moments ago gone.

"Hello? Harvey? That you?"

He paused, listening. The first real smile she had seen twitching across his face as he ran his free hand through his hair rapidly. "Aye, fair enough. Should have known better than that. Sorry." Pause. Enthusiastic nodding. Then sudden laughter, sounding all the more surreal in the charged aftermath of their argument. "Fuck off, you're no' getting a quote from me." Another pause, chin dropping to his chest. "Really? That…" A glance up, shy, apologetic. "That would be great, Harvey. Thanks. Thanks a lot." Silence as the other end of the line spoke. "Tomorrow. Yeah, tomorrow. Give Esther my love, too. See you."

He clicked the phone off, let his hand drop slowly into his lap. Chewed his lip for a moment, then downed the whisky in a gulp. When he looked at Susie, she felt a jolt of cold shock as she saw tears glisten in his eyes.

"Who the hell was that?"

Doug shook his head, the smile returning to his lips. "I'll get to that in a minute," he said as he reached for the whisky. "But first, let me ask you a question."

"What?" she said, trying to keep the frustration out of her voice.

"Ever been to Skye?" he asked, eyes dancing with mischief as he reached for her glass and downed her whisky as well.

14

Charlie Montgomery loved the morning. He loved to rise early and work while the world roused around him. He loved the thought of his opponents stirring from their warm, soft beds, sleep-addled and slow, groping for coffee, while he was already in top gear, ticking along with the precision of a fine watch, already well on the way to beating them.

The thought made him smile as he finished his morning ritual of press-ups and coffee, the first sunlight paling the darkness outside to a deep burgundy that made it look as if the sky was a huge stage curtain draped in front of his windows.

Home was a penthouse flat in Leith, tucked behind the Ocean Terminal shopping centre. It had been overpriced when he bought it seven years ago, and the crash a few years back had done nothing to help its value, but it was worth it. Charlie loved the open-plan design, the space and the balcony that, on a good day, gave him clear views across the Forth to Fife and beyond.

It was a long, long way from the council house he had grown up in with his parents and brother in Bonnybridge. He had a picture on the partition wall between the kitchen and the living area of him and his brother aged about twelve standing in their garden, the house a pebble-dashed monstrosity sitting squat and ugly and grey behind them. He hated the picture, hated his brother even more, but he kept it there as a reminder.

And a warning. *You came from this. Don't go back*, the picture screamed.

By the time he had showered and dressed, the sun had rolled

back the stage curtain. The sky was cool and clear, heavy with the promise of another day of fine weather that put Charlie's teeth on edge. Sun in Edinburgh at this time of year meant only one thing. Tourists. And with the High Court sitting across the road from St Giles' Cathedral on the Mile, that meant he'd have to dodge clumps of the camera-wielding, chattering idiots on his way. He sighed. A small price to pay.

He left the flat and started to walk into town. It would take him about an hour and it was uphill all the way, but Charlie enjoyed the time, and the chance to put his thoughts in order. By the time he reached the court, he would be warmed up and ready for action.

He headed up North Junction Street, passing a pub that was already open for business. Caught a whiff of stale beer and old cigarette smoke cut with the harsh tang of cheap whisky and thought, as he always did, of his dad. Slumped in his chair in the living room, beer belly spilling over his trousers after it was released from the prison of his starched uniform shirt, jacket and hat discarded on the dining table at the back of the room. PC Edward Montgomery. Local bobby and pillar of the community. Lousy father, insipid adulterer and alcoholic. He had died three years ago, a massive stroke taking him out of the confused misery of dementia he had lived in for the last fifteen years. Charlie wished he had lived a little longer. He hadn't suffered enough.

Reaching the top of Leith Walk, Charlie kept climbing, passing St James Centre on his right and then turning along Princes Street, which was, as ever, choked with buses, taxis and cars. He turned left at Princes Street Gardens, just as a tram slid by, already busy with commuters. Charlie watched it for a moment. He had fought against the trams, taken the council to court over them, commented in the stories that decried them as "Edinburgh's shame" and "Capital's billion-pound folly". And yet, now that they were running, they were an accepted, even grudgingly loved, part of life in Edinburgh. They were busy every day, and there was even talk now of finishing what had been started and extending the line all the way down to Leith. Charlie smiled. Let them. It would clear the streets for him in the morning and, who knows, there might be a few cases in it for him as well.

He walked down to Market Street then turned up as if his destination was the Mound, heading for the News Steps that cut up the hill and led to the back of the court. He was heading for the small café that sat on the side street beside the court. It was a rarity in Edinburgh for two reasons – it wasn't a high street chain and it served food that was actually fresh and not vacuum-packed. Charlie took the stairs two at a time, mentally putting the finishing touches to Kevin Malcolm's defence. He smiled slightly, pleased by his plan to use "psychological trauma" and the stupid little shit's drug problems as justifications for his actions. It wouldn't get him off, but it would hopefully cut time served. Which Charlie would take as a victory.

So what if a violent little ned with anger management issues was back on the streets early? He would win the case. And that was all that mattered.

He was so engrossed that he almost didn't see the figure on the landing about halfway up the staircase, where it twisted around to follow the contour of the hill. Swaddled in a dirty blanket and backed into the corner with head down to their knees, he had almost thought it was a pile of rubbish in front of him. He moved to the other side of the stairs to avoid any pleas for change and bounded to the landing, reached out to put his hand on the rail to steady himself before launching himself onto the last flight of stairs and…

The agony was sudden and complete, flashing through him as though the handrail had been electrified. He looked down, eyes bulging with incomprehension at the knife that had been plunged into the top of his hand. He staggered back as he reflexively tried to pull his hand away, felt blackness rush in as a fresh wave of cold agony lanced up his arm as the blade ground against bone. A hot, clammy hand clamped around his throat and squeezed, throttling his scream and making his eyes bulge in air-starved terror as steely fingers dug into his windpipe.

"Hi Charlie," a shrill voice whispered in his ear, hot with hatred and breathless with effort and excitement. "Nice to see you again after all this time. Got a wee message for you."

The fingers dug into Charlie's windpipe more forcefully as the knife was wrenched free from his hand in a rocking, twisting motion, the sound of bones splintering echoing in his ears.

A sharp kick to the back of the knees buckled his legs, and he felt crushing weight as his attacker bore down on him and forced him to the ground. A sudden moment of freedom as the figure backed off. Charlie hugged his ruined hand close to him, hot blood plastering his shirt to his chest, tears rolling down his cheeks.

"Wha...?" he croaked through his ruined throat, the effort excruciating. "Wha...?"

The kick whipped his head back, dark stars exploding in front of his eyes as blood flew from his nose in a spattering arc. He fell backwards, crying out as he hit the cold stone stairs. Soft laughter in front of him. Taunting.

Pain exploded in his midsection, white and flaring, as a boot was driven into his stomach. He gasped, choking and gagging, eyes bulging in terror as blood roared in his ears and he tried to breathe with lungs that felt like deflated balloons. The next kick was harder, his attacker grunting with effort. He screamed through blood-stained teeth as he felt a rib snap like a brittle twig.

"Wh..." he gasped, tongue jabbing against jagged stumps of broken teeth as he tried to speak, his breathing a ragged hiss. "Wh... why are...?"

A face suddenly filled his blurring, dimming vision. A nightmare leering at him from the past, carrying rational thought away with it on a crushing tide of terror and panic.

"Here's the message," the nightmare whispered, holding up a glinting object and rolling it in the weak morning light. "Hope you like it."

Something cold was jammed into Charlie's mouth, blunt needles of pain gouging into his gums as it clattered off his ruined teeth. More punches now, driving the last air from his chest as the darkness rushed in and wrapped itself around him like a warm blanket. Charlie dove for it, feeling the pain ebb, replaced by cool numbness as he drifted...

...drifted...

Pain screamed from his scalp as his head was wrenched back by the hair and he was dragged back to his knees. A bolt of scalding ice lanced across his throat and he clawed for it instinctively. Blood erupted from the wound in a torrent, spattering the walls and the dirty concrete. The world began to list and sway, almost as if he was on a boat at high tide. He was looking back down the stairs he had just come up, the stairs that led all the way down to Market Street.

And suddenly he was flying. Tumbling head over heels, bones snapping and disintegrating as he hit the stairs and bounced. On the landing above, the nightmare watched with cold amusement.

He came to rest about three quarters of the way down, legs and arms jutting out at unnatural angles, blood from the stab wounds to his chest starting to glisten as it seeped into the dark material of his perfectly tailored suit.

The nightmare bounded down to him, checked briefly for a pulse. Found a weak one thrumming in his ruined neck.

"Fra... Frankie..." Charlie coughed around the object in his mouth, blood spilling from what was left of his lips.

"Yes, Charlie, that's right. Frankie," the nightmare whispered.

The knife was driven into Charlie's brain just at the temple, a quick, sudden stab, the sound of a dozen eggs being cracked at once. He made a grunting snort then collapsed forward – air driven from his lungs in a wheeze as his body hit the concrete and bounced slightly. He twitched once, weakly, then was still, the smell of shit rising into the air as his bowels gave way, mingling with the sound of soft, contented laughter.

15

Doug let out a burp that was part wind, part nausea, and fought back the sudden wave of acidic bile that clawed at the back of his throat. The whisky last night had been a very bad idea. He took a quick swig of Coke then grasped the wheel tightly, pushed down on the accelerator a little harder. Driving faster would force him to concentrate more, get him there more quickly. Take his mind off Greig.

Pick a lie, any lie, he thought.

He still couldn't quite believe Harvey had got in touch, after all these years.

Who is he? Susie had asked after he put the phone down. The response that flashed through his mind was, *The man who made me who I am today.* And though it was a cliché it was, at its core, true.

Harvey Robertson was senior reporter at the *Capital Tribune* when Doug started there on work experience. It began as a fortnight, part of his HND course. Thanks to Harvey, it became a career. Doug was assigned to shadow Harvey, who was to "show him the ropes". From the start, Harvey liked him. While he made Doug do the usual gopher-jobs – "shit-end-of-the-stick duty" as Harvey called it – such as getting the coffees, going on the lunch run or getting the papers, he also made sure Doug was involved in the process of putting a paper out. Thanks to Harvey, Doug spent time with all the departments in the *Tribune*, from advertising and subs to backbench, newsdesk, reporters and even conference. He gave him the big picture.

And to Doug, it was a revelation. He'd been born to his parents ten years too late. It wasn't their fault, blame late marriage and hectic careers, but it marked him out as different from the start. He was always the least fashionable kid in class; as fashions and haircuts changed around him, he was always dressed in a range of sensible cords, jeans and smart shirts. Hardwearing shoes as, after all, "trainers were only for gym class". His haircut was a copy of his dad's – slicked back, hacked into submission by the local barber, an amateur who inherited the business from his own father and kept it going on a clientele of pensioners and kids whose parents didn't see the sense in paying any more than the price of a round at the bar for a haircut.

At school, Doug was a social misfit – the quiet, badly dressed kid in the corner who kept his mouth shut, blushed when a girl spoke to him and squinted out at a world he loathed from behind a pair of cheap NHS prescription glasses. He had cried when the optician said he needed glasses to read the board in class: it was just another reason for him to be picked on by the "cool kids".

So when he told his parents – his father an accountant and his mother a nurse – that he wanted to be a journalist and write for a living, the response was predictable.

"That'll no' happen, son."

"Get a proper job, you can do better than that,"

"Why don't you go work with your father?"

It was a leap too far for them. They were practical people whose son wanted to follow an impractical career. They tolerated it when they saw how focused he was, but Doug could almost feel the disappointment radiating from them over his "silly choice" and the ruined dreams of Dr Doug prowling the wards of the ERI, or Douglas McGregor QC, scourge of the Scottish courts.

But with Harvey, it wasn't silly any more. This was serious work being done by professionals, back when newspapers were run by people who judged a paper and its content by more than what it cost the publisher to produce.

Doug poured his heart into the work experience placement and, when it was over, Harvey pulled a few strings and got him his first journalism job, subbing the obits for the *Tribune*.

The pay was shit and the hours terrible, but Doug didn't care, he was doing what he wanted, with people who thought about writing and language the same way as he did.

Over time he became a general reporter and, again, Harvey took him under his wing. Taught him the tricks of the trade: how to get into a story, how to work the angles, who to make contacts of, who to make friends with, who to watch closely. Made him work on his shorthand for endless hours until he got it right and, incredibly, legible.

"There are no new stories, Doug, just new angles," he had said once when they were enjoying a traditional lunchtime pint in a small pub tucked up a back alley just off the Royal Mile. "The trick is finding the angle, and making it work for you."

When Harvey got wind that Andrea McKenzie, the crime reporter who had taken over from him at the *Tribune*, was moving on to the small screen, he pushed Doug to take the NCTJ exams he needed to get the job. At first Doug had shied away from it, terrified, if he were honest, that he wasn't up to it. But Harvey kept pushing him until, eventually, he relented.

And, sure enough, by the time Andrea appeared on her first six o'clock bulletin, sporting a makeover so striking it made Doug wish he had paid more attention to her when they worked together, he was sitting at her old desk, the newly appointed crime reporter for the *Capital Tribune*.

Harvey had retired about six years ago, sickened by what he called the "bean-counters who were cutting the guts out of the industry". When there was a redundancy offer at the *Tribune* he took it, and ploughed the money in to a small bed and breakfast on the Isle of Skye. It was where he had met his wife, Esther, years ago while on holiday, and he "always wanted to go back for the women and the great beer".

Doug hadn't heard from him since. Until last night.

"Sorry it took so long to track you down, Douglas," he had said, his voice as soft and even as ever. "Saw the story on the news, called the *Trib*, got Walter. He told me what happened. Didn't for a second think you'd be in morning conference, thought I'd taught you better than that."

"Aye, fair enough, should have known better. Sorry."

"What you sorry for, Doug? Just means I get some great first-person stuff to sell to the agencies."

"Fuck off, you're no' getting a quote from me."

Doug heard an inhale on the other end of the line, pictured Harvey taking a draw on the cheap, gnarled old pipe he thought made him look distinguished.

"Look, Doug. Esther's worried sick about you, and I'm no' so happy about all this myself. You know it'll be a shitstorm there for the next few days, so how do you fancy coming and seeing us for a bit? I'll show you some of the women and let you drink some of the beer."

"Really? That… that would be great Harvey. Thanks, thanks a lot."

"So we'll see you tomorrow? I take it finding the place won't be too much of a leap for a crime reporter as good as you?"

"Tomorrow. Yeah, tomorrow. Give Esther my love, too. See you."

He had clicked off the phone, feeling like a drowning man who had just been thrown a life jacket. Tried to tell Susie about Harvey and what had happened. She'd laughed off the offer of a trip to Skye, wondering why he didn't find it funny.

The feeling of relief the call had given him lasted all the way back to Musselburgh and the living room of his flat. Sitting there, thoughts of Greig's death pressed in on him, clawing, insistent, demanding attention like a petulant child.

The terror in his eyes as the blood gushed from his neck…

Look at me.

Greig whipped round by the force of the first shot…

Look at me.

The way his knees buckled and he collapsed, cracking his skull open on the table…

LOOK AT ME.

The whisky was poured and in his hand before he knew it. He drank about a quarter of the bottle in a hopeless attempt to drown out the thoughts and images before he passed out from sheer nervous exhaustion, only to wake up in his chair cold and stiff and hungover.

And now, here he was, feeling like he was about to puke any at moment and hammering the car up the road to the Isle of Skye, his mind full of questions about Greig, the future, Susie, Rebecca.

Pick a lie, any lie, he thought again as he urged the car even faster.

16

By the time Susie arrived at the scene, Burns was already there with the usual supporting cast of detectives, uniforms and scenes of crime officers. Police cordon tape rustled in the fresh morning air, glinting occasionally as it caught the light.

She nodded a greeting to the uniforms who were standing at the bottom of the staircase, where Burns had told her to come when he called her ten minutes ago. Which was odd. It would have been easier just to step out of the court, round the side and onto the News Steps that way, rather than coming all the way round then down Market Street, but she wasn't in the mood to argue. Blame too much wine last night with Doug.

She pushed through the growing scrum of gawkers, tried to stay out of shot of the photographers and cameramen who had arrived, ducked under the tape and started up the staircase, yesterday's gym session setting off dull pain in her legs and butt as she moved. Ahead, Burns spotted her and moved to meet her.

"Morning, sir," she said, noticing the thin sheen of sweat on his forehead. The outdoors didn't suit him, especially when stairs and bright sunlight were involved. His natural habitat was the CID suite or the pub, best viewed under artificial light.

"Drummond," Burns growled. "What do you know?"

"Not much more than you told me, sir. Victim was found by a female heading for the National Library on George IV Bridge. Her screams alerted an officer heading for the court at the top of the steps, he radioed it in about thirty minutes ago."

"Hmm. Hmm." Burns nodded agreement. "And you've not

heard any chatter on the radio about this yet?"

"No sir, I've not checked it. Why? Should I have?"

Burns grunted. "No real reason. Except it wasn't quite as routine as you said. You see, young PC Burnett, who responded to the screams, recognised the victim. Got a bit agitated when he made the call to Control. I'm pulling the recording to beat him to death with later, but I think the phrase he used was, 'Someone's kebabed Charming Charlie Montgomery.'"

Susie felt her mouth drop open, shock hitting her in the stomach like a left jab. Her head darted up to where a knot of forensic officers dressed in their white jumpsuits were wrestling with a pop-up tent behind another length of police tape that had been draped across the width of the staircase. She couldn't see the body.

"What? Sir? You don't mean?"

"Oh yes, Drummond, I do. Go and have a look for yourself. Hope you didn't have a big breakfast though, he's in a hell of a state." Susie searched Burns's face for any trace of gallows humour. When she didn't find it, her stomach gave another queasy lurch.

She climbed the last of the stairs, pain in her legs forgotten, until she reached the second, inner cordon that was designed to protect the immediate crime scene. She peered over, the forensics staff shuffling out of her way to give her a clear view. Swallowed back the sudden tang of bile in her throat as she looked down at the dead eyes of Charming Charlie Montgomery.

It took a force of will to tear her eyes from the knife that jutted out of his temple and consider the scene as a whole. His face was a ruin of blood and dusty-purple markings that looked like birthmarks. She realised with a sudden twist of revulsion that they were imprints from the boot that had been smashed into his face again and again. His nose was mashed against his cheek like a blob of plasticine, obviously broken by one or more of the kicks. His limbs were arranged at crazy, disorienting angles beneath him, broken and wrenched from their sockets by the fall. His perfect hair, which Susie noticed he always patted down at the back just before he made a comment in the courtroom, was ruffled and slick with blood and, Susie thought, flecks of bone.

"What happened?" she asked, directing the question into the crowd of SOCOs. One of them Susie recognised, Amanda Paterson, who stepped closer to the cordon, picking her steps gingerly so she didn't disturb anything.

She nodded a small greeting, looked at the body again, then back up the stairs. "Best we can tell, he was stabbed on the landing halfway up – there's a hell of a lot of blood up there and the spatter patterns and pooling show that's where most of the damage was done. Looks like he was beaten up there too; there wouldn't have been enough room to get the force into those blows on the steps here, too confined."

Susie saw a picture she didn't want to look at form in her mind. Charlie being attacked, stabbed to the ground then beaten before…

…before…

She blinked rapidly to clear the image. "Then he was thrown down the stairs? That's how he ended up here?"

"Either that or he fell when trying to get away, yeah." Amanda nodded, glasses winking. "But he was dead by the time he landed. No way anyone could survive that type of blood loss, even without the knife wound to the head."

Susie was dimly aware of Burns's heavy breathing as he came to a stop beside her. Forced herself to focus on the job, screen out the acrid tang of blood in her nostrils and the caustic taste tickling her gag reflex at the back of her throat.

"Robbery, sir? He fought back, attacker pulled a knife? Secluded staircase, just the place for a dumb shit to jump an unsuspecting passer-by."

"My first impression, too. But his wallet, watch and other personal belongings are still on the body. And besides, this was deliberate. Look at the knife – a simple mugger would have scarpered, not hung around and left the murder weapon. And whoever did this left us a message."

Susie felt her legs twitch, either to run or buckle, she wasn't sure.

"What message?" she asked, amazed how calm her voice sounded, especially as she was talking through numb lips.

"Not sure yet. But the doc says something's been rammed in his mouth. We'll know more when he gets Charlie back to the lock-up for the post-mortem. But it's not your average mugger's MO now, is it?"

"No sir," Susie mumbled, "it's not. But what…?"

"Haven't got a fucking clue," Burns said, his voice heavy with disgust. "But that's a journalist and a lawyer dead in the space of twenty-four hours. What's next, a banker?"

Susie glanced over his shoulder to the HQ of the Bank of Scotland that sat on the Mound, a massive, castle-like building that dominated the view over Princes Street.

What next? Good question.

She turned again, the Scott Monument coming into view. A flash of Charlie Morris leering over her, pushing a gun into her face. The terror. The impotence. She blinked rapidly, forced herself to breathe. Wished she had taken Doug up on his joke offer of a road trip after all.

17

The acid begins pumping through my legs and lower back ten miles outside of Dumbarton, so I pull into the first layby I can find and take a hit from the wrap. It races up my nose and stabs into my brain like a shard of hot ice, the warm, velvet perfection spreading through my body in a wave that carries away the pain and exhaustion.

I sit slumped in the seat, hands resting on the steering wheel. Ruined, ancient things, skin the colour of wax stretched over gnarled knots of knuckle, mottled with nicks and scars and liver spots. They hurt every time I move them, wake me from my nightmares with bolts of searing agony if I clench them in my sleep.

But still strong when they need to be. Still steady.

Still killers.

I muster the energy to haul myself forward and reach into the glove compartment for the map. It's an old and tattered thing, just like me, but it serves its purpose. Right now, it's camouflage, just in case an overly enthusiastic copper decides to take an interest in why I've stopped. I unfold it on the steering wheel and stare at it, colours blurring and running into one another as I let my eyes defocus and concentrate on my breathing. I don't need to look at that map, I know exactly where I'm going.

I grunt what passes for a laugh and feel a lazy smile play across my lips. "Over the sea," I whisper in a voice I barely recognise as my own. It's funny, I always wanted to see more of Scotland, but I never had the time.

But I do now. And I have something more, something I've not had for a very, very long time.

A mission to believe in.

I blink my eyes back into focus, take another deep breath and flex my hands as I wriggle in the seat and get my legs moving. Not bad. The pain is there, as it always is, but the wrap has numbed the worst of it. I shake my head, make a mental note to pick up some Red Bull at the first service station I come across and get back on the road.

I drive very, very carefully. Not too slowly, not too fast, just another driver on the tourist trail. I feel the urge to press the accelerator down, race to the goal and get on with the mission, but I resist it.

Discipline. Patience. Control. I've waited this long. A little longer won't hurt. I can see the end destination now – my arrival is as inevitable as the death and suffering I will bring.

18

The morgue was at the top of a slight hill overlooking the Cowgate, a small, squat building the police had nicknamed "the lock-up". It was concrete-grey, listless and anonymous looking, just another utilitarian structure forced upon Edinburgh's Old Town during the Seventies.

Susie had always hated the building. The harsh, astringent whiff of disinfectant, the overly bright strip lights dancing over the tiles and chrome, the rooms kept cold for obvious reasons and, below it all, the feeling of death seeping from every surface.

She was sitting in Dr Williams' office, which was little more than a small anteroom off the main surgical bay where the post-mortems were carried out. She was nursing a bad coffee and a worse headache, and neither of them looked like they would improve in the near future.

It had started at the CID suite after she had seen Charlie's body. Burns had called a meeting and, as there were now two murders, divided up the detectives into teams for the Greig and Montgomery inquiries.

Only one problem – Susie wasn't on either team.

She waited for the rest of the officers to file out of the room, counting very slowly and deliberately to ten in her head as she did, ignoring the dull ache from her jaw as she ground her teeth – an old habit that had cost her hours and hours in the dentist chair growing up.

When the last of the officers had left, she walked to Burns's office. Paused at the door and knocked, trying not to imagine the noise the glass would make if she shattered it.

One... two... three... fo-

She was through the door and in the office before Burns's barked "Come!" had faded from her ears.

He was standing at the window in the corner, making a half-hearted attempt to disguise the butt of the cigarette he had just smoked. As with all public places these days, smoking in police premises was frowned upon, but the reek of old smoke and the nicotine stains that ran around the top of the dull magnolia walls like a scum ring in a dirty bath told another story.

Observe the law. Just don't always enforce it, Susie heard one of her lecturers whisper in her mind.

Burns took a moment to look her over as he settled back into his chair. From the squealing it was making, Burns's latest get-fit kick wasn't going so well.

"Drummond," he said with a small nod at last, as if confirming that, yes, that was still her name. Arrogant prick. "Something I can do for you?"

Susie settled her gaze on his, vowed not to look away. "The duty split, sir. I noticed I wasn't assigned to either the Greig or Montgomery case. I was wondering if you could tell me why?"

Burns contorted his features into what Susie guessed was his version of empathy and understanding. It looked more like he wasn't getting enough fibre in his diet and the shit train was about three days late.

"I thought we had been through this? I can't put you on the Greig case, and you were a witness in the trial Charlie was working on when he died. So I can't use you on either of them, can I? But there is something I need you to look at, a suspicious death at the ERI."

Susie felt cold fury prickle between her shoulders, fought to keep her breath even and her tone low. "With respect, sir, I don't think that's the best use of my expertise. You've got two high-profile murders in two days. I would have thought that…"

"You would have thought?" Burns snapped, his eyes growing dark as his cheeks and neck flushed an angry purple. "And just who, Detective *Sergeant,* said that you were entitled to have a fucking thought or opinion about any of this? I've already told you that the high heidyins are looking at you very, very closely, so the last thing I need is for that to turn into problems on the Greig case. And you know as well as I do that you can't investigate the death of a man who you were facing off against in court. So what exactly do you want me to do?"

The words were out of Susie's mouth before she could stop them, tumbling from her, each as hard as the lump in her throat and as acidic as the tears scalding her eyes. Fuck this. Fuck this right off.

"How about you use me, sir… you know, let me do my actual job? I'm a good detective, I've shown that time and time again, even with all the shit and sneering behind my back. I put in the hours, do the job and get the results. I understand about Charlie's case, but to keep me away from the Greig murder purely on the basis of my alleged connection to a reporter at the *Tribune,* who may or may not have witnessed the murder, and because of some scrutiny from senior officers is, frankly, cowardice. If I mess up, then I mess up and I'll take responsibility for that. But if you want to sideline me then…"

She let the sentence drift off, partly because she couldn't be sure she could keep her voice level, and partly because she didn't know what came next. She'd thought of quitting before, especially after the whole Christmas party nightmare and in the aftermath of the Buchan case. But would she?

Could she?

Burns slid a file from the corner of his desk in front of his looming gut, eyes never leaving Susie. His breathing was deep and heavy, almost like snoring and, for a moment, Susie was sure he was building up to an explosion. She was about to get the Third

Degree Burns treatment, both barrels. The quitting question was about to be taken out of her hands.

"Drummond," he said, fiddling with the edges of the file as if he wanted to crush it into a ball at any second. His voice was flint: cold, unfeeling, razor sharp.

"This is the file on the unexplained death at the Edinburgh Royal Infirmary. Happened yesterday afternoon, got a little lost in the hoo-hah surrounding the Greig case. A twenty-two-year-old male, hospitalised with serious head injuries, found dead by his nurse. Williams is doing the post-mortem as a favour to the director of the hospital, an old colleague of his. So you will go and see Dr Williams and get his report. I suspect his office will be more welcoming than this place for the next few hours."

Susie gulped. So that was it, she was fucked. Might as well go all the way then. "Sir, I…"

Burns raised a hand. "And when you have finished with Dr Williams, you will review all the statements from the Greig case, including that of Mr Douglas McGregor, see if King and co missed anything, offer your thoughts."

Susie let out a sigh, felt her legs go heavy from burned-out adrenalin. "Thank you, sir, I appreciate the opportunity to…"

Burns waved his hand again, swatting away an imaginary fly. "Don't give me the shit, Susie. You're right, you're a good copper, I should be using you, no matter what those fuckwits upstairs say. But one thing. Talk to me like that again, ever, and you won't have to worry about the brass fucking your career over, understood?"

She nodded, feeling like an over-grateful puppy. "Yes, sir. I apologise. And thank you."

"Don't thank me, Drummond. Get the fuck out of my sight. And get me some results."

Susie took the hint and headed straight for the morgue. So now she was sitting in Dr Williams' office, waiting, hoping he had finished the business end of the day and she could just get his thoughts or, better yet, a first draft of his report.

Her phone beeped. A text message from Rebecca. *Hear you got assigned to the Greig case, congrats. Give me a call when you get a minute, need to go over lines, R.*

Susie clicked the phone off, downed the last of her coffee. Grimaced.

Bitter and cold.

19

Doug's hangover cleared just as he swung out of Kyle of Lochalsh and down onto the long sweep of road that took him over the Skye Bridge. He realised that he had been driving on autopilot most of the way, taking corners by instinct, ignoring the sparse, rugged beauty of Loch Lochy, Ben Nevis and the Cairngorms as he left Fort William and the towns and cities behind, the landscape seeming to decompress and stretch out to fill the horizon with stunning mountains that jutted defiantly into the sky.

Instead, he spent the journey trying to think through the whisky-induced fug about what had happened. Tried to look at it rationally rather than as a witness. See it like any other story, just as Harvey had taught him to.

Okay, so, the facts. Someone wanted Greig dead. Someone who was obviously a skilled sniper, able to shoot through a window and hit him twice dead centre with only three shots. But then that was a problem. If the killer was as proficient as Doug thought he was, why such a public killing? Why not just lie in wait for Greig down a quiet alley, or get him as he left the *Trib* at night under the cover of darkness?

The answer was simple. Because whoever did this, didn't want it to be a quiet death. Being splashy was the whole point. This was a message, clear and simple.

But to whom? And what was the message?

Doug sighed with frustration, hauled his mind back to the task of driving. Felt his hangover snarl again as the steep climb and pronounced camber of the Skye Bridge gave him a brief stab of vertigo and a stunning view of Loch Alsh below.

He came off the bridge and followed the signs for Broadford. According to the map, Harvey's hotel was on the Sleat peninsula, a bulge at the bottom of the island that pushed back out towards the mainland. And the best way to get there was to come off the bridge and head for Broadford. The road was quiet, better kept than Doug had been expecting, white-bricked homes and small knots of houses clustered together sliding by.

His phone pinged and he reached for it, giving the road ahead a brief glance. Rebecca. *Off the record, Susie on the Greig case. Speaking to her later. Rx*

He frowned, tossed the phone aside. He had called her this morning, apologised for not being in touch since the hospital, explained where he was going. What he didn't explain was she was part of the reason for him deciding to go.

It had started a couple of weeks ago, when Doug had been at a press briefing on a spate of pick-pocketings around Morningside. The MO was simple enough – identify a likely target, normally older and less likely to know what was going on until it was too late, jostle them on the street and grab their wallets and valuables in the confusion. Not original and, in the days of identity theft, cyber crime and card cloning, Doug had to admit a grudging admiration for the retro nature of the crimes.

A couple of the incidents had been caught on CCTV cameras outside shops and in the streets, giving police a fairly good look at the suspects, hence the press briefing to get the word out, alert locals and try to track them down.

So far, so routine. Except that, supporting the CID officers at the briefing was a new face. A face who wasn't impressed by the antics of one Douglas McGregor, who was happily baiting DI Burns into an early heart attack by asking why Police Scotland couldn't track down what looked like Morningside's equivalent of Oliver Twist and the Artful Dodger during the height of tourist season.

Burns was just building to a truly volcanic explosion, Doug could tell by the way the colour was draining from his face as his neck turned scarlet, almost as if his tie was too tight and the blood was pooling around the blockage.

Doug only felt a little guilty at goading Burns into giving a juicy quote – he was generally a good copper, but the way he was side-lining Susie on some of the bigger cases recently rankled.

But before he was able to get out an expletive-laden putdown, the new face stepped in. Rebecca Summers, a fresh recruit to the new corporate affairs and media team, brought in to give Police Scotland a professional face after some difficult headlines over the Chief going lone ranger and armed police officers prowling the aisles of local supermarkets around the country.

"Well, Mr McGregor," she said, "we'd love to hear your suggestions. Oh, and if you've got a phone number for Fagin or Nancy, I'm sure that would help – who knows, maybe they could help us hit the Bullseye? Now, is that enough literary allusion for you, or can we get back to the serious business of the press briefing?"

Doug opened his mouth to give a witty retort, found he had nothing to throw at the woman now giving him a small, amused smile that almost offset the calm, cold fury that was radiating from her dark brown eyes.

He was dimly aware of a ripple of laughter running through the other reporters, felt his face turning as red as Burns's neck.

Doug hustled out meekly when the briefing ended, headed back to the *Tribune* and wrote up the story then got to work trying to forget his humiliation.

It wasn't helped by the fact that Robbie Alexander, one of the snappers the *Tribune* used to cover police stories, took a picture of Doug at the perfect moment, mouth hanging open with stunned incredulity, the look of shame written over his face like rouge applied by a five-year-old.

Doug, read the note attached to the print of the picture Robbie had stuck to Doug's computer, *thought you might need a new byline pic. Think this one really captures the inner you. Robbie.*

Bastard.

Doug bundled the picture into his drawer, hoping not too many people had seen it, then made a fuss of looking busy on the feature he was writing. He was almost fooling himself when his mobile rang. He frowned when he read the display. No caller ID, which probably meant a call centre trying to give him the good news on the fortune he was owed in unclaimed PPI. Against his better judgment, he answered it, vaguely hoping for someone to take his frustration out on.

"Doug McGregor."

A woman's voice. Soft, with a gentle undercurrent of Belfast taking the edge off the consonants and exaggerating the vowels. "Mr McGregor. Yes. Hello. My name's Rebecca Summers. We, ah, met at the press briefing in Fettes."

Doug sat up in his chair, felt the heat rising in his cheeks as his mouth dried out. Shit.

"Aye, yes. Yes, we did. You're the Dickens lover, right?"

She gave the comment a laugh more polite than it deserved. "Yes, that's me. I just wanted to call to, ah, apologise, if I embarrassed you. The last thing I want to do is get off on the wrong foot with anyone in the press."

Doug coughed back a laugh in spite of himself. "Ms Summers, don't take this the wrong way, but I've been a lot more embarrassed than that on jobs before. That said, if you feel you want to make it up to me by giving me an exclusive, then I'm not going to try and stop you."

A chuckle down the line, a lot more genuine than the first. "It's Rebecca. And I hardly think you need our help getting splashes Mr McGregor, given the work you did on the Katherine Buchan story last year."

Doug forced back the sudden image of Katherine Buchan plummeting towards the earth from the top of the Scott Monument, head exploding as she hit the ground below. It had been a hard story to work on, harder still to forget. He still looked up every time he walked past the Monument, imagined what she saw and felt as she fell, the wind screaming in her ears as her heart hammered its last frantic beats in her fragile chest.

"Call me Doug. And I had a little help with that one. Got lucky with a few contacts."

"Oh yes, I've heard you've got some very good sources here."

"I couldn't possibly comment," Doug said, his voice hardening. Pleasantries over, here came the main course. Find his source, warn him off.

Another chuckle down the phone, throaty, warm. Doug could imagine those dark eyes flashing with amusement. "Don't worry, Mr McGregor, I'm not going to tell any stories out of school. Susie already told me all about it. Who do you think gave me your number?"

"I, ah, eh…"

"I can tell you've got a few questions. So how about we meet for a coffee? Say Sam's Cafe on Broughton Road? Maybe three o'clock this afternoon?"

Sam's Cafe. The same place Doug had first met Susie when he found out about her little mistake with a married senior officer at the office Christmas party.

Christ, how much had Susie told this woman?

"I'll be there," Doug said, anxious to get the call over and speak with Susie.

"Great. And Doug, Susie says save yourself a phone call, she's coming too."

Before he could think of a reply, Rebecca cut the line, leaving Doug sitting at his desk, lost for words. Again. He was just glad Robbie wasn't around for another profile picture.

Sam's Cafe was deserted when Doug arrived, save for a tired-looking woman he knew was called Iris wiping at a table half-heartedly and Susie sitting in the corner with Summers. Doug approached slowly, not sure what to say or do. He felt like he was going for an interview without his normal preparation. He'd had enough time to find one card to play, but he was sure he wouldn't be holding the best deal in the room. Not a pleasant experience. Normally, it was the other way around.

Susie looked up and smiled a greeting, mischief glittering in her eyes and a small smile pulling at the corners of her mouth. "Doug, glad you could make it. I hear you've already met Rebecca."

Doug took Rebecca's hand and shook it. Small, warm, perfect manicure, strong grip, no jewellery. "Hi," he said weakly and slid into the seat beside Susie. "So, is someone going to bring me up to speed here or what?"

A brief glance exchanged between Rebecca and Susie. *You go.*

Rebecca placed her hands on the table in front of her, spreading her fingers. "Susie and I used to work together, Doug, back when we were both down at Galashiels. I got in touch when I got the Police Scotland job in Edinburgh, Susie was good enough to fill me in on the lie of the land with the press around here, though I had a pretty good idea of how things worked from the way the Buchan story played out. Nice work, by the way."

Doug nodded his head. He wasn't about to argue. "And let me guess, Susie also told you to watch for the cocky little shit from the *Trib* who likes to wind up Third Degree?"

"Guilty as charged," Susie said. "And that's DI Burns to you, Doug."

Rebecca leaned forward slightly. "Anyway, I thought it would be a good idea if we met. I want to get to know the usual suspects around here, and you seemed like an obvious place to start. So if you need anything, let me know. Hopefully, me knowing Susie means you won't treat me like a normal press officer?"

"You mean ignore you completely and go straight to my sources for anything interesting?" Doug replied, regretting how harsh his voice sounded. "No comment. But..." He trailed off, noticing another look between the two women. "I'll keep you in mind."

"Good enough," Rebecca nodded. Slid a card across the table

to him. Doug considered it for a moment, then slid it back to her.

"Thanks, but don't need it," he said, fishing out his phone and calling up a contact listing. It contained Rebecca's work numbers, along with her private email address, LinkedIn account and Twitter handles – professional and private. It also had her home phone number and address, both of which were classified. Fairly standard for anyone working for the police. And, just to show off a little, he had added her National Insurance number as well.

"How? How did you…?"

Doug smiled, glad to be back on more familiar territory. "Contacts," he said, getting back up. "Good to meet you, Ms Summers, I'll be in touch. Susie."

"See you later, Doug," she called as he left.

More as a courtesy to Susie than any real need, Doug called Rebecca on a few stories over the next few days. And as they spoke he found she had a dry sense of humour that he appreciated, and a refreshing scepticism about her bosses. If the line they were trying to spin was shit, she would tell him – off the record, of course.

"There's no point in selling you shit," she said. "You won't run it and won't respect me for trying in the first place, so why bother? If they want to ignore my advice and make themselves look like morons, so what?"

All of which had culminated in an almost accidental invitation for a drink two nights ago. Doug frowned. Two nights ago. Before…

…before…

He had called for an update on an ongoing sexual assault investigation, getting to the story later than he would have liked because he had spent the bulk of the day covering the desk for Walter. She had sounded tired and frustrated when she answered, so on impulse he had suggested a drink to wind down. They found themselves in an overly fashionable wine bar near the foot of Leith Walk and…

Doug yanked the wheel suddenly, tyres squealing as he slid

round the turn-off to the Sleat Peninsula that he had almost missed. Ahead, the road snaked away between the mountains, twisty and narrow, just as Doug liked.

He dropped down a gear and hit the accelerator. Fuck it, he could worry about this later. Right now, there was driving to be done.

20

The corporate affairs and media team for Police Scotland East Division worked out of Fettes down at Crewe Toll, in the building that had once been the headquarters of Lothian and Borders Police. The building hadn't changed much, apart from the rebranding and usual chess moves as old departments moved to make way for new ones that did more or less the same thing with half the staff and a name twice as long. At its core, it was still a cop shop, which meant that the press, and those who worked with them, were more tolerated than embraced.

Susie could sympathise.

She was sitting with Rebecca in a small office that was part of a refurbished suite for the corporate affairs and media team. It looked like the designer had been given a gift voucher for Ikea and strict instructions to buy the most utilitarian and offensive furniture they could find. Susie was perched on a polished plastic seat, nursing a glass of water, trying to flush the hangover, exhaustion from her stand-off with Burns, caffeine and aftertaste of the morgue out of her mouth. It wasn't working.

"You okay, Suze?" Rebecca asked, hands wrapped around a cup from which delicate wisps of steam snaked, carrying with them the scent of whatever herbal tea it was that Rebecca had fallen in love with this week. As ever, she looked camera-ready, hair and make-up perfect, her TV lighting-friendly neutral blue business suit hanging off her like it was tailored. Which it might have been: Rebecca loved her labels.

"Yeah," Susie said, lying. "Fine. Just been a long day, that's all."

Rebecca nodded. "I can imagine. First Charlie Montgomery, then the suspicious from the ERI. How did that go, anyway?"

Susie shrugged. She had been lucky, Williams had finished the post-mortem by the time she arrived. Unfortunately, he had insisted on showing her the body, the Y-incision that he had made to scoop out the internal organs freshly sewn up and puckered on the mottled greying flesh of the kid's chest.

"Fairly routine," she sighed. "Subject was Daniel Pearson, aged twenty-two. Lived across the water in Rosyth, Fife. Admitted with head injuries two days ago when he tried to get too close with his camera and ended up giving an oncoming tram a header on St Andrew Square. He had a fractured skull and bleeding on the brain."

She shuddered slightly, the image of the other set of stitches that scrawled across his head flashing across her mind. "He hadn't regained consciousness since, prognosis was fairly grim."

"So why the question mark? No chance it was natural causes?" Rebecca asked.

"The nurse who found him said the heart monitor had been disconnected," Susie replied. "Which, in the event of cardiac arrest, would have tripped an alarm at the nurses' station in the main ward. But that didn't happen. Plus, Williams found what he calls petechial haemorrhaging in the eyes."

She saw Rebecca's puzzled expression, cocked her head in apology. "Sorry, it's when the tiny blood vessels in the whites of the eyes rupture and bleed under stress. Classic sign of strangulation or suffocation. Add that to the fact the SOCOs found the kid's saliva on one of the pillows and bang, instant suspicious death. It's not conclusive, but…"

Rebecca nodded, scrawling notes on a pad in front of her. "I'll give the hospital press office a call, see if I can help. What's your next step?"

"The mother, Diane, has already been interviewed by the local office across in Fife, but I'll head over and talk to her myself.

Father apparently isn't on the scene, hasn't been for years."

Rebecca sighed heavily, shook her head. "What a bloody week," she said. "With Charlie, Greig and now this, what the hell is going on?"

"Wish I knew," Susie said. "But I'll be damned if I let Burns use this as an excuse to keep me away from the Greig case."

Rebecca looked at her for a moment, a smile playing across her lips. Nothing changed. They had met when she was working in the press office at Galashiels and Susie had been a PC. Rebecca had worked on the local paper, decided to make the leap to media relations when the previous press officer left on maternity leave and didn't come back.

They were both members of the force running club, taking advantage of working and living in the Borders to run up and down hills in an exercise of controlled masochism. But while Rebecca saw it as a pastime and a more entertaining way to keep fit than trips to the gym or workout DVDs, Susie was always focused on the finish line. She ran to win, and once she decided she was racing, nothing would stop her.

"Speaking of the Greig case," Susie said slowly, "you spoken to Doug yet?"

"Texted him a while ago, when I heard about your little chat with Burns. That okay?"

"Fine, saves me a job," Susie said, a half-beat too quickly for Rebecca.

"Look, Susie," she said. "I know you said there was nothing with you and him, and I believe you. I mean, I know you're friends, he said that much himself, but if this is too weird, if…"

Susie snorted a laugh that poked a stick into the headache still lurking in the corner of her mind. "Doug? No, Rebecca. Seriously, no. I'm not sure we're even friends. Truth is, I'm not sure what we are. The Buchan case did something, but romantic? No. Not at all. It's just…" She flailed for the words. "I'm worried about him, you know?"

Rebecca nodded sympathetically. But she was sure this was more than concern for a friend. The way Doug had looked at the hospital, cored out by shock and disbelief, the way he had sounded on the phone, his normally calm, measured voice stretched tight and thin and off-key by what had happened. She was worried, too. But why? She barely knew him. They were little more than acquaintances. And yet, the other night, when they had got past the professional suspicion and mutual reticence…

Susie's phone buzzed on the cheap Formica table, loud in the silence. She grabbed it and hit *Answer*, held it to her ear tight enough that Rebecca could see her knuckles turning white. And she realised in that moment that she was also worried about Susie.

"Drummond." She straightened in her seat. "Yes, sir. No, sir, I've not had the time to review anything yet, too busy getting up to speed with the ERI case. Why?"

She listened, nodded. Then her eyes grew wide, the pupils glittering with almost feverish intensity as she ran an unsteady hand over her face as the colour drained from it.

"Yes, sir. Understood." She glanced at her watch, a quick, convulsive twitch. "One hour. Yes, sir. Thank you."

Susie clicked off the phone and laid it on the table, then looked up at Rebecca, eyes full of questions.

"What?" she asked, torn between curiosity and concern. "Susie, what the hell…?"

"That was Burns," she said slowly, as though she was digesting the words as she spoke them. "Williams found out what was stuck in Charlie's mouth."

She shook her head, chewing her lip, gaze turning inward in the hunt for answers.

"And?" Rebecca prompted, her voice almost a shout. "What?"

"A bullet casing," Susie said, almost to herself. "Ballistics ran a cross-check due to the unusual nature and calibre of the bullet. You see, it was from a high-velocity rifle. The type snipers use."

Rebecca rocked back in her chair. "Wait. Snipers. But…"

Susie nodded. "Yes. The casing matched the bullets they dug out of Greig and the wall of his office. Whoever shot him also killed Charming Charlie." Susie grunted a laugh devoid of humour, dropped her head to her chin and closed her eyes, trying to screen out the screaming questions and think clearly.

"Looks like I'm working both cases, after all."

21

Harvey Robertson was a traditionalist when it came to his journalism. No sensationalism, no over-egging a story, no short cuts. No exaggeration. Which is why, Doug thought, he shouldn't have been surprised when he discovered that the "little B&B" wasn't so little after all.

He was parked in a small layby just down from the main gate, glancing between his sat-nav and the discreet, tasteful sign nestled amongst the foliage of a perfectly manicured hedge, verifying that he hadn't made a mistake somewhere.

Behind the sign, the hotel it advertised, Robertson's Retreat, sat like a king on his throne at the top of a gentle slope of lush green lawn that looked as if it could double for a bowling green.

Who knows, Doug thought, maybe it did. Wouldn't be the biggest surprise of the day so far.

It was a converted manor house, massive bay windows staring out over the Sound of Sleat and to the jagged horizon of the mainland in the distance. The granite facade was pristine and seemed to glitter in the afternoon light, while the window frames and guttering glowed with the sheen of fresh paint and fastidious care. In the small car park to the right of the building, Doug could see a cluster of high-end saloons, tourers, Range Rovers and what he was sure was a Ferrari neatly parked up in individual bays. At a rough guess, he thought there was more than a million-and-a-half worth of automobiles sitting in the lot.

The other side of the house was dominated by a huge glass sunroom in which Doug could see tables dotted around, making the most of the views. The dining room obviously, offering the spectacular views as a free appetiser or dessert.

With a bemused chuckle, Doug started the engine and bumped his car slowly over the cattle grid set into the tarmac at the gate and crept up the driveway, suddenly aware that his pride and joy – a Mazda RX-8 he'd bought after his previous car was lobotomised by a hired thug with a grudge and a penchant for knives – wasn't the king of the road he thought it was.

He parked up as far from the main body of cars as he could and killed the engine, suddenly nervous. What the hell was he doing here anyway? He should be back home, chasing the story, no matter what Walter said. Since when was a little thing like seeing someone murdered in front of his eyes going to keep him away from the front page? Was this a test? Had he failed Harvey by quitting the story and coming here?

He jumped out of the car, hoping movement would quieten his thoughts and the images of Greig's silent scream. Turned and stopped dead when he saw Harvey standing at the main entrance, lounging against one of the sandstone pillars that framed the door and watching Doug with a look of cool amusement in his eyes.

He was greyer than Doug remembered, the hair was thinner and the waist was thicker, but the face hadn't changed. Round cheeks and a thick jaw hidden behind a dark beard that was flecked through with white. "My Tipp-Ex stains," Harvey had called them. "Danny DeVito's grumpy Scottish uncle Harvey", the reporters had called him back at the *Tribune*. Looking at him now, Doug couldn't argue with the comparison, or his own private nickname for Harvey – "Scrooge McFuck".

Harvey leaned forward, held up a slender walking cane with what looked like a silver handle. "You going to stand there gawping all day, Douglas, or are you going to make an old man come to you?"

"Time it would take you, deadline would be passed and we'd all be in the shit," he replied, striding forward, hand outstretched.

Doug's slender hand disappeared into the warmth of Harvey's paw-like grip. Harvey shook vigorously, patting Doug on the shoulder as he did – classic Scottish male shorthand for a hug.

"Good to see you, Harvey," Doug said.

"Likewise, son," Harvey replied, his eyes darting over Doug's face, seeming to read every line and blemish. "How you holding up?"

Good question. "I'm fine, Harvey. Now. Not sure it's totally sunk in yet…"

The silent scream on Greig's face.

(Look at me.)

The feel of his blood, sticky, hot, between fingers.

Harvey gave him another tap on the shoulder, breaking him from his thoughts. "Aye, right," he grunted. "'Mon inside. Esther's desperate to see you. Then we can have a drink and catch up. Some things are better talked about when you're not totally sober."

• • •

Seeing Esther was the second surprise of the day and, after the discovery of the hotel, it was like a kick in the teeth.

Doug remembered her as a vital woman, with hair so black it shone, delicate features, porcelain skin and a figure that had almost made him call her Mrs Robinson the first time they met. Now she sat propped up in a bed, skin a sickly grey, hair bleached white with age and the stress of illness, her features subsiding as if the foundations beneath them were starting to decay.

Which, in a way, they were.

"Douglas," she said, her pale blue eyes dancing with the old amusement he remembered so well. "Good to see you. You well, son?"

Her hand scrabbled over the sheet for his. He almost flinched away from the suppurating cold when he took it.

"I'm fine, Esther, really," he said, giving her his best empathetic smile and realising it was Harvey who taught him it in the first place. *Make the interviewee trust you, Douglas.*

"More importantly, how are you? Harvey told me the doctors say you're doing better?"

She snorted, the sound of diamond being run across glass. "Aye, it shows, doesn't it? Good days and bad days, Douglas. The chemo was awful but they think they've got all of it now."

Harvey had filled Doug in on the way up the grand double staircase to the suite of private rooms he called home. Bowel cancer. They had found it a couple of months ago, after she'd started to have stomach pains and noticed blood in the toilet. Tests followed by an operation to remove the tumour, then chemotherapy to destroy anything they may have missed. Now it was a waiting game as she recovered before going back for a follow-up check. It was hanging over both of them, the unspoken axe waiting to fall.

"Well, if there's anything you need…"

She smiled, patted his hand. It was like being caressed by slivers of ice. "You're a good 'un Douglas, always were. I'm fine. What I need is for you to take this one to the bar and buy you a drink, give me five minutes' peace."

Doug gave a small salute. "Happy to oblige, Esther," he said, feeling his stomach lurch and his mouth go dry at the thought of more booze.

"You heard the lady, Harvey, buy me a drink. And make it a double."

22

The car bumped across the Forth Road Bridge, a steady thump-a-thump of percussion as the tyres' contact with the tarmac was interrupted by the steel expansion joints set into the bridge at regular intervals. On the right, the railway bridge dominated the skyline, a jutting sculpture in red steel like a giant's Meccano creation, trains crawling over its back as they ran from the Highlands all the way down, across the Forth estuary and on to Edinburgh and further south. In the beginning, trains had been an elegant form of travel; steam engines and dining cars and the adventure of the journey. These days they were overpriced, under-maintained steel boxes crammed with weary commuters forced out of Edinburgh by ever-rising house prices.

To the left, the skeleton of another bridge was emerging from beneath scaffolding and cranes – a new Road Bridge to help ease congestion and take the strain off the original. It didn't take a genius to figure out which of the three would still be considered a wonder of the industrial world another hundred years from now.

After the connection was made between Greig's and Charlie's murders, Burns had called a conference of all the CID officers working the cases and briefed them. Everything was now to be cross-checked, to see what and where the connection between the two men was. One killer, one motive, two deaths. Simple maths.

"And," Burns said, his voice more blunt and doom-laden than normal, "the Chief is now taking a personal interest in this case, so I do not want any fuck-ups. Clear? Do the job and do it right."

"Nae wonder the Chief's interested," DC Eddie King muttered under his breath. "Course he is. Guns involved now. Sexy."

Susie arched an eyebrow. She hadn't thought King capable of anything that came that close to insubordination. Or humour, for that matter.

Assignments were given out and the officers went back to their work. Including Susie, whose first job was to drag herself across to Fife and interview the mother of the dead kid from the ERI.

Burns cut her off on the way out of the CID suite, walking slightly in front of her and craning down to whisper in her ear, his breath heavy with the crappy peppermints he used to try and disguise the lingering fug of stale cigarette smoke.

"You heard what I said, Drummond, and I meant it. You're working the cases, both of them. But the Chief looking at this puts a whole different level of shit on the table, so I need to be seen to be playing by the rules. Which means keeping you out of the way for a while. Clear?"

His gaze was boring into her, unblinking, something halfway between fury and pleading in his eyes. The Chief must have given him a hell of a talking-to about this. And suddenly, Susie felt a wave of gratitude for Burns. He was a grumpy bastard and impossible to please, but here he was playing a high-stakes game with his bosses to make sure she got the chance to be a detective rather than an embarrassment better forgotten.

So she headed for Rosyth, which sat just across the bridge, on the shore of the Forth. She vaguely remembered something Doug had said about calls to rescue a ferry link from the port at Rosyth to Zeebrugge – he had mostly grumbled about being given the story when there were more important stories he could be covering – but other than that, the town was alien to her. It was her first visit. She wondered if it would be her last.

She followed the sat-nav, driving past a small row of shops and a petrol station, traditional buildings slowly petering out as she crossed the no man's land where old Rosyth gave way to the new-build housing estates that seemed to creep into every bit of empty land in the country.

Diane Pearson lived in a small, anonymous terraced house in an estate that looked identical to about three others Susie had driven past. The small front garden was neat, bordered with a riot of flowers and shrubs that meant nothing to Susie. Her dad would have been able to name every one of them, though. He was a keen gardener, a passion he had tried, without success, to pass on to Susie.

Another disappointment for him. A daughter when he wanted a son. A police officer when he wanted a lawyer. A gym bunny when he wanted a gardener.

She sighed. Old wounds.

She bumped the car up on to the pavement at the front of the house and parked up. Saw the blinds in the front window of Pearson's house twitch.

She had called ahead and made an appointment, so she was expected. Question was, what type of reception would she get? In Susie's experience, calling on the relatives of the recently deceased got three main reactions – shock, sorrow or fury. Susie was hoping for fury. Shock and sorrow had a numbing effect, made people forget things, made them near-impossible to talk to. But fury had to be expressed. And that meant talking. Maybe shouting. Maybe swearing. Susie didn't care what it was. At least if Diane Pearson was talking, she might say something useful.

The door swung open before Susie was halfway up the drive, Diane Pearson standing framed there. She was a tall, rangy woman, long blonde hair shot through with streaks of silver. The file Susie had read before leaving put her age at fifty-two, but she looked older. Deep wrinkles had been worn into her forehead like grooves, probably from the squinting she did through the thick glasses she wore, while the morning sun, which should have made her look better, gave her a sickly, almost translucent sheen. It made Susie think of her mother and the long years before her death, the endless trips back and forth to the hospital as the Parkinson's slowly corrupted her body, leaching away her strength and dignity, coring her out and leaving her a hollow, empty shell; a cruel parody of the vibrant woman Susie had known growing up. She died of pneumonia, lying in a hospital bed surrounded by machines and doctors, her skin sallow, a corpse being forced to live.

When she went, Susie was ashamed to admit that her overriding reaction had been not grief, but relief.

Diane offered a smile as Susie walked up the steps to the house, noticing the grab rail that had been fitted to the wall, there to help with Daniel. He had been born with what the file described as "severe medical and learning difficulties", specialists putting his mental age at around eight. It made Diane Pearson's appearance make sense to Susie. A single mum working a full-time job and looking after a child with the strength and impulses of a man and the control of an infant? Not a life she would choose.

"Detective Drummond?" Diane asked, holding out a thin hand. Susie shook it. It was surprisingly warm, the grip strong and assured, making a lie of Susie's first impressions of the woman. She should have known better – being the sole carer for Daniel would require all kinds of strength, mental and physical.

"Mrs Pearson? Yes. And, please, it's Susie. Thank you for seeing me, especially at the moment."

Diane took a deep breath. "Yes, ah… well. Please, come in, Susie."

• • •

The living room was small and cluttered, a thin patina of dust draped over the knick-knacks, ornaments and toys clustered around the bookshelves and mantelpiece, which framed an old-style gas fire. An old television sat in the corner of the room, the DVD player below stacked high with DVDs featuring *Batman,*

Spider-Man and a range of other multi-coloured heroes Susie couldn't name.

The walls were covered with pictures of Diane and Daniel, as though she was displaying a visual history of his life, from the first days in hospital to the man grinning at the camera, open smile showing a row of small, incredibly white teeth, the streets of Edinburgh behind him. He looked like his mother, Susie thought. Something in the shape of the face and the mouth. And the fine blonde hair that seemed to glow in the picture. It was, Susie knew, the way Diane Pearson's hair would have looked a decade ago. None of the pictures featured anyone who could have been Daniel's father.

Diane gestured towards a small couch jammed against the wall of the room, bracketed by coffee tables crammed with yet more ornaments.

"Please, Susie. Have a seat. Can I get you a drink? Tea? Coffee?"

"No, Mrs Pearson, thank you," Susie said, sitting down. The couch was hard and unforgiving. She made an obvious glance towards the door. "Are you on your own, Mrs Pearson? I thought a liaison officer from the local station was sent to sit with you?"

"Oh, you mean that PC, eh, Mathers?" Diane replied, easing herself into a chair to the right of the couch, facing the TV. "I sent her away. I wanted some time to myself."

Susie nodded. "I'm sorry to intrude, Mrs Pearson, I understand this is a difficult time for you. I just have a few questions, then I'll be on my way."

Diane nodded, wearily. "I've been a social worker and counsellor for more than thirty years, Susie, I know how this works. Procedure. Though I'm not sure how I can help. Danny was in an accident, a bad one. They took him to the hospital, operated. Then I got the call saying..." Her voice hitched in her throat. "Saying..."

Susie gave her best understanding look. She hated this part of the job, intruding on private grief, asking questions that meant the bereaved had to face up to horrible possibilities and thoughts at the worst moment of their life. Bad enough to lose a loved one. But to even acknowledge that it might have been deliberate, that someone had meant harm to the person who meant everything to them?

Why the hell had she wanted this career again?

"So, ah, Mrs Pearson, what did happen to Daniel?" She knew the answer, the hospital report told her that much, but she wanted to hear it in Pearson's own words.

Diane shifted in her seat, fiddled with her glasses. Her gaze came to rest on the dead TV screen, as though she were watching what had happened replay on it.

"As you no doubt know, Susie, Danny had some health issues. Learning difficulties due to autism. I work in Edinburgh, so made sure he was in day care when I was there. He loves going through on the trains every day, riding over the bridge. He counts the beams, you know, knows how many there are off by heart." She smiled. A mother's pride. Susie picked up on her using the present tense, felt a pang of regret when she realised Diane would become aware of it herself all too soon.

"Anyway, he was out on a day trip with the carers, in Edinburgh. Normally Danny hates the crowds, but he loves the trams – the idea of trains in the city seemed to light up his imagination." She pointed a finger to the ceiling. "You should see his room. Lego models of the city, with the trams running through it. According to Lee, Danny's carer, they were on St Andrew Square. It's the best place for Danny to see the trams as there's a stop there and the park is just opposite if the crowds become overbearing and he needs a break in an open space. Lee says he wanted to get a picture of a tram running down the hill onto Princes Street with his phone, so he gets out in front of the tram, leans in too far into the road and…" She glanced at Susie, face full of pleading. *Don't make me say this*, her eyes said.

Susie nodded. "And he leaned in too closely, lost his footing and his head was hit by the tram as he fell." She'd read the incident report. It was a cruel, freakish accident. He'd stumbled forward just at the wrong moment, hit the tram at precisely the wrong angle. A few months earlier, a tram had clipped a girl who was running across the road, messing around with her pals. She'd more or less bounced off the carriage, escaping with a bruised bum and a dented ego, while Danny had paid a much higher price.

Senseless.

"I got the call at work," Diane continued, voice growing colder. "He was taken to the ERI. Had bleeding on the brain, which meant they had to operate to ease the pressure. And then..."

Susie let the words hang in the air for a moment, feeling their weight fill up the room, making it stuffy, oppressive. She spoke in a near-whisper. It felt like she was shouting in a church.

"Mrs Pearson. Diane. Can you think of anyone who might have wanted to hurt Danny for any reason?"

Diane's head darted up, glasses flaring in the light. Her hands clamped down on the arms of the chair. And when she spoke, Susie finally knew what her reaction to the death of her son was.

Rage.

"Who the hell would want to hurt Danny?" she sneered, her pale skin blotching with hectic patches of colour. "He was a child. Innocent. His world revolved around me, his friends at the care centre and trains. Why would anyone want to do him harm?"

Susie held up her hand. "I'm sorry, Mrs Pearson, but I have to ask. You know how it is. Procedure." She made a point of glancing around the pictures on the walls again. Took a breath. No point in delaying.

"And Danny's father, ah..." She made a show of going through her notebook. "He's not around at all?"

Diane's mouth worked in a chewing motion, as though she were getting ready to spit out something rotten. "No. Hasn't been around for years. Stupid bastard got himself locked up just before Danny was born. Made no effort to stay in touch. Don't even know if he's out or not. If he is, we've not seen him, and that's fine with me."

Susie nodded. Made sense. A severely disabled kid and a convicted criminal for a father. No wonder she looked old.

Susie made a note to follow up on the conviction, not wanting to give Diane a distraction to rant at, and track down this Lee at the day centre. His contact details would be on the accident statement he gave to the hospital, but it would be worth talking to him. She took a moment to scan over what they had covered so far. She was aware of Diane's cold gaze on her, a challenge to ask more idiotic questions.

"Well, thank you for your time, Mrs Pearson. And, again, my condolences for your loss and intruding at this time. Danny looked like a lovely boy."

A twitch of a smile, like a crack racing along the surface of a melting glacier. "Thank you, Susie. He was."

Susie stood up, made a step for the living room door. "We're reviewing the CCTV from the hospital, talking to the nursing staff. I'll be in touch, okay?"

Diane looked at her, unanswering, just long enough for Susie to feel uncomfortable. "Fair enough," she said eventually. "I'm going back to work tomorrow, you can get me there."

Susie blinked, confused. "Work? But isn't that…? I mean…"

"What am I going to do here, detective?" Diane replied, her voice a forced casual tone. "Sit and stare at the walls? Better to stay busy. There's work to be done. Nothing else I can do for Danny now, is there?"

Susie glanced at the front door, glad to step into the fresh air. "Well, no, I… I suppose not. But if you need anything, the liaison officer is on hand and there are people we can put you in touch with…"

Diane smiled, this time almost genuine. "Detective. I'm a counsellor. I'm the one people call to talk to. I know what they'd say. Take time to grieve, work through your loss. Talk to people. Well,

I'll best work through this by going back to work, rather than rattling around here, with reminders of Danny on every wall."

Susie nodded, passed her a business card. "Okay, but here's my number if you need it."

Diane took the card and disappeared back into the house. Susie had a sudden image of her walking through the living room to the kitchen, tearing up the card before dumping it into the bin.

She headed for the car, trying to make sense of Diane Pearson and their conversation.

There's work to be done, she had said.

At least on that, they agreed.

23

Doug sat across from Harvey in a small snug in the hotel bar built around one of the bay windows that overlooked the front of the grounds and the Sound of Sleat beyond. The bar was boutique hotel casual; mood lighting, deep carpets, leather seats and bar stools. An array of exotic whiskies, local beers and wines arranged like ornaments on the glass display shelf behind the bar, glittering in the soft downlights trained on them. Overall the place oozed class, sophistication and, with the view of the seven-figure fore-court out front, affluence.

A long, long way from the *Tribune*.

Harvey set down a bottle of malt, which had too many conso-nants in its name for Doug to even try to pronounce, along with two glasses and a small jug of water. He slid into the seat across the table from Doug, pulled the stopper and poured two generous glasses. Doug swallowed, trying to get the bilious taste out of his mouth.

Harvey raised a glass, tipped it towards Doug. "Here's to old friends, Douglas, sorry it had to be like this. *Slainte.*" He downed it in a shot. Doug hesitated with his own glass, feeling the fumes of the whisky tickle his nose and prickle his eyes. Thought of Esther upstairs and the promise he made. Downed it.

Harvey rocked back and laughed. "Ever the poker player, Douglas," he said. "I wasn't sure you were going to manage that one, you went green as soon as I put the bottle down. Rough one last night?"

Doug smiled, pushing the glass back across the table. "Just a bad day, Harvey. Needed something to help me sleep."

Harvey grunted an acknowledgement, topped up his own glass. Tipped the bottle to Doug, who shook his head. "Hell of a thing," he said. "I saw the reports, obviously, but what actually happened, Doug?"

Doug took a shaky breath. Closed his eyes. Focused on the detail and building the story – the who, what, when, where and how, just as Harvey had taught him. There was another element, the crucial one that evaded him. The why. Why would someone execute Jonathan Greig. Any why so violently, so brutally?

Doug opened his eyes, took a deep breath and swallowed down the cold terror in the back of his throat. Slowly, he started talking, taking Harvey through everything that happened, from getting ready for conference to the first shot, the moment of stunned silence as the window cracked, Greig clawing for his throat as it was torn open, and then…

Look at me.

…then…

"Shit," Harvey whispered, his face tight, eyes unreadable. "I'm sorry, Doug, really. What a fucking mess. You heard anything about how the investigation is going?"

Doug shook his head. "Not a thing. Walter D-listed me from the story as soon as I was out of the hospital, ordered me to take a holiday. Makes sense. Can't have a witness investigating a murder before he gives evidence about it in court. Still, I…" He fidgeted with the glass, spun it in his hands. "Doesn't feel right, you know? Greig was a shit, but he deserved better than that. And there's something else, something…"

Three shots. Two hits. One fatality.

"What?" Harvey asked, glass paused halfway to his mouth, intense concentration on his face, as though he were trying to read the thought in Doug's eyes. "What is it, Douglas, you got something?"

Doug grunted in frustration. "No, not really. It's just there's something… niggling… about this, you know? And it's like I can't see it because I'm too close to it. Because I can't get the look in Greig's eyes out of my mind."

He moved for the bottle out of frustration. Harvey reached out, strong hand wrapping around his, eyes boring straight into Doug's.

"Not the answer, Douglas. Believe me. I almost fell into a bottle when we found out about Esther's cancer. And it worked, for a little while. Until I realised I wasn't sleeping at night but blacking out, that the hammering heartbeat and queasiness in the morning weren't the angina but the hangover. Until I realised whole conversations were being deleted and I couldn't remember things I'd been told five minutes ago." He smiled ruefully. "And then Esther confronted me at the back of the hotel. And the shit really hit the fan."

"Back of the hotel?" Doug asked, taking his hand off the bottle.

"Yeah. You see, we've got recycling bins here, local businesses get a rebate if they do their bit. Nothing big, but everything helps, especially with a place like this. But then Esther noticed that the glass bin was filling up a little too quickly, especially as we were in off-season and the tourists who love to buy a 'traditional Scotch whis-KAY for an evening dram' weren't around. It's a scary thing, Douglas, to see how much you've drunk laid out in front of you like that. So please, take a telling. Don't go down that road. You want to enjoy a drink with me, fine. But don't use it as an escape. Please."

Doug smiled, the relief from Harvey's initial call flooding back. Still the teacher. No matter what had happened, Harvey would help. He always did.

"So," Doug said, leaning back. "Esther, how is she? Really?"

Harvey's gaze twitched to the bottle then back to Doug, that same unreadable look in his eyes. He leaned forward, hunching his shoulders, staring at the table, tracing a pattern only he could see on the surface with the base of his glass.

"You saw her, Douglas. Good days and bad. She's in a lot of

pain, and the chemo took a hell of a lot out of her. But, like she said, there's the doctor to see next month and…"

"But the prognosis is hopeful?"

For the third time, Harvey gave Doug an unfathomable look. Contemplative. Speculative. Appraising. Doug suddenly realised it was the type of look he used during interviews when he was trying to push the subject that little bit further. Then the look was gone, replaced by something altogether more familiar. Determination.

"Look, Doug. The thing is…"

He was cut off by a jingle from Doug's phone, an app on it alerting him to breaking news from the BBC, relayed by the hotel WiFi. Reflexively, he pulled the phone from his pocket, opened the app – and froze as he read the headline.

"Jesus," he whispered, running a numb hand through his hair. "Fucking Jesus Christ."

Harvey craned forward, trying to see the screen. "Doug? What? What the hell is it?"

Doug looked up, eyes wide with incomprehension. The feeling from the Skye Bridge was back – the forced vertigo, the lurch of the stomach. This couldn't be happening. Couldn't be.

"Charming Charlie's been murdered," he whispered, hand clenching down on the cold glass, dimly aware of the dull sparks of pain shooting up his wrist from the effort.

"Who? Charlie Montgomery? Really? Fuck's sake…"

Doug nodded, felt his head kick into gear. Thoughts started to race in at once. Who to call first? Walter. Walter, to say he was on the way. Or Rebecca, to get the press line, something to give Walter when he called him. Or Susie, to get the line beyond the official bullshit? Or… or…

He was standing up before he knew it, Harvey rising with him, alarm clear on his face, but his voice calm. "Douglas, no. You can't. You've just seen one murder, the last thing you want is to get mixed up in another one. Besides, Edinburgh is a five-hour drive away, and you're in no shape, especially after a drink. Let someone else cover it, Doug. Please."

"But Harvey. I… It's my job, I don't…"

Harvey held up a quietening hand. "Okay," he said. "Why not make some calls, see what's happening? If you want to, leave tomorrow. But not now, Doug. You'd spend most of the day on the road, the editions would be out and done by the time you got back. And besides, Esther would be heartbroken."

Doug sat back down, deflated. It struck him that the old Harvey would have leapt at the story, done anything to be the first to have his byline all over it. A tickle of concern whispered through his mind as he realised how much Esther's illness had changed the man he thought of as the best reporter he had ever known. But still, it was wrong. He should be there. Covering the story, doing his job. Getting the headlines and the bylines. Not sitting in Skye drinking whisky with his old boss and hiding like a kid from the class bully. Harvey had taught him better than that.

"All right," he said. "But I'm going to make some calls, okay?"

"No problem," Harvey said, pouring another two whiskies. "But go into the garden below the sun-room to do it, phone reception is shit in here. And take this with you, you look like you need it."

Doug offered a weak smile. "What was it you said about falling into the bottle?"

"Doesn't apply when you're on a story, Douglas, you know that. Now go on, make some calls. You can tell me about it later. Who knows, maybe we can share a byline."

Doug snorted a laugh. "Aye, right," he said, heading for the exit, Harvey watching him go.

• • •

I follow him with the sight as he walks out of the room, a fluid right-to-left motion, the red dot in the centre of the sight never more than a few millimetres from his temple. I feel the old itch in my trigger finger, apply a little more pressure to make it ease. The temptation is great. Paint the bar with his blood and brains, watch the chaos and terror and confusion unfold like a breaking storm in my wake.

But no. No. Patience. Discipline. Control.

I recognise him from the Capital Tribune offices. He was with Greig when he died. But unlike the others, he didn't run screaming from my work. No, he took a moment to look at it, bathe in it. Accept it.

Admirable. And, potentially, useful.

It was a simple matter to ascertain who he was – his picture byline was all over the paper's website. Doug McGregor, the paper's crime reporter. Ironic. And apt.

Following him was almost too easy.

I track him out the door then swing back through the restaurant to the bar. Mr McGregor can wait. He may be the perfect witness to what comes next, to chronicle this monstrous crime, or he may be another monster to slay.

After all, he is guilty by association to Greig, at the very least.

My cheek presses into the stock of the rifle as I smile. The thought of confronting Mr McGregor with the choice will keep me warm through the night as I prepare a gift for him.

24

The sweat was pouring off Paul as the bus crawled along Princes Street, plastering his T-shirt to his back, like steel wool being pulled over raw skin, as the waves of cramp rolled across his body.

He was heading back into the city centre after paying a visit to Matty in Dalry. He lived in a small flat just around the corner from Tynecastle, the Hearts FC ground. Growing up, Matty had been a fan of the other team in the city, Hibs. The rivalry between the two was like a microcosm of the Old Firm rivalry that existed between Rangers and Celtic in Glasgow. After a particularly bad-tempered season a couple of years ago, the government had woken up to a slew of bad headlines about "Scotland's shame", panicked and rushed in legislation to outlaw sectarianism and "stamp out this blight on the national game". Arrests were made, fines handed out, cases quashed. None of which stopped Paul from hawking back and spitting every time he passed the road-end that led to Tynecastle.

Matty had been his usual languid self, the flat sickly sweet with the smell of old hash and fresh alcohol. He ushered Paul into the front room, the light bruised by the fight between the black-out curtains and the lamps dotted around, and dominated by a glass case that Paul hated – inside two huge snakes coiled lazily, tongues flicking the air for a taste of him. He dimly wondered if snakes could get stoned. If they did, they were in the right place, though the image of a snake getting the midnight munchies made him shudder.

As ever, Matty was wearing an unbuttoned blue shirt, trousers, no shoes. The cueball appearance of his head was only ruined by the shaving nicks from where he'd cut himself, probably because he was permanently stoned. McHeisenberg, Paul thought suddenly, biting down an urge to laugh.

Matty produced a wrap with a theatrical flourish, promised Paul it was "the best shit in the city, guaranteed" and would put him "on another planet".

With the hunger snarling in his veins, Paul hadn't quibbled about the price, handing over most of what he'd earned the night before, and left. He took the wrap in the tenement stairwell, huddled in the shadows beside the door to the communal garden that no-one ever used.

Now here he was, coming back into town, fresh from his all-too-brief trip to Planet Matty. From the burning in his nose and the jangling in his teeth, it was obvious Matty had cut the wrap with something, crushed ibuprofen most likely.

Paul ground his head against the cool of the bus window, squeezed his eyes shut. His options were limited. He'd used up most of his cash, and the last thing he wanted was another night tricking up at Calton Hill. If Carol ever found out about that…

His phone rang in his pocket, startling him out of his reverie and making him slam his head into the window with a dull thump. Cursing, he fumbled for the phone, fingers feeling clumsy and numb. Felt a stab of hope that cut through the pain when he saw the caller ID.

"Frankie? Frankie, that you?"

"Who the fuck else would it be?" the voice on the line hissed. "Where are you?"

Paul glanced up. "In town. Just passing HMV on Princes Street. Why?"

"You sound strung out, Paul. Have you been taking Matty Simpson's poison again?"

"Yeah," Paul mumbled, hot shame pouring into his cheeks like boiling water. "But Frankie, I couldn't reach you, and I needed…"

"Stop snivelling, Paul," Frankie said, the voice cold and harsh. Paul folded himself tighter into his seat, felt his bladder loosen. Frankie's rages – the quiet control of them, the lack of any emotion but hatred and fury and resolve – terrified him. "I've spoken to Stevie Leith, you know, on Leith Walk? He's going to take care of you until I get there. You'll find his stuff much better than that shite Matty Simpson punts around. And I'm sure the surroundings will suit you better."

Paul felt a rush of gratitude and tears began to roll down his cheeks. He didn't care. Frankie would look after him. Stevie would look after him. No more tricking. No more lying to Carol. Just the sweet relief of the hit and the joy and...

The words tumbled out of his mouth, as fast and desperate as his tears. "Thank you, Frankie, thank you. I'll do what you ask, I'll be good, I'll..."

Frankie's voice was cold and final, a steel gate being slammed shut. "Fine. Fine. And Paul, if you're contacted, you know what to say, don't you?"

He sniffed back tears, wiped at his eyes with a dirty sleeve. Another wave of cramp twisted through him, nothing to do with the withdrawal or the poisonous hunger.

"Yes, Frankie," he whispered into the phone, glancing around the bus. "I know exactly what to say. I won't let you down."

"You better not, Paul. You better not. Stevie. One hour. Don't keep him waiting."

And then the phone clicked and Frankie was gone. Paul looked out at the pedestrians on Princes Street, envying them their ignorance as they bustled around the streets, heading for the shops or work or home.

He wished he had that choice.

25

Rebecca was prepping her notes for the afternoon press conference when her phone went. She reached for it without taking her eyes off the screen, annoyed at the interruption. She glanced up at the clock. Twenty minutes. This better not be another agency call asking for advance sight of the release and one-on-ones with Burns, the Area Commander or the Chief.

"Press office, Summers."

"Rebecca? Rebecca, it's me."

She straightened in her chair, a cold prickle running down her back.

Calm, Rebecca. Calm.

"Doug? How's Skye?" Tone light, casual. Good.

"Great, you should have taken me up on my offer," he said, his voice hesitant but, she was glad to hear, sounding more like himself. The stress she had heard when he called this morning, like the creaking of a guitar string being over-tightened, was gone, replaced by something perhaps even more worrying.

Excitement.

"Maybe next time," she said, her voice sounding harsh in her ears. "Anyway, why the call? Wasn't just to say hello, was it?"

He gave that laugh that only he thought was shy. "Ah, no. 'Fraid not, Rebecca. Look, I heard about Montgomery, wondered if there was anything you could tell me. Don't think I'm going to make the press conference."

She swallowed back the anger, resisted the urge to snap the pen she was holding. Just. "Don't worry, it's covered. I got a call from Angus about twenty minutes ago, he's covering it for the *Trib* with Robbie."

"What, the Dynamic Duo? You'd be lucky if they could write a once-upon-a-time story, let alone this. Come on, Rebecca, please. If there's something, anything…"

"Why, Doug?" she snapped, surprised by the sudden anger. "Why ask me? You're not working at the moment, Walt's orders, Angus told me. So who are you writing this for? And why call me? It's not like we can go out for a cosy drink and chat it over afterwards, is it?"

Silence on the other end of the phone. For a moment she thought he had hung up, wasn't sure whether she felt disappointment or relief. Then his voice, slow, hesitant. She could see him running his hand through his hair, spiking it up in that way he did.

"Look, Rebecca. I'm sorry about this. Really, I am. Sorry about the other night, sorry if things got out of hand and I crossed a line. But it's not like it's been a normal week for me, is it? I'm a reporter, I want to report. I…" He coughed, frustration as he fumbled for the words. "I *need* to. If you can't, or won't help, I understand, I'll check the wires and my other contacts and do it that way. But if there's anything you can do, please…"

Rebecca chewed her lip, torn. She hated this. He hadn't crossed any line she didn't want him to, so why did she feel he had? Why was she at once hurt and elated when he called, why the flash of anger when the call turned out to be all about the work. It had only been one drink, one night, but still…

Other contacts.

She sighed. "All right. But this is strictly on embargo until the press conference is over, okay Doug? I'll send you the release and the copy of the statements by Burns and the AC. But that's it, okay?"

"Okay," Doug said. He sounded like a kid being given a puppy. "That's great, thanks Rebecca. And listen, I… I really am sorry about all this. Guess it was a bad week to go for a drink."

"You can buy me another one to make up for it," she said, instantly regretting it.

"It's a date," he replied, a little too quickly.

Fuck it, she thought, go for broke. He owed her. "Look, Doug. I know this is a tough time, and I really hope that seeing your old boss is what you need. But I don't want to be messed around. Happened too many times before. If that's that, fine, but don't string me along, okay?"

"I wasn't," he said. "Really, Rebecca. It's just, I…"

Her mobile pinged, no doubt another reporter. Funny how she was everyone's best friend when there was a big story breaking.

"Doug, I have to go. I'll send you that stuff across, let you know how the presser goes." She closed her eyes. Took a breath. Jumped. Added: "For all the good it'll do you."

"Oh, I'll talk Walter round," Doug said, the old practised charm in his voice. "Angus can butcher the presser, I'll do the follow-up when I get back tomorrow."

"It's not Walter you have to worry about Doug, it's *my* boss. And the courts, if and when this goes to a trial. Can't have a witness for the prosecution being cited as a reporter in the pre-trial media storm."

"What? Burns? Look, I know Third Degree doesn't like me, but he can't stop me on this one…" His voice trailed off as the penny dropped. Must have still been in shock. It took him longer than Rebecca would have supposed.

"Wait, Rebecca. Trial? *A* trial? You're treating these two murders as one case?"

"I never said anything, Doug. Just be careful about the questions you ask, okay? And call me when you get back tomorrow, I think we should talk."

She cut the line before he could reply, stared blankly at the screen. Hit a few keys and sent him the press release and statements before she could change her mind then rocked back in her chair and thought about two nights ago, when the wine had flowed and the talk had been a world away from murder and press conferences and work. Wondered if that story was over, found herself not wanting to know the answer.

26

After leaving Diane Pearson, Susie headed for the police station in Rosyth, which she found – after much swearing at the sat-nav and three passes of a hotel called the Gothenburg, a bookies and a pool hall – was a small, single-storey structure trying and failing to blend into its residential surroundings on Crossroads Place.

It was probably a waste of time, there was nothing in what Pearson had said to indicate she was lying, but Susie hated loose ends. And an ex who had prison time in his past seemed like a very big loose end. Better to check.

She showed her warrant card to the desk sergeant – a huge, florid-faced man with sideburns he'd brought from the Seventies and a voice too soft for his massive frame – and asked for PC Mathers.

"She's no' in, hen... ah, Detective Sergeant," the Man Mountain replied, his face, remarkably, going a shade redder. "She's at a school visit in the toon. You want the address?"

Susie shook her head. The last thing she needed today was a visit to a high school. "Nah, but can you give her a message? Ask her to pull the family details on Diane Pearson and send them to me. And ask her to call me when she gets back." Susie pushed her card under the glass barrier of the reception desk.

The sergeant picked it up in a hand that looked like a baseball glove, turned it delicately in his fingers as though it was some rare and precious jewel.

"No problem, guv," he said. "Will do."

Susie nodded and headed for the car. Sat in, stuck the key in the ignition and paused. What now? Burns said he wanted her "out of the way", meaning she would be about as welcome as a priest at a soft-play centre back at the CID suite. But she was damned if she was going to let that stop her doing her job. He had said she was on the cases, all of them. Fine. She made a quick mental calculation, decided Burns would be out of the CID suite, prepping for the press conference with Rebecca. Called DC King's number from memory.

As she expected, King wasn't there, but a voice identifying herself as PC Chambers answered the line.

"Hi, Anna? Anna, it's Susie. Listen, need a favour. I'm on my way to an interview and I need the Montgomery and Greig case files. Yes, yes, I know, I shouldn't ask for copies, but Burns will have my ass if I'm not prepped for this witness. Could you get a set down to the front desk for me, ready for pick up in, say, forty-five minutes? Great, thanks."

She cut the line, smiled. Perfect. As long as Chambers didn't run screaming to King or Burns, she could scoop up the files, read them at home.

She drove out of the car park, hit the bypass and hammered her foot to the floor. Forty-five minutes to get back was cutting it fine, and she didn't want to keep Chambers waiting.

The phone chirped on the passenger seat just as she was crossing the bridge. She flipped it over, saw the caller ID – *Doug-mobile*. She glanced at the dashboard clock, smiled. 2.51pm. The press conference was due to start at three. So obviously he'd heard about Charlie and was calling for the lowdown. But, she thought, he was leaving it kind of late, especially if he wanted some kind of line he could spin to his newsdesk.

Unless, of course, she wasn't the first person he had called.

Susie turned her attention back to the road, concentrated on driving that bit faster. It was another unanswered question. And right now she had enough of those to deal with – the last thing she needed was another.

27

"Come on, Walter, I'm only asking for a look at Charlie's obit, no' a peek at the secret archive of Margaret Thatcher's dildos. Where's the harm?"

Doug was pacing back and forth on the driveway at the front of the hotel, feet scrunching on the gravel, phone pinned to his ear, mind spinning. If what Rebecca had hinted was right, then there was some kind of link between Greig's and Charlie's deaths. Question was, what? A journalist and a lawyer. Not the most popular of professions, but hardly a prime target for would-be serial killers. Especially not serial killers proficient with sniper rifles. So, what? There must be something to link the two of them, something that made them a target.

What?

His first instinct had been to phone Susie and see what, if anything, she knew. No answer, which didn't surprise him as much as the relief he felt when the phone clicked over to her voicemail.

He glanced back at the hotel, saw Harvey calmly watching him, lifting his glass to toast him through the window. Doug nodded back. Facts, he needed facts. And the *Tribune* seemed a good place to start.

At the other end of the line, Walter grunted. "Look, Doug, ah told you. Take some time off, get away. Last thing you need is to be working a story."

"No, what you said was the last thing I needed was to be working *Jonathan's* story. And I'm not…" *As far as you know,* Doug thought. "So come on, Walter. I'll be back tomorrow, do the follow-ups then. So what's the harm in me looking at what you've got, getting a bit of background on the guy?"

Walter gave a resigned sigh. "Aye, a'right. I'll ping you Warren's obit up when he's finished it. But nae shit Doug, okay? I've got coppers crawling all over this place, camera crews begging for interviews. Last thing I need is you blundering in and stirring up the shit with the cops over this one, okay?"

"Who? Me? Walter, as if I would."

"Aye, right. See you tomorrow." And the line went dead.

Doug was heading back to the hotel, casting longing glances at the parked-up cars, when his phone beeped, telling him he had mail. He flicked open the email app, smiled.

Here you go, the obit. No shit, Doug, or the next masterwork obit will be about the poor crime reporter that didn't listen to his boss. Drive safe. See you tomorrow. W.

Same old Walter. A soft, warm core of molten rage hidden underneath that rough exterior.

He skimmed through the copy, nodding approvingly. It was a good piece, although it was obvious Warren had been forced to pad a lot to hit the wordcount. Lots of detail, not a lot of character.

Charles Edward Montgomery, born 1960 in Bonnybridge, UFO capital of Scotland, to Edward and Helen Montgomery. One younger brother, Angus. His father was the local bobby, his mother a teacher. Leaving school, he headed for Dundee University to study law. Showed a passing interest in student politics, with references to him being a part of the student Lib Dems during his time there. He graduated in 1981, worked at a couple of small firms in Stirling before being headhunted by Wallace and Dean, one of the bigger legal firms in Edinburgh at the time. He handled a few high-profile cases, soon became known as the defence lawyer no-one wanted to need. Made a name for himself by campaigning against the trams when they were proposed, going so far as to offer free legal advice to any shop owners on Leith Walk who were affected by the work, which was, ultimately, abandoned. *Trams go off the tracks as Leith link derailed*, was one of the better headlines at the time.

There was scant information about his personal life in the obit, which only stated that he was survived by his brother. No wife, kids, girlfriend or boyfriend named, and some glowing quotes about his "dedication and professionalism" from Matthew Wallace, the co-founder of Wallace and Dean.

Doug swore under his breath. Useless. He opened up the internet app, started Googling Charlie's name, but the pages came back cluttered with news reports of his death and pictures of the News Steps, where he died.

News Steps...

Doug stopped dead. Stood up straight. Strained his ears as though listening for a whisper. Something hot and prickly and ancient crawled across the back of his neck and whispered in his ear and he whirled round, feeling the pressure of someone's gaze on him. Looked up at the hill to the back of the hotel, nothing there but the trees swaying gently in the wind.

He shook his head. Still jumping at shadows. No surprise really given...

Look at me.

...what he had seen.

He fumbled to regain his train of thought. Something about the News Steps where Charlie had died.

News Steps...

No, not News Steps. News.

"You fucking moron," he whispered to himself. Why had he wasted time phoning Walter? Charlie Montgomery was a lawyer in Edinburgh when the reporter who taught Doug the trade had been working the beat.

The reporter now sitting quietly drinking whisky in the bar of his hotel.

Doug hurried inside, eager to ask Harvey a few questions, and wondering how, after all these years, he was going to interview him.

28

PC Chambers had been as good as her word, getting the copies of the Greig and Montgomery files to the front door of the station without bumping into Burns or King. They were waiting for Susie when she arrived, double-parking and hopping out of the car. She swapped the desk sergeant's world-weary scowl for a grateful smile as she took the files, dropped them on the back seat and then headed for her flat on Broughton Road. From the station, it would only have been a twenty-minute walk, but she wanted the car with her, just in case Burns got it into his head to send her on another wild goose chase.

She ran up the stairs to the flat two at a time, partly because she was eager to get reading, partly because she knew it was likely to be about the only exercise she would get for the day. With all the background reading she had to do on the Greig and Montgomery cases, and Diane Pearson's notes to write up, the gym was off the agenda.

She was breathing heavily when she got to the front door of the flat, a small tremor in her hand from the exertion as she unlocked the door. Dropping her bag and kicking off her shoes, Susie dumped the files in the living room and headed for the kitchen. She boiled the kettle and made a pot of tea, then carried it back to the living room and dumped the lot on the coffee table. Paused for a moment when she saw the discarded Chinese menu from last night, briefly thought about calling Doug back. She got as far as fishing her phone out of her pocket and starting to dial before she tossed the phone across to the couch he had sat on.

Doug could wait. If he was desperate, he would get what he needed from Rebecca, just like every other reporter. In the meantime, she had work to do.

She poured a mug of strong tea – paint stripper, Doug called it – then curled up on the couch and pulled the sheaf of files to her. She decided to take them chronologically, starting with Greig before moving on to Charlie. Aside from being the rational approach, it also, she thought, gave her a little time to prepare for the sight of that knife sticking out of Charlie's temple again.

She saw her mistake as soon as she flipped open the file. The pictures were a nightmare of violence, frozen moments of terror and blood screaming silently from the glossy paper. She had met Greig a couple of times, most notably when he had hauled Doug over the coals in front of her for keeping vital information from the police during the Buchan story. Her overall impression was of a man who valued control, respect, dignity.

There was no dignity in the images in front of her now. Greig was lying on the floor, his head twisted at a horribly improbable angle, eyes forced wide by agony and terror and disbelief, flecks of blood covering his pale cheeks like freckles. A long, deep gash ran across his forehead like a bloody zipper, and Susie shuddered as an image of Danny Pearson and the stitches running across his head flashed into her mind.

She flicked back and forth through the reports, finding the key details. No real surprise. Cause of death was massive blood loss coupled with catastrophic damage to internal organs. The first shot had clipped his carotid artery in the neck as it tore out part of his windpipe, the second had pierced his heart before depositing what was left of it and the surrounding organs onto the desk in front of him. According to Williams' report, he would have been dead before he cracked his skull open on the desk.

She rifled through the pages, coming to the report on the sniper's nest. Pulled the pictures out, flicked between them and the reports from ballistics and the SOCOs.

She was looking at a small patch of flattened grass nestled in between two jutting outcrops of rock, only about ten feet across by eight feet long. Another establishing shot of Arthur's Seat – the extinct volcano that loomed over the Edinburgh skyline like the grass-covered back of a sleeping giant – showed the area highlighted. It was on a slope about a third of the way up Samson's Ribs, the gravel walkway that led up and around the main body of Arthur's Seat. It was a steep path, with sheer rocks on the left and a grass bank leading back down to Holyrood Park on the other. At the time of the killing, and with the weather, it would have been exceptionally quiet, giving the killer all the time they needed to take the shots.

And what shots they were. Whoever the killer was, they were extraordinarily skilled, both reports agreed on that. More than a thousand yards out, in a cross-wind, and he had hit the target not once, but twice, in vital areas of the body. A precision job. Obviously a professional, and Susie was glad to read that "cross-checks with local armed military units were ongoing". She didn't think for a minute that a soldier had casually walked off Redford Barracks in Corstorphine with a smile on his face and a sniper rifle over his shoulder, but at least the bases were being covered.

Twice, Susie thought. *A professional. Two hits. Three shots. What...?*

She flipped back to the SOCO reports, cross-checked them with Doug's own witness statement. Doug talked about three shots, ballistics confirmed three bullets recovered. The most likely theory was that the first was a calibration shot, to ascertain wind direction and pull, and take out the large window that might have been distorting the sights. Yet there was something about it, something Susie couldn't quite see, like a 3D image that had yet to jump out of the random pattern on the page.

Three shots...

She shook her head. Dismissed it. Went back to reading the files and, in particular, the forensics on the bullet. Analysis had matched it to the casing that was found in Charlie Montgomery's mouth. While the damage to the head of the bullet dug out of Greig was too severe to ascertain whether it was the actual casing, ballistics could confirm it was the same calibre and make – a .308-calibre bullet, specifically designed for sniper rifles. There was a stock picture of an unused bullet, along with images of compatible rifles. They were long, deceptively slender items, almost too delicate to be lethal. But all you had to do was flick back to the pictures of Greig to see the truth behind the illusion.

They were instruments of violence and death, perfected and honed for one purpose alone.

Susie took a gulp of tea, forced back the memory of the last gun she had seen, the muzzle jammed into her face, a psychopath with the face of a monster leering at her down the barrel. Charlie Morris. It felt like a lifetime ago.

It felt like yesterday.

She flicked forward, to the background files on Greig, started reading. There was nothing to indicate an obvious motive. Initial searches showed he had been divorced ten years, with the wife now living in Liverpool. Local officers had been sent to talk to her and ascertain her movements at the time of the killing, but Susie found it doubtful that an assistant head teacher at a city comprehensive would have the motive, or skill, to assassinate her ex-husband.

Of course, this left the possibility of a contract hit, someone paid to do the job, but it didn't feel like that to Susie. This was too violent. Too public, too personal. There was something…

intimate

…visceral about the killing. In his own office, in front of his staff, just at the point of the day when he was most in charge? No, there was something else.

On the couch opposite, Susie's phone began to ring, startling her from her thoughts. She unfolded herself from the couch, wincing at the pins and needles in her legs, and reached across for the phone, ready to hit the *Call end* button if it was Doug again.

But the caller ID showed it was a Fife number, she recognised it from looking up the details of the Rosyth station. She hit *Answer*.

"Hello, DS Drummond."

"DS Drummond?" a woman's voice, hesitant. "This is PC Carrie Mathers, Rosyth? You, ah, you asked me to dig out the Pearson file for you?"

"Ah, yes, Carrie. Thanks for getting back to me. You find anything?"

"Yes, ah, yes I did, ma'am. I'm sending it over to you now."

"Much appreciated. Anything interesting?"

"Seems fairly run-of-the-mill, ma'am," Carrie replied. "Gavin Franklin Pearson, born 1968. Sentenced to twenty years in 1993 for the murder of a student in a club in Edinburgh. Seems he was working on the door, an altercation kicked off and this student..." – a rifling of papers down the line – "ah, Martin Everett, came at Pearson with a broken bottle, ended up with it in his neck, bled to death on the dance floor."

Susie paused for a moment. Odd. "And it was a straight murder conviction? No culpable homicide plea?"

"No, ma'am," Mathers replied. "If there was, I expect it was thrown out before the trial anyway."

"Oh, why would that be?"

"Well," Mathers said, voice dropping as though sharing a secret. "You know how it is when ex-soldiers are tried for murder. They put in the culpable homicide plea and the prosecution throws it out. After all, they're trained to fight, trained to kill, aren't they? Prosecutors go for the throat, say they should know better."

Susie felt her legs buckle, as though someone had cut the tendons. The words screamed into her mind as though they were aflame.

Trained killer.

Ex-soldier type.

Should know better.

"Ma'am? DS Drummond, you still there?"

"Oh yes," Susie whispered.

"You okay, ma'am? Went a bit quiet there for a minute."

Susie closed her eyes, forced herself to breathe deeply, focus. "I'm fine, thank you, Carrie. Good work on digging the file up."

Susie hung up and tried to slow down her racing mind. Gavin Pearson suddenly seemed to be much more than just a loose end. It was clear to Susie she'd have to speak with Diane again – she was definitely going to want a word with her about her ex.

29

Night fell gradually on Skye, the fading light matching the mood of the evening as guests returned from day excursions, shopping or sightseeing for dinner and an evening of relaxation.

Doug sat in the dining room of the hotel, peering into the blackness. He had never seen anything like it. In the city, the nights were always stained orange from the streetlamps or stabbed white by headlights from passing cars and buses. Here, there was nothing. Even the sound seemed smothered, drowned out by the enshrouding dark. When he had stepped outside earlier as Harvey flitted between tables, greeting guests and checking they were happy, the silence had made his ears buzz, threatening to give him a headache as he strained to hear anything other than the polite undercurrent of noise that drifted from the hotel behind him.

He got back to the table just as Harvey was completing his touring circuit. Esther had joined them for dinner earlier, hardly eating anything, arranging the meal into tasteful patterns on her plate and distracting Harvey with a well-timed laugh or an anecdote about their time in Edinburgh. She excused herself after the main course, saying it was "time to give you boys some time to catch up", walking to the door just a little too quickly to be casual. Doug watched her go. She only reached out for the wall as support when she thought she was out of sight.

They sat across from each other now, table cleared and coffee served in a flurry of waiting staff so well drilled they could have been military. Doug was keen to get back to his "interview" with Harvey – their earlier conversation had been interrupted when Harvey made for the kitchens to prep for the dinner rush. Not that there was much to tell, from what he had said. He'd run into Montgomery a few times on the court beat. Covered stories where he'd got the defendant a reduced sentence or pleaded out to something minor on a technicality. Had written up the story when Montgomery tried and failed to get selected for a seat at the Scottish Parliament. And that was that. Scant information.

"Sorry, Doug," Harvey had said before excusing himself. "I can go through my cuts if you want, see if there's anything else, but he honestly didn't make that much of an impression. He was just another lawyer to cover."

Doug mulled over Harvey's words, took a sip of coffee. Strong, hot and very, very black. Like everything else in this place, it was tasteful, discreet and expensive. He remembered an old line Harvey had told him – *There are no new stories, Douglas, only new angles* – and smiled. Decided to take a new angle.

"So, what about Greig? What was it like to work with him at the *Trib*?"

Harvey leaned back in his chair, toying with his pipe. Doug could tell he was itching to light it up. The reek from his jacket and the yellowing stain on his thumb and index finger from tamping the tobacco down told him he did so every time he was out of the main house.

"Not much to tell, Douglas," Harvey said. "As you know, we were reporters together at the *Tribune* back in the day. He started in, oh, '81, I think, I started in '82 after working freelance. I'd been happy enough, but Esther wanted the stability of a steady income and a staff job. Suppose she was right. Eight years of putting up with me working when I liked, wondering how much I'd make in a month – it was long enough for her to have to worry." He paused for a moment, a wistful look flitting over his face. "Anyway, we were both general reporters back then. I moved into crime, he moved onto the council beat, then tried his hand at the foreign desk and features."

Doug nodded. That much he knew. He'd first encountered

Greig when he was doing his work experience. He had been on the desk then, doing the job Doug had been doing only a day ago. Rounding up stories, assigning them to reporters, checking the facts and figures. Going into conference, telling the editor what the stories of the day were…

Look at me.

He swallowed down a mouthful of coffee. Grimaced. "So how come he ended up in the editor's chair and you ended up here? I remember Greig being on the desk when I first started, I was shit-scared of him. Those fucking suits and that patronising manner always made you felt as if you were a half step behind him. You would have been a better editor. What happened?"

Harvey leaned forward, poured himself some of the coffee from the cafetière. Shrugged. "He wanted it, simple as that. I only ever wanted to be a reporter, get the stories. But Jonathan, well, Jonathan was a career journalist, always wanted to get to the editor's office, no matter what."

"You think that…?"

Harvey laughed a little too loudly, the sound a shrill note of discord in the hushed, civilised quiet of the dining room. "What, that someone blew him away because of something he did climbing the greasy pole to the editor's chair? Douglas, I thought I taught you better than that. This was the *Capital Tribune*, not Watergate, for God's sake."

Doug nodded an apology. "Sorry, Harvey. It's just… just…" He paused, flailing for the words. "There has to be a reason for this. You don't shoot someone…

His eyes wide and glittering with fear, blood and internal organs dripping from the conference table in gelatinous globs.

"…without a reason. Greig must have done something to someone to explain this. Was there a story he worked on that you remember, a court case, something that might have…?"

Harvey downed his coffee, nodded to a waiter. Went back to staring at his pipe as if it was a crystal ball.

"Douglas, I'm sorry, I just don't know. I worked with the man, he moved up, I stayed reporting. When it was time for me to go, he signed off on the redundancy deal that helped Esther and I get this place. If there's more I could tell you, about Greig or Charlie, I would. But I can't. I'm sorry, Douglas, I truly am. I know seeing him killed like that would have been a hell of a thing, but I don't have the answers you need."

Harvey smiled, and, for the first time, he looked old to Doug. When he spoke, his voice was small. "Maybe I'm not a reliable source, after all."

Doug leaned back as the waiter produced two glasses of something amber and pungent. "Look, I'm sorry, Harvey, really. You've got enough on your plate, what with this place and Esther. The last thing you need is me here, going off the rails. Maybe I should head back tonight, after all…"

Harvey looked up at him, that old, unfathomable gaze in his eyes. His voice was casual. His eyes were stone. "Don't you dare, Douglas. I invited you here, remember? And Esther will want to see you in the morning, spoil you with breakfast. You know what she's like. And it's not as if…" He trailed off, voice cracking, sorrow bleeding in like oil into a clear spring pond. The sound made Doug's stomach lurch.

"Harv? Harvey. Esther. How bad is she? Really?"

Harvey looked up, his eyes red-rimmed and bloodshot. He glanced around the dining room quickly. Drew himself up, bolted a smile that didn't hit his eyes onto his face. "She's fine, Douglas, really. Ignore an old man. It's just the news about Greig, seeing you again. It's all been a bit much."

He pushed away from the table, arranged his cane and stood up. Raised his voice just enough so the room would hear. "Now, excuse me, I need to check on my guests, make sure everyone's having a little too much to drink and ordering desserts they can't justify. Enjoy the drink, Douglas, and sleep well. We've got you in suite four, you should like it."

"Harvey, I..."

Harvey took a half step, put his hand on Doug's shoulder. The weight surprised him. He dropped his voice. "Don't worry about it, Douglas, just remember what I told you about the drink, okay?" With that, he reached over, picked up his glass and clinked it off Doug's. Crystal, definitely.

"To Esther," he whispered in Doug's ear before tossing the drink back in one. "I'll see you later, Douglas."

He moved off, the cane a forgotten affectation in his hand, before Doug could reply. Doug watched him closely. Harvey Robertson. The best journalist he had ever seen. The man who had shown him it was important work, that it wasn't just a headline or an exclusive but a responsibility. To find the story. Hold those in power to account. To report in the public interest. And now, here he was, entertaining millionaires and affluent tourists, the very people he used to love putting the awkward questions to, in a hotel that wouldn't look out of place in the newspaper luxury living sections he once sneered at. Harvey Robertson, playing a part to the world as his wife lay upstairs, counting the hours until her death sentence or her release.

Doug reached for his glass. Stared at it. Thought about Susie and Rebecca. About Greig and Charlie Montgomery. Was what Rebecca had hinted true? Could there be a link between the deaths? If so, what the hell was it? And why the hell was he sitting here when the story was five hours away?

He flicked the glass, listened to the musical tinkle it made. Thought of the blunt, harsh crack as the window of Greig's office shattered, the bullet hammering into the wall beside him. Felt his heart race as the moment flooded back to him, the terror, the confusion, the horror.

Three bullets. Two hits. One death.

One death...

The incomprehension in Greig's eyes. The violent, spasmodic jerk as the bullet drove through his chest.

Doug tossed the shot back before he knew what he was doing, the burning clawing up his throat. He headed for the bar, telling himself the stinging in his eyes was only from the fumes. It wasn't tears for Esther. Or Greig. Or himself.

Not at all.

• • •

I'm already in position by the time he steals out of the side door that leads from the kitchen to the bin store at the back of the hotel, toying with that shitty old pipe of his and trying not to spill the whisky he carries like a trophy.

I watch him light up, the dot of flame flaring like a bright green jewel in my night-sight, then move forward slowly, silently, the stabbing pain as I breathe and the grinding agony in my legs forgotten as I close in on my prey.

I crouch behind one of the industrial bins just in front of him, close enough to smell the pipe and the whisky, close enough to hear his greedy, suckling breath as he gums at the pipe, coaxing it into life. The knife is in my hand, cold, heavy, lethal, as I lunge forward, hand snaking around his throat and pinning him to my chest. His glass falls to the ground and the sound of it shattering in the silence is thrilling, intoxicating.

He mewls and thrashes against me. I punch him once in the ribs, hard, the brass handle of the knife giving me extra force, feel the hot breath rush out of him against the hand I've clamped over his mouth to silence any screams.

"Shhh," I whisper into his ear, "you don't want to disturb your guests. Especially Mr McGregor. Imagine what he would think."

He thrashes against me, weakly. It's only a gesture, he knows he's mine now. Completely. I close my eyes, fight back the sudden glorious image of the knife plunging into his chest, ribs splintering as I twist it inside him and hot blood spouts into the night, trailing steam in its wake.

But no, no. Control. Control.

"I didn't realise you had such interesting friends, Harvey," I hiss. "Mr McGregor's going to be a very, very interesting man to get to know. And I will get to know him. After all, I've got a hell of a story to tell him, haven't I?"

A moan escapes him and he claws at my hand, trying to prise it away from his mouth. I smile in the darkness, shake my head.

"That's all right, Harvey, you don't have to say anything. I understand. And we'll have the time to talk soon enough. But in the meantime, you know I'm out here. And if you say anything to Mr McGregor, I'll kill everyone here, starting with Esther. Clear?"

He freezes in my arms. The sudden sting of ammonia on the breeze tells me he's pissed himself.

Excellent. Message received.

I kick the back of his knees, forcing him down. Tighten my grip on his throat, ignore the pain shooting up my arm. Give him one last asphyxiating tug then let him go and slip back into the shadows.

He collapses to the ground, gagging, coughing, spluttering.

"Leave them alone!" *he barks, his voice a ruined agony thanks to my grip. He sounds like me.* "You want me, fine. I know the deal. But they were never part of this. Never!" *The anger fades from his voice, replaced by a pleading so pathetic I feel a fresh urge to gut him there and then.*

"Please, they don't deserve this. Please…"

"No, Harvey. They didn't. But they do now. Funny how the innocent suffer, isn't it?"

I steal back into the night, eager to be back to my nest to watch his next move. Just one more job to do, then I can enjoy what comes next.

Padding silently through the dark, the pain and the fear and the uncertainty lost in the thrill of the night and the purpose of my mission, it takes me a moment to recognise what I'm feeling.

Pleasure.

I smile, juggle the knife from one hand to the other. The night is dark and there are monsters to slay. But there's far worse than monsters out here tonight.

Tonight, there's me.

30

Burns had given up on any pretence of obeying the no-smoking rule and sat behind his desk, cigarette clenched between his teeth. At the door, a fan wafted from side to side lazily – his small concession to keeping up the illusion. Above his desk, the smoke alarm hung from the ceiling like an eyeball popped from its socket.

Susie swapped a brief glance with Rebecca, who gave a small, grim, shake of the head. *Bad news,* the gesture said. Susie had seen it a lot recently.

After hanging up on Mathers, she had called in to the CID suite, found that Burns, the Chief Constable and King were still at the press conference. She settled for sending a text to Rebecca – *Get wrapped up ASAP, need to speak to Burns, got a lead* – and jumped in the car.

She had been in the CID suite for about five minutes, poring over the Pearson file again to see if there was anything she had missed, when Rebecca marched in, grim-faced and muttering curses under her breath. She grabbed Susie without breaking stride, hurried for the kitchenette alcove off the main suite where an ancient, toxic fridge hummed in the corner and a coffee urn bubbled lethargically on the worktop.

"Bad?" Susie asked.

"Fucking bloodbath," Rebecca replied. "Chief made the decision not to overtly link the cases, wanted to keep that back in case the nutcase who did this decides to contact us. Keep it as critical information to flush out the lunatics from the genuine perp."

Susie nodded. Made sense. "So?"

"So, nobody bothered to tell the reporters it was our little secret, did they? They were all over it the moment Burns had made his opening remarks."

Rebecca paused for a moment, thought back to her conversation with Doug.

For all the good it will do you...

It's not Walter you have to worry about, Doug, it's my boss...

She had implied to him that the cases were linked, and he'd obviously got the hint. But had he then stitched her up? Told some others at the press conference, got them to push Burns's buttons?

Had he? Could he?

She shook her head, aware Susie was talking to her. "So what happened?"

"Like I said, bloodbath. Question after question about public safety." She adopted a sarcastic tone. "'What are you doing to assure the people of Edinburgh that they're safe from the knife-wielding, gun-toting killers who are free on the streets?' 'How do you respond to those who say this shows that the decision to routinely arm officers was no effective deterrent?' 'Can you confirm that the murders of Charles Montgomery and Jonathan Greig are linked?' 'What are you doing to identify other possible targets?'" She rubbed her temples. "Christ, Susie, they just wouldn't let up."

"And I take it Burns didn't take kindly to it?"

"I honestly thought he was going to stroke out at the lectern. Luckily, the Chief stepped in and stopped it from being a total car crash, but still, all those questions about guns and armed cops hurt. Fuck, the headlines are going to be shit tomorrow. Please, tell me you've got something to help with this, something..."

"Summers, Drummond, my office, now," Burns barked, his voice rough with swallowed-down fury.

They followed him in and Susie laid the file on his desk as he rummaged in a drawer and pulled out a packet of cigarettes. Outlined her thoughts and what she had found on Gavin Pearson.

"Which is why I asked for Rebecca to join us, sir. If there is a link, we're going to want to handle the press on this closely."

Burns looked up at her, face twisting into a grotesque conspiratorial look as he threw her a slow wink that made her at once nauseous and furious.

"And you know all about handling the press, don't you, Drummond," he said, flicking open the file.

Gavin Franklin Pearson had been jailed for murder in 1993, after a bar fight had gone wrong. According to the report, he was running the door team that night at a club on the Grassmarket, Edinburgh's main drinking strip, when a fight broke out on the dance floor. He and his team had intervened, and Gavin had taken exception when one of the punters decided a quick game of bottle-the-doorman was in order. The bottle had ended up in the jugular of the punter – Martin Everett, a third-year law student at Edinburgh University with a dad whose name was familiar to those in the car trade – and he bled to death right there and then. Pearson was sentenced to twenty years, no pleas entertained. So far, so run-of-the-mill, until you got to the service record.

Pearson was former military. Signed up after school, did his training at Glencorse Barracks just outside a small town called Penicuik in Midlothian. Instructors stated he was a capable, tough recruit, physically fit, adaptable, disciplined.

He joined the infantry, was just in time to be shipped out to the first Gulf War, Operation Desert Storm, in 1991. He was one of thousands of allied troops to move in to Kuwait to kick Saddam Hussein out, back in the days when a war in the Middle East wasn't based on sexed-up dossiers or the private agendas of a leering megalomaniac and a would-be cowboy with Daddy's-boy delusions and the inability to chew a pretzel without almost choking himself. Pearson's service record up to that point had been nothing special: "acceptable and satisfactory" was the way the reports put it. But once he put his boots in the sand, Pearson's reports went off the chart. He was charged with equipment maintenance, not an easy task when guns fell apart in soldiers' hands and boots melted in the heat. But he proved to have an aptitude, especially with rifles.

Part of the problem was the desert sand getting into the mechanics and jamming the weapons, so Pearson was put in charge of a strict regime of stripping and cleaning the rifles. He cycled the guns in service with those of soldiers coming off watch, making sure there was always a weapon available and stripping the others as soon as they came in. And, being a good soldier, he tested his work on a rudimentary rifle range he set up. Extensively. Over the five months he was there, Pearson was practising with a range of high-powered rifles every day. The benefits of this practice was clear in his record – he won the inter-forces sniper tournament that was organised to celebrate the end of Desert Storm in the May of that year.

He stayed in the Army another six months, his once exemplary record starting to show signs of wear and tear, misconduct charges started to pop up like rust patches on a highly waxed car. He was medically discharged in November 1991, his confrontation with Everett just over a year away.

Burns closed the folder slowly, as though it were a fine novel he was taking a moment to digest. He ground the cigarette out onto his desk very slowly and deliberately, then looked up at Drummond.

"Suggestive," he said. "But hardly conclusive."

Susie felt her cheeks flush as though she had been slapped. Took a moment to make sure she had heard him right. "Sir? Sir, I'm not sure what you mean. He's trained in the use of high-power weaponry, including the Springfield M1A that ballistics think is the most likely weapon used in the Greig murder. He's got the skills, he's got the form. Surely..."

Burns stood up from his desk, arranged his belt around his pendulous gut. "All circumstantial," he said, with a sigh that was half burp. "He's not the only former soldier in Edinburgh, you know. For Christ's sake, there's an old soldiers' home on the Royal Mile."

"But sir, his record, the timescale, they fit. Surely the least I can do is…"

"Ah, and that's the guts of it, isn't it, Drummond? What *you* can do. As I said, it's suggestive, and we should and will follow up on Mr Pearson, but what are you actually saying? That he blew away Greig, then visited his son in hospital and killed him before deciding to polish off Montgomery for breakfast the next morning? Jesus, Susie, if that's true, he puts Charles Manson and Freddie Krueger to shame. And there's nothing in there to tell us why. Why would he go on such a killing spree – especially his own son? Why now?"

Susie glanced between Rebecca and the file on the desk. She had been so sure when she had received the information. But now…

"Sir, I'm merely suggesting that this is significant new information. Surely it's no coincidence that Greig, Montgomery and his son were all killed within twenty-four hours of each other. There must be a link, sir."

"Oh, and why's that?" Burns asked. "Because it makes sense? Or is it because you're so desperate to be involved in these cases that you're seeing links where there aren't any, merely to prove how valuable you really are?"

Susie felt a sudden flash of anger – cold, hard – rush through her like ice water. She was aware of the dull ache in her hands as she bunched them into fists and squeezed as hard as she could. She was staring so hard at Burns that the rest of the world began to fade out. She was dimly aware of Rebecca saying something, trying to interject about handling this for the press, making sure the line was…

"Sir," she said slowly. "It is my opinion that the discovery that Daniel Pearson's father is a former soldier with experience of weapons similar to that likely used in the Greig murder is highly suggestive and relevant to several other inquiries. It is my belief that we should make Gavin Pearson a person of extreme interest, either to identify him as a suspect or eliminate him from our inquiries." She heard a small voice in her mind: *Enough now, Susie, you've made your point. Enough.*

But no. Too late. Fuck that. She was sick of everyone second-guessing her professional opinion, thinking of her as little more than the daft lassie who fucked her boss and now fucks around with the crime reporter – who's probably also fucking her pal.

Fuck. That. She swallowed, made sure she enunciated every word. "It is also my opinion that this gives the Chief a perfect opportunity to pursue his pet project of keeping as many armed officers on the streets as possible. It is further my opinion that by keeping me on the sidelines of this case, you are depriving the investigation of a valuable asset. Sir."

Burns studied her, ignoring the horrified looks from Rebecca and the cold fury in Susie's gaze. He pulled the file to him, flicked through it again. Then closed it, up-ended it, and tapped it on the desk like a newsreader at the end of a bulletin.

When he spoke, his voice was almost fighting the whisper of the fan to be heard.

"Drummond, what did I say would happen the next time you spoke to me like that?"

Susie felt the world open up under her, reality rushing back in and extinguishing her fury like water thrown on a fire, leaving nothing but smoke and ash. "Sir, I…"

"I said you wouldn't have to worry about upstairs killing your career, didn't I? Well, now you don't have to worry." He slid the file over to her slowly, deliberately. "As I said before you decided to go off on me, this is suggestive, but not conclusive. So find me a conclusion. Either rule out Pearson, definitively, or find me a link between him and Greig and Montgomery. And do it quickly, Drummond. Because if you don't get me some answers – and show you can do some proper police work without fucking things up for me – then I'm going to let upstairs do what the hell they want. Understood?"

Susie lurched forward for the file. "Completely. Thank you, sir. Will that be all?"

He nodded, eyes never leaving hers. "Yes. Oh, and Summers…" His neck turned slowly, like an old millstone grinding round in a forgotten mill. "This conversation remains off the record, understand? Because if I read one word of this in tomorrow's press, just one, I'll be forced to ask how the press knew we were looking at a link between Pearson and the murders. We look for him, but we do it quietly. No shit in the press, no leaks to your reporter pal."

Rebecca took a half step forward. "Sir, I can assure you I…"

"I don't care about assurances, Rebecca," he said. "Keep this quiet, or you'll find the press aren't the only one who can spread rumours and false stories. And believe me, my audience is a lot, lot scarier than theirs."

He reached for another cigarette, clamped it in his mouth and leaned back in his chair. Watched them leave the room, then put the cigarette back in the packet slowly and tossed it into the bin.

31

I stagger my way through the trees back to my impromptu camp, hardly feeling the branches that claw at my face and arms in the dark. The pain is back and snarling; acid races through my legs with every step, scalding, agonising, as my lungs turn to lumps of burnt wood in my chest, blackened, spent, unable to take in the cool night air that taunts me with the promise of relief.

Finally, I make it to the clearing, feeling the notch I cut into a tree on the perimeter to know I'm in the right place and it's safe to use my penlight. I flick it on, the sudden light stabbing my eyes and filling my head with a cold fist of pain that presses against my temples, threatening to push my brain straight out of my skull. The hunter from earlier is gone, replaced by the shambling abomination I am now – a broken, spent shadow of the man I once was.

I collapse into the snug I've dug for the tent and zip it shut tightly. Lie on my back for a moment wheezing, tasting bitter, hot blood in the back of my throat. I fumble into my pocket for another wrap, desperate for the cool, sweet oblivion it will bring.

I pull the wrap out of my pocket and train the light on it for another moment. Force myself to pause and take stock while my mind is clear, ensure I've not missed anything and that discipline and control have been maintained.

The car was more time-consuming that I would have thought, complicated by the lack of light and the constant threat of one of those cackling idiots leaving their over-priced meal and under-educated conversation for a smoke or, more common these days, to check their phone. Luckily, I was left in peace to do my job, which was relatively simple. Car alarms and security systems are simple, vulgar things, designed only to protect cars from obvious threats, not the more subtle dangers I have in mind. The main purpose of the car alarm is to make a lot of noise. But noise can be silenced. You just have to know how.

I grunt a laugh too painful to enjoy as I remember Robertson, his empty threats and the way he screamed to leave McGregor and his wife out of it. Pathetic. Surely he realises the choice was made years ago, that they became a part of it the moment he took them into his life?

Empty noise, I think to myself as I fumble at the wrap, just empty noise.

I take the wrap in one glorious snort, feeling it race up my nose and into my brain like a trail of ice, cooling, numbing.

I collapse back onto the floor and close my eyes. And, for the first time in years, I realise that the thought of opening them again does not fill me with dread.

There is a mission to complete, monsters to slay and promises to keep.

32

After the bollocking from Burns, Susie and Rebecca weighed up their options. They had rejected hitting the pub or getting a carry-out – Susie guessing that drinking would make her angrier and more liable to do something she regretted – instead opting for a quick visit to the gym and a chance to unwind in the spa. Which is why they found themselves sitting in the jacuzzi, sharing an arch glance and stifling grunts of laughter as a man with the upper body of Schwarzenegger tottered past in a pair of budgie smugglers on legs that a ten-year-old would have been proud of. His skin almost glowed with false tan, which gave him a strangely orange hue.

"He jumps into the water, it's gonna be like dropping a Bisto cube into the pool," Susie said with a shake of the head.

Rebecca snorted. The muscles-on-muscle look had never appealed to her, she preferred men who were lean, fit and could think beyond reps and sets. Having their natural skin tone was a bonus, too. A thought of Doug flashed through her mind, the pale skin, high cheekbones, hair that was permanently unkempt. Eyes that always seemed to be searching for what you hadn't said, the way he sounded when…

She shook her head, felt heat that was nothing to do with the jacuzzi. Susie glanced over at her, tilted her head in a question.

"Nothing," Rebecca said. "Just thinking about today. What a fuck-up. And Burns, who the fuck does he think he is suggesting we'd leak anything? What, does he think we're that stupid?"

Susie gave an exasperated sigh, ran her hands down her face.

"I don't know," she said. "It's obvious he's getting it from upstairs, especially with all the heat around the use of firearms, and the Chief will be shitting bricks now there's a link between the two murders. But I would have thought the information on Pearson would have given him more than an aneurism. There's got to be link there, Rebecca. It's too much of a coincidence not to be."

"Any luck with it?"

Susie sighed. "Nothing definitive yet. Diane Pearson was at work in Edinburgh at the suspected time of her son's death – claims she was with clients all morning. CCTV from the hospital is inconclusive – there's a fair bit of activity in the main hall at the supposed time of death as it's near the start of visiting hour. A couple of potential matches with Pearson's description in the footage, but the video quality isn't great and there's no facial recognition given the angle of the cameras to 'protect the rights of patients.'"

Rebecca nodded. Not a good news story. "Anything on Pearson himself?"

Susie shook her head, ponytail whipping lazily in and out of the water. "Again, nothing concrete. Last known address was in Union Place. He must have been taking casual work, as there's no list of him taking benefits or registering for the dole. His Army pension was paid into his account as normal, records show he was making fairly regular withdrawals, keeping himself quiet. We've got officers asking neighbours, but nothing conclusive. Seems he kept himself to himself. Hasn't been seen for a couple of weeks."

"So, what's next?"

Susie shrugged, stood up, sleeked her hair back and waded towards the steps of the jacuzzi. "Keep watching. Look for known associates, though there's not many of them, put a quiet bulletin out to all areas asking for them to be on the lookout. We've got his car registration, so if he's using that it should help. But still..."

"Not great." Rebecca paused, a thought she didn't want to have occurring to her. "Have you thought about asking...?"

Susie shook her head. "Yes, I have. But no. He's in Skye, trying to get his head together. I've already got one missed call from him, last thing I need is to call him back and give him an excuse to get involved in this."

Rebecca thought of her own call with Doug, before the shit hit the fan at the press conference. Surely he couldn't have, wouldn't have?

"But if he could help?"

Susie chewed her lip, stared at Rebecca. Seemed to be on the verge of saying something then turned and dove into the pool. Rebecca watched her, feeling that familiar pang of jealousy as Susie cut through the water almost effortlessly, long toned limbs moving like the parts of a machine as she swam.

When they'd first met down in the Borders, they were both new to their jobs; Susie was freshly promoted to plain clothes, and they bonded over their shared awkwardness. As time passed they became friends, sharing their frustrations at the job and the inbuilt sexism they faced. From the start, Susie's attitude had impressed Rebecca. She wished she had her confidence, the ability to go for what she wanted no matter what, to take no shit, whether that was from colleagues or superiors. Coming from a farming background, with three brothers and a father whose idea of week-end fun was a trip to the church followed by *Songs of Praise* on the TV, Susie's attitude was a revelation.

And now there was Doug to consider. Yes, Susie had introduced them, ostensibly so they could work together, but still, was there something more to it? She could see how worried Susie was about him – she felt the same way – but there was something else. Something about the way she silenced her when she suggested calling him to help find Pearson.

Susie had told her about the Buchan case, about how Doug had found leads that she couldn't as a police officer, so what was the problem? After all, Doug had told her about their night, hadn't he? She had told her that he called to say he had had fun. But still, there was that nagging feeling of an invisible border about to be crossed. What was it Doug had said? *It's a date.* But was that what she wanted? Is that what Susie wanted?

With a sigh, Rebecca hauled herself out of the jacuzzi and jumped into the pool. To hell with it. They were going for a drink after this, no matter what Susie said. And while they were drinking, they were going to have a talk.

33

Doug woke with a start, temporarily disorientated. There was an awful moment of vertigo when he didn't know where he was, couldn't figure out why nothing in his room was where it should be, why his bed had sprouted four posts and ornate carvings overnight.

He reached for his habitual glass of water where he thought his bedside table would be, swore as a glass hit the floor and the smell of whisky stung his nose. Slowly, realisation slipped into his mind as the fog of dreams rolled away. Skye. He was on Skye. After saying goodnight to Harvey last night he had gone to the bar, ordered a whisky and come to bed. Lain down and closed his eyes, tried to force his thoughts into some form of order as he avoided remembering...

Look at me.

...what had happened to Greig. He must have blacked out then, from sheer exhaustion. He remembered now. The whisky he had just knocked over had been full when he spilled it.

He stood up, stretched, still not quite able to believe he had slept after the events of the last couple of days. Walked over to the bay window and swept back the heavy velvet curtains that kept the room in unnatural gloom.

The mini-suite Harvey and Esther had put him in was spectacular. It was dominated by a huge four-poster bed, which was separated from a small living area by one of two couches that sat in an L-shape. The layout was similar to his own flat in Musselburgh, but much more tastefully done.

The front of the room was taken up by a floor-to-ceiling bay window, which looked out to the Sound of Sleat and back over to the mainland. The sky was like the blurred palette of a water-colour artist, swirling greys and blues shot through with bronzed fingers of sunlight, as though God was shining a flashlight through the heavy cloud. The light flecked the water with silver, threw the mountains and water into sharp relief against the horizon, highlighting them against the glowering shadows of the clouds.

Not bad for an old hack, Doug thought with a smile. He found his jeans and dragged them on, patted the pockets to make sure the car key was there. He had left his laptop in the boot last night, but he would need it this morning. The view, and a night's sleep that wasn't filled with flashes of terror and images of blood, had revived him, woken up the reporter. Harvey's words from last night came to him – *I thought I taught you better than that, Douglas.*

He had. And now Doug was going to prove it. No more hiding. This was the biggest story in years. He was damned if his byline wasn't going to be all over it.

Downstairs, the lounge was quiet, the last of the breakfast dishes being cleared away. Doug glanced at the grandfather clock ticking patiently in the corner of the room – 9.40am. He had slept late.

He ordered coffee and fell into an absent conversation with a woman sitting at the table opposite him, head buried in a book that, reading upside down, Doug thought was about Egypt or something similar.

"Wrong part of the world for that, isn't it?" he said.

"What, huh?" She looked up at him, startled. She was slim, with high, prominent cheekbones and long brown hair that trailed over the pages of the book as she looked up at him. He could see the slight marks of glasses on the bridge of her nose. Either short-sighted or she had spent a lot of time wearing sunglasses. He looked at her exposed arms, neck and face. Tanned, with a slight blush of red from too much sun. Sunglasses it was.

"Sorry," Doug said. "I noticed your book about, ah, Egypt. I was thinking it was the wrong side of the world for that, unless you're reading a very different tour guide from mine."

She studied him for a moment, as though making a decision, then smiled, accepting the joke. "Ah, no, no. Egypt's just a fascination of mine. I'm actually on Skye to see An Corran, Mr...?"

"Sorry, Doug, Doug McGregor," he said, standing up and offering a hand.

She took his hand, shook it firmly. "Pleased to met you, Doug. I'm Kathleen. Kathleen Kendrick. Now tell me, do you always read other people's books upside down?"

He smiled shyly. "Occupational hazard, Kathleen, sorry. So, who's Anne Corran?"

She snorted a laugh. "Not Anne Corran, Mr McGregor, *An Corran*. It's a historic site, from the Mesolithic Age, thought to be the oldest site of human habitation on Skye. And," – she leaned forward, clasping her hands together – "if you believe in monsters, you can see dinosaur footprints on the beach."

Doug felt an awkward smile arrange itself on his face. Monsters he knew all too well. "Ah well, just as well I've not got time to visit then," he said. "I hated *Jurassic Park*."

She nodded, as though disappointed. "Your loss, Doug. Why are you here on Skye?"

Doug cast his arm around vaguely. "I know Harvey Robertson, the owner of the hotel," he said. "He asked me to visit him from Edinburgh."

"Wait," Kathleen said, "Edinburgh?" Realisation dawned in her eyes. "I thought I knew that name. Doug McGregor. You're the reporter from the *Tribune*, aren't you? I heard what happened. No wonder you're on Skye. Are you all right?"

Doug waved a hand away...

Dark blood seeping through Greig's fingers, like oil glistening in moonlight.

…glad that the waiter had arrived with his coffee. "I'm fine, thanks," he said, pouring a cup with a hand that only shook slightly. "Actually, I'm heading back today."

"Well, you take care, Doug," Kathleen said. "And remember, those footprints are always there when you're ready to see them."

Doug raised his mug in a farewell toast, then headed for the front door of the hotel.

He paused on the front step, took a few deep breaths to steady himself, surprised by the sudden surge of anger he felt. What the fuck was wrong with him? If he was going to cover this story, and he was, then he was going to have to toughen up and face what had happened, not piss his pants and have a panic attack every time he thought about it. This had all started with Greig's murder, with the blood and the terror and the pain, and if he was going to figure it out, he was going to have to confront it.

He took a swig of the coffee, strong, hot, smooth, and headed for the car. He was about halfway across the courtyard when his phone started to beep in his pocket, pinging with the emails and messages it missed while in the blackout zone of the hotel. He paused and dug it out from his pocket, scrolling through. It was mostly what he expected, mails from other reporters asking him for quotes on the story, his view of events, and a warning email from Walt about "not getting any ideas and stirring up any more shit". He skimmed through four messages from his parents – all variations on the same *Are you okay?* theme. Thumbed in an equally generic response and hit send.

There was also a missed call from Susie, no message. He paused, looking at the screen for a moment. No message. Odd. He looked up at the car, as if seeking an answer. If she couldn't get him, she normally left a message, or at least sent a text.

The phone pinged again, and he smiled, a vague feeling of relief whispering in his mind. Typical Susie, alwa…

He frowned as he looked down at the phone and the message. Not what, or who, he was expecting. At all.

Doug, saw what happened on the news. Called around, know you're ok, but wanted to check in. If there's anything I can do, give me a call. Off the record, of course. X

Doug shook his head as he hit *Redial.* Cheeky bastard.

The phone rang in his ear, followed by a click as it was answered. Then a soft, cultured voice on the other end of the line, comforting, reassuring. The voice that took control and told you everything was going to be all right in a time of crisis. The voice that said his side of the story was the only one you ever needed to hear.

"Hello, Hal Damon."

"Hal? Hal, it's Doug McGregor. How you doing?"

"Doug? Doug! Good to hear from you! And shouldn't that be my question? I saw what happened. You okay?"

Doug sighed down the phone. "I'm getting there, Hal. It's not been a fun couple of days though." He heard the sound of a child burbling in the background. "That Jennifer I hear? How's she doing?"

"She's great, Doug, great. Crawling now, into everything. Driving Colin and I crazy trying to keep up with her, but at least she's sleeping more at nights. Now stop trying to change the subject. You need anything? I can be there today if you need me in Edinburgh."

Doug smiled into the phone, typical Hal. Mr Efficiency. They had met last year when Doug was working the Buchan case, and Hal was hired by the Tories to handle the PR around the death of the daughter of one of their MSPs. The story had become a little harder to sell when Doug found out that the MSP in question, Richard Buchan, was an incestuous rapist and murderer, but Hal had mitigated the worst of the damage to the party. He had also given Doug a very juicy lead on a wider cover-up involving Buchan and the former Chief Constable of Lothian and Borders Police.

That story had earned Doug a "Scoop of the Year" nomination at the Scottish Press Awards, and a new friend in Hal in the process. They had kept in touch since the case, Hal's new profile winning him Scottish clients and Doug giving him coverage where he could. And, over time, they had come to respect each other's abilities and strengths. They met whenever Hal flew into town from London, sometimes with his husband, Colin, and their daughter, Jennifer. The family was so picture-perfect it made Doug more jealous that he would care to admit.

"No, I'm fine," he said, dragging himself back to the present. "Thanks, Hal. Though I'm not in Edinburgh at the moment, I'm up in Skye visiting an old friend."

"And why do I get the feeling that's a temporary situation?" Hal asked.

Doug laughed. "Yeah, okay. You're right. I'm heading back home today, going to get on the story, see what I can find out." He paused, a thought occurring to him. "Actually Hal, you could do me one favour."

"Name it."

"Walter's being a bit more cautious than usual with me covering this one, seeing as I'm a witness to the crime. But, and this is off the record, I've been given a strong tip that there might be a connection between Greig's murder and the killing of a lawyer in town, Charlie Montgomery, you hear about that?"

"Hard not to," Hal replied, "it's all over the news. But connected? How?"

"That's what I don't know. Do you think you could run a cuts check for me, see if there are any stories where Jonathan Greig and Charles Edward Montgomery connect? If there's something that ties them together, it might help me make sense of this."

Hal's voice was muffled and Doug could see him standing – tall, shoulders back, body sculpted by long hours in the gym – with the phone wedged into the crook of his neck and a notepad in his hand as he wrote the names down. "No problem, Doug, I'll get that started now. Want me to send what I find to your private account, just in case Walter is watching?"

Doug smiled again. Ever the professional. "Yeah, thanks Hal, that would be great. And if you find anything, give me a buzz, will you? I'll be driving but I'll use the hands-free, honest."

"Yeah, right," Hal said through a snort of laughter. "You take it easy, Doug, and if you need anything else, just call, okay? Colin's worried about you, so am I."

"Thanks, Hal, but I'm fine. Give Colin and Jennifer my love, will you?"

"Will do, Doug. And give Susie a kiss from me, will you?"

"Away and fuck yersel," Doug said with a laugh, and cut the line. Typical Hal. He was relentless in pushing Doug about Susie, convinced he was a matchmaker to compare with Cilla Black and that they were the couple he should buy a hat for. It was a running joke between them, but somehow, this morning, it didn't seem so funny any more.

One missed call. No message.

Doug stood for a minute, looking out at the water as it glinted silver and grey. Then he dialled Susie's number and clamped the phone to his ear.

34

"Stevie?"

Stevie took the phone to the window, glanced down at the street below. He was on the third floor of a new development just off Leith Walk, all laminated floors, designer kitchens and "well-proportioned rooms, offering an oasis of calm in the hustle and bustle of the city". To Stevie, it was all marketing bullshit – he preferred the character of a tenement any day – but tenements didn't tend to have video entry, security card-activated elevators and five-bolt deadlocks on the doors of the entrance halls and flats themselves. All of which he found handy in his line of work.

"Frankie? Frankie, that you?"

"No, it's your mother. Who the fuck you think it is?"

Stevie flinched at the venom pouring down the line, gave the street below another nervous glance. The last thing he needed was a visit from Frankie today, especially in this mood.

"Sorry, Frankie," he whispered. "But it's not the best line. Where are you?"

"Never mind where I am," Frankie hissed, voice carried on a wave of static. "The only person you should be worried about now is Paul. You are taking care of him, aren't you?"

Stevie let out a sigh. Paul had arrived last night, not long after a call from Frankie that left Stevie in no doubt that he was getting a house guest for a few days. It was the last thing he needed, but it didn't pay to say no to Frankie – especially at the moment.

Paul had been a mess when he arrived, strung out and hurting, skin the colour of wallpaper paste and glistening with sweat.

His eyes were huge, sparkling black pits that twitched around the room in time with the spasms racking his body.

Stevie bundled him into the shower, ignored the screams and pleading as he turned it up as far as he could and forced Paul to stand under it. By the time he came out, pigeon chest hitching and gasping as he clawed for breath, emaciated muscles clenching feebly with every spasm, Stevie had the present Frankie had told him to prepare waiting. Paul glanced at the needle in his hand, ran a thick, slug-like tongue over cracked lips, then took a step back, almost falling back into the shower.

"Ho... hold on a minute there, Stevie. Thought Frankie told you to look after me? I've no' shot up for years, don't do that any more. Sure Frankie wouldn't want me to..."

Stevie shook his head, bit back the impatience he felt and the urge to just stab the little cunt with the syringe and leave him on the floor. "Paul, it's fine," he said, forcing his voice to be calm, reassuring. "Why do you think Frankie asked me to have this ready for you anyway?"

Paul's eyes darted to the needle then back to Stevie. Fear and hunger fought for control in that gaze – it was like watching a sea churned by a storm. "What? Really? But I thou... Frankie said..."

Stevie took a half step forward. "Look, Paul. Frankie sent you here so I could look after you. This is what you need. So trust us. If you can't do it yourself, I'll do it, okay? But you need this. Frankie says so."

Paul bit his lip slightly, then raised a thin, pallid arm, like a child expecting to be given a sweet. Stevie took Paul's arm just above where the bicep should have been, his arm so skinny he could almost get his hand all the way around it, then squeezed, trying to coax a vein to the surface. After a moment, a thin, purple-green line popped up from the skin and Stevie drove the needle home.

Paul winced and let out a moan as he drew his arm to his chest. Gave a smile so grateful and sickening it made Stevie want to cave in the ruined stumps of his teeth with a hammer. Stevie nodded

143

and led him to the spare bedroom, where he'd set up towels, water and a pot to be sick or piss in. He hadn't had time to put a rubber sheet under the bed. Fuck it, just have to run the risk.

Paul collapsed in a heap on the bed and Stevie lifted his feet onto it. He pulled the wet towel off him and threw the quilt over him, listening as his whispered *thank yous* grew quieter and his breathing grew deeper. He had waited until he was sure he was out and then went back to the bathroom, dug through his clothes until he found Paul's wallet, which he held in his hand now.

"Paul's fine, Frankie," he said into the phone. "He's still whacked out in the bedroom, just like you wanted."

"Good. Did you find what I was looking for?"

Stevie opened the wallet, pulled out a small, tattered business card from between a condom and a ruined picture of a woman who, he guessed, had once been attractive before the weight of life had hit her like a right hook.

"Yeah, Frankie. Right where you said." He read the card. The name on it meant nothing to him. "Work address is right here. You need something sorted out?"

"Not yet," Frankie said, suddenly sounding tired. "Just keep that card safe for now. And as for Paul, you know what to do?"

Stevie shuddered. How the fuck had he let it get to this? "Yes, Frankie, I know."

"Good. Don't let me down, Stevie. It'll just be like he went to sleep. If you do it right, he'll never know. If you do it wrong, then I'll know. And I'll be very upset. You don't want that, do you?"

"No, Frankie," Stevie mumbled, pressing his head against the cold glass of the window and looking down at the sheer drop. "I don't want that at all."

35

It had rained through the night, the cobbles of the street gleaming in the morning sun, framed by sandstone buildings that bled moisture marks from their eaves and window frames like sweat patches, and pavements that always looked dirtier after a downpour.

Susie stood on Cockburn Street just off the Royal Mile, outside Diane Pearson's office. Across the road was Fleshmarket Close, a small, dark vennel that ran down the hill to Market Street and the entrance to Waverley Station. Halfway down the lane was Doug's favourite pub, the Jinglin' Geordie. He loved it because it was a reporters' pub, or had been before redundancies, closures and cuts became almost weekly events in the newspaper industry. From what Doug had told her, the *Tribune* hadn't fared much better, hence the sale of their office complex on the edge of town and the move into their city office.

But still, Doug loved the Jinglin'. He was, Susie thought, more of a romantic than he cared to admit.

She shook her head, focusing on the job at hand. She had arranged to meet Diane to learn more about Gavin, see if there were any clues she could give her to his location. Burns had been right about one thing, they needed to find him. Now. And not just because Burns had threatened to throw her to the wolves if she didn't.

She was about to press the buzzer on the office door when her phone rang. *Doug-mobile*, it flashed.

She paused. Torn. After her conversation with Rebecca last night, she had called him, not sure of what she was going to say, only that it was going to be loud. And angry. If Rebecca was right, then he had jeopardised both their jobs by leaking the possible link between the Greig and Montgomery murders. And, on top of that…

Being put through to his answerphone was like being slapped in the face. The anger bled out of her, leaving only a dazed exhaustion that left her unable to think. She had clicked the phone off, resolving to give him a piece of her mind later.

And now, here was the perfect chance, with him paying the bill, and she wasn't sure what to do.

Fuck it.

"Doug? How's Skye?"

"Great, Susie, how you doing? Burns still making you look bad?"

She ground her teeth, bit back her anger. "It's not Burns that's making me look bad at the moment, Doug, it's you. Nice work. Fucking me and Rebecca over at the same time. That a new record for you?"

Rebecca? Doug felt a hot flush rush through his cheeks. "Susie, I don't know what you… Look, I'm sorry, I…"

Susie's voice grew dull and cold. "*Sorry?* Sorry! She tries to help you out, and the first thing you do is leak a potential link between the two biggest murders in Edinburgh in the last ten years? Putting both of us in the shit with Burns and the top brass – and for what? To show you're still the big name in town, even though you're not here? 'Sorry' doesn't seem to cover it, Doug."

Doug took a breath. Susie at full tilt was like a force of nature – when the fury broke through that veneer of control and discipline she had constructed, it was like standing in the path of a hurricane. Doug had seen it a few times, been the focus of it more than once and hated every second of it. And yet, despite that, Doug felt something different this time. Not fear. Not intimidation. Not even the usual admiration. No, this was something totally new to these meltdowns.

Relief.

"Susie," he said tentatively, eager not to wake the volcano between eruptions. "Look, I'm sorry. But I promise you I didn't leak the link between Montgomery and Greig. Honestly. Rebecca only hinted at it – until now, I didn't know it was an established fact. So thanks for confirming that for me. Care to tell me what the link was?"

A moment of silence on the line, long enough for Doug to wonder if she'd hung up on him. Shit, that last smart-arse comment had been a mistake, but he hadn't been able to resist.

"Susie, after the last few days, the last thing I'm going to do is lie to you – or Rebecca. I promise, it wasn't me."

"Shit," Susie whispered over the line. Doug could almost picture her, head dropping, hand massaging the stress rash she got at the top of her neck. "You better not be fucking around here, Doug."

"I'm not. Promise."

"Shit," Susie whispered again. "But if you didn't, then who did?"

Bingo. Thoughts tumbled through Doug's head. All of them giving him the same answer. And the same opportunity.

"Only two options," Doug said. "Either you've got a leak at Fettes, or..." He paused, strangely thrilled and horrified by the idea at the same time. "Or, whoever did this decided to have a little fun, put you on the back foot and let the press know."

"Jesus, you mean the killer?" Susie whispered.

Doug shrugged, looked out to the horizon. "It's possible. There're only a few people who know of the link between the murders, even less who would want that information out there before you were ready. So yeah, it's a thought. How'd it get out, anyway?"

"Don't know," Susie replied, voice vague and distracted. Clearly, he had got her attention. "All Rebecca said was that the press were ready for the Chief and Burns, that they went for the jugular the moment they opened up for questions."

Doug nodded. Predictable. He'd have done the same himself.

Time to play his card. "Okay, I'll look into it. Ask around. See if I can find out where this came from."

"Hold on, Doug, just wait a minute. You're not meant to be anywhere near this, remember? If Burns finds out…"

"He'll do what? You've already said you're in the shit with him. Maybe if I can find something out, it'll give you something to take to him, get him off your back. It's not going to hurt Rebecca if she can find the leak and plug it, either. And besides, we both know there are people out there that won't talk to you but will pick up to me."

Susie paused. *People that won't talk to you.* Shit, he was right. The Buchan case had, ultimately, rested on Doug's ability to get information from sources that would run a mile from Susie or anyone with an official title. It had been useful in the past. Could it be useful again?

"Okay," she said. "But be quiet about it, Doug. And if you find anything, I want to know about it first, not read about it in the *Trib*. Clear?"

He almost laughed. "Promise. Anything else you need me to look in to while you're at it? I'm heading back today, but I've got to say some goodbyes, make a couple of calls and get things started before I go."

People that won't talk to you…

"Well, there's… No. No. It's nothing."

"Susie? Susie, what? If there's something I can help with, let me know. I promise, I won't use anything without telling you first, okay? But if I can help, I want to. After the other night, I owe you."

Should she? Burns's words echoing in her ears now. *If you don't get me some answers, I'm going to let upstairs do what the hell they want.*

People that won't talk to you…

"Susie?"

She started, remembering he was on the line. She rubbed furiously at the base of her neck, at the hot, insistent itch, like something clawing at her chest. She took a breath, took a step off the street into a small alleyway that ran up to the Mile.

"I might have a suspect," she said, not quite believing what she was doing. Had Burns really left her this desperate?

"What?" Doug's voice was urgent and pleading – a child desperate to know what happened next. "Who? How? Why aren't…?"

"Burns is playing it cool, by the book. Seems he's getting a world of shit from upstairs. A kid died at the ERI the same day as Greig. His dad is a former soldier, served in the Gulf first time round. Did time for murder, got out a couple of years ago, disappeared. I need to find him."

"What? Wait. Gulf War. You mean…?"

"Yes, Doug. Guns. He knew all about guns. Including the rifle which uses the ammunition that killed Greig."

"Fuck," Doug whispered. "And I take it there's no record of him since he was released?"

"Nothing at all," Susie said.

"And no obvious link to Greig or Charlie?"

"Would I be telling you if there was?"

Doug grunted, too distracted to rise to the jibe. "Okay, give me the name. I'll ask around. Rab might be able to help, a few others."

She gave him Pearson's full name and date of birth. Reached out to touch the granite wall of the alleyway as she did. Cold.

"And Doug, I meant what I said. No fucking around with this. I need a result, not a fucking byline in the *Trib*."

"Understood, I won't use a thing without your say-so." He was appalled by how convincing he sounded. He almost believed it himself. "Susie, just one more thing…"

She held her breath, knew what was coming.

"What?"

"The link. What was it? How did you put the murders together?"

Susie paused. How desperate was she?

Let upstairs do what the hell they want…

Find me a conclusion…

149

Kill your career…

Fuck it.

She retreated deeper into the alley then slowly told Doug about the bullet they found in Charlie's mouth and the match with Greig's murder. The silence from the other end of the line was complete, oppressive, almost a living thing that seemed to bleed from the phone and wrap itself around her, pierced only by the rasping sound of Doug fighting to breathe through the growing panic and nausea as he counted the shots in his mind and saw Greig staring lifelessly back at him from a growing pool of his own cooling blood.

36

Rebecca spread the papers out on her desk, casting her gaze across the headlines. They were as bad as she feared. *Link in Capital killings, Police hunt for one suspect in Edinburgh killings, Killer evades city police* and, her favourite, *Minister demands answers as city killer evades police.*

It was inevitable really. With this level of coverage, it was only a matter of time before the politicians got involved. Especially in an election year, with the referendum aftermath still fresh in the memory and the controversy about routinely armed police officers on patrol only a Google search away.

The news websites were similarly grim reading, with the added dimension of video clips from the press conference, with Burns spluttering and stuttering after every question.

She sighed, pushed the papers aside. What the hell was Burns thinking? With all this going on, the last thing they needed was him to be ignoring a potential suspect, merely because it was Susie who had turned him up and she was in shit street with the top brass. And just what had she done in the Buchan case that pissed them off so much anyway? From what Rebecca had managed to piece together from the coverage – and what little Susie would tell her – she had faced down a gun-toting psychopath, brought in a convicted rapist who, while not guilty of murder, had notched up an impressive tally of crimes, and helped expose an MSP as a paedophile whose main form of relaxation was raping his daughter and prostitutes. All of which didn't exactly reflect badly on the police. Doug's follow-up – on the link between Buchan and the then-Chief Constable and a cover-up of a hit and run – wasn't the happiest of reading, but from what Rebecca had seen, the press team at the time had managed to put the best spin they could on it... this happened years ago, the force was different then, it would never be tolerated now, any allegations will be fully investigated.

And maybe they were, but Rebecca had heard nothing else about it. So what was the nerve Susie hit? Surely they still weren't holding a grudge about her fuck-and-forget with her former boss? Police officers could be an unforgiving, tribal bunch, but surely they weren't going to kill her career over it.

Were they?

She looked back across the papers again, then called up the holding line she had drafted and released on the computer. *Officers from Police Scotland are currently investigating the suspicious deaths of Jonathan Greig and Charles Edward Montgomery in Edinburgh. Both investigations are proceeding. As with any investigations which run parallel in a close geographic area, departments will be liaising closely to maximise local knowledge and resources to expedite the identification of any suspects. Updates will be given in due course.*

She turned away from the screen in disgust. A no-comment comment, dictated by the Chief after the press conference with the grim warning that it was to be issued "word for word, comma for comma". She checked the news agency websites and a couple of the bigger media outlets and, sure enough, they had tacked it on to the bottom of their copy. She'd be amazed if anyone read that far to be bothered by it, and it would do nothing to stem the fresh tsunami of queries she would no doubt face over the day. It was like being told to fight a fire with a water pistol.

She stood up, walked around her desk, stretching her back, which was complaining from too many hours hunched over a computer and too little relaxation. She stood at the window, looking at the TV satellite vans parked outside, dishes all swivelled to the sky expectantly. She thought briefly of Burns, sitting in his office two floors up, glaring down at the vans, no doubt blowing smoke from his cigarette at them, wishing it would choke every one of the little fuckers.

Burns. A thought flashed across her mind, like the ghost of a bright light that strobes across your vision after you've looked at it for too long. Burns. If he was going to put her and Susie in the shit like this, why couldn't she do the same to him? The holding line was shit, the press would be hungry for something, anything, new. She could leak the possible suspect line, emphasise enquiries were in their early stages but a positive avenue is being explored, then hint that top brass had ignored it. It would create an unholy shitstorm, but at least it would move them away from this holding pattern, focus their minds and get Susie some of the help she needed.

Nice fantasy. Pity it wouldn't work in practice. Burns and the Chief would know exactly who had tipped the press off, plus it could prejudice any chance of a future trial if Pearson really was involved. And, on top of all that, there had already been too many leaks.

She thought again of Doug, of last night's conversation with Susie and the vow to let the bastard have it both barrels the next time she spoke to him. But now, in the harsh light of another morning of bad headlines and bosses breathing down her neck, Rebecca wasn't so sure. Oh, she was certain he would leak a story if it suited him, but she couldn't see what he got from this. She had only hinted at a link, not confirmed it, so his initial line was fairly weak to start with. His byline wasn't on any of the copy she had seen today, except as a factual mention as being on the scene when Greig was murdered. So what did it get him? A chance to show off? Get the other reporters to dance to his tune via remote control? He had a grudge against Burns, mostly because of the way he had treated Susie, but this had just made it worse for Susie. *And, if it's a consideration,* Rebecca thought, *me as well.*

She turned away from the window. No. Whoever had leaked

this, it wasn't Doug. Which wasn't as comforting as it should have been. Because if he wasn't responsible, then someone else was.

Rebecca grabbed her jacket, headed for the door. If Burns wanted her, or a reporter wanted the line again, they could get her on the phone. Right now she needed to be out, away from this claustrophobic office that seemed full of questions.

Now, she needed to go get some answers.

37

The phone's screen cracks easily, a cheap brittle thing that shatters into an intricate kaleidoscope of colours as I push my fingers down on to it. I slip out the SIM card and hold it up, the small gold chip winking in the light. I snap it and pocket it to dispose of later. Not that there's any real risk of it being traced – the phone is a pay-as-you-go that I bought for cash at an anonymous shop, and no-one has the number unless I think they need it.

I could have kept the phone, but there's no point. With the final call made, there's no need for it any more. It's obsolete, like I will be in a few short hours.

Only one last monster to slay.

One more mission to complete.

Then we can all rest.

38

After the call with Susie, Doug threw himself into work, desperately trying to outrun the memories of Greig as he walked aimlessly around the hotel car park, circling his car as though he were its moon.

His first port of call was Rab MacFarlane. With his security business covering most of the doors in the city, if anyone could get a line on what happened with Pearson, Rab would be it. When he called, it was his wife, Janet, who answered, and he was forced to run the verbal gauntlet of *how-are-yous* and "When ye comin' tae visit us, son? Rab's fair woond up aboot a' this – and I'm no' so happy 'bout it either."

Doug promised he would visit as soon as he could, listened to the clicks as Janet transferred the call. He knew she would be listening though, hunched over her desk in the small reception room that led to Rab's office, her skin not so much as tanned as varnished by the salon treatments she was addicted to, hair coiffed and frozen into position with enough hairspray to put a hole in the ozone layer.

"Doug? Doug? How you doing, son? You decided to let one of the boys look after you yet?"

"No thanks, Rab, I'm big enough and ugly enough to look after myself. Besides, I'm in Skye, a long way from any hassle."

Rab grunted. Unhappy. They had met when Doug had done a feature on the licensing of doormen in the city; Rab had given him the inside view of how the industry worked and Doug had mentioned him favourably in the copy. Since then, they had developed what Rab called "a mutually beneficial relationship", with Doug running the odd helpful story and Rab helping him with some of the less-legitimate lines of inquiry he needed to chase up.

Case in point, Gavin Pearson.

"Well, listen, you change your mind, come see me when you get back. And do it oanyway – Janet's doin' my heid in asking after you."

Doug smiled. When he first met Janet, he had fallen into the role of cheeky young man, all harmless banter and studied compliments about her appearance. But over time, the banter had given way to a real affection. He was under no illusions, the steel in Janet was razor sharp and lethal, but there was also a warmth to her that he liked. Almost like the aunt who made the rude jokes at family get-togethers and snuck you an extra drink when no-one was looking. And he knew she liked the attention. After all, family was everything to her. Even if they were journalists.

"Tell her I said thanks. Listen, Rab, I was wondering if you could do me a wee favour?"

Rab's voice grew cautious. "This something to do with what happened to your boss?"

Doug swallowed. "Maybe. Look, I need to find someone. Name is Gavin Pearson, done for murder in an Edinburgh nightclub in 1993. Released a couple of years ago. Fell off the radar since then."

"Fuck, don't make it too easy for me, Doug, will you?"

Doug closed his eyes, ground his fingers into them. Heard Susie's voice whisper in his ear. *No fucking around with this, I need a result.* He thought about Janet listening, hanging on every word. Janet, the Lady MacBeth of Edinburgh's security industry. If you wanted a broken jaw or a shattered ribcage, you pissed Rab off. If you wanted to go to the morgue, probably by the scenic route, you crossed Janet. Or someone she cared for and "did Rab's heid in" about.

And yet…

I need a result.

A flash of Greig standing, paralysed, mouth open in a silent scream, blood spurting from his mouth. The echoing crack as his head hit the table. The feel of his blood oozing between his fingers.

Fuck it.

"Pearson's ex-military. First Gulf War. Spent a lot of time in the desert looking after firearms, including the type that was used to kill Greig. He comes home, might be a lot of call for his kind of skills in certain circles. So anything you can find out would be appreciated, Rab. Really."

From the other end of the phone, Doug heard a soft swallowing sound, saw Rab down the whisky he no doubt had on his desk. Whisky and business: Rab's favourite tipple.

"And you think he might be the man who killed your boss?"

"It's a theory, I'm checking it out for a friend."

"By friend, you mean that copper you're determined to help out all the time?"

"Yeah, Rab, that's her. Drummond. Susie Drummond. She's one of the good ones. She knows not to ask where I get my information."

Rab grunted, the sound of stones being chewed. He had a natural distrust of the police, tolerated Doug's closeness to Susie only because of Janet's fondness for the boy. The fact that he had a direct line to the ear of a police officer via Doug was mere coincidence.

Honest.

"Any threat to you?" he asked.

Doug shook his head. "No, I don't think so. I'm in Skye, best bet he's in Edinburgh or thereabouts; no indication he's overly mobile. If it's him. Besides, whatever the reason, this was personal. Whoever killed Greig fucking hated him – and I don't think I've pissed anyone off that much yet." Doug winced, the joke sounding like an off-key chord in his own ears.

"Give it time, Douglas," Rab said, deadpan. "I'll look into it, see what I can find. In the meantime..." He let the sentence drift off, quiet menace dripping from the phone.

"Thanks, Rab, I owe you. Again. I'll come and visit when I get back."

"Make sure you do. Oh, and Douglas?"

"Yeah?"

"Bring Janet something back from Skye. You know she likes her souvenirs."

39

Diane Pearson's office was on the first floor of the Department of Social Care and Community Support on Cockburn Street. To get there, Diane had met Susie in reception and led her down a long, echoing corridor with walls painted an industrial green, old double doors with safety glass panes and a battered concrete floor that was pitted and marked with the passage of countless pairs of shoes.

It reminded Susie of her high school.

The office itself was small and cramped, stuffed with an over-sized sofa, a small table, a bookshelf and what looked like a reclining chair that had escaped from the Seventies. Various posters adorned the cream walls, advertising everything from the Samaritans to a quick call from the police if "our staff aren't allowed to work free from the threat of violence".

Diane ushered Susie to the couch and folded herself into the chair opposite. Susie struggled to sit upright, the cushions were so soft and encompassing she felt as though it was trying to suck her in.

"So, Susie, how can I help you?" she asked, flicking away a strand of her white-blonde hair from her too-thin face. Susie wondered if that was the standard line she used with everyone who came to see her.

"Ah, just a couple of follow-up questions, Mrs Pearson, shouldn't take too long."

Diane held up a pale hand. "No problem, I'm out of my office for meetings elsewhere this afternoon, but I've cleared my diary this morning, so take as long as you need."

Too good to refuse, Susie thought. "Well, thank you," she said. "But if you don't mind me asking, what exactly is it you do? I know you said you were a counsellor and social worker, but I've never heard of this place before."

Diane nodded, flashed a small, understanding smile. Perfectly friendly, perfectly practised. Perfectly empty. A smile she'd given a million times before in this room.

"I'm not surprised," she said. "We're a relatively new department, helping those identified with additional mental or physical support needs and trying to help them to lead productive, fulfilled lives in the community."

Susie nodded. So far, so press release. "Additional needs? You mean like Danny?"

The smile flashed across Diane's face again, this time looking like a grimace. "Sometimes, though, Danny's physical needs meant it was more appropriate for him to be cared for at the centre. We're more concerned with those who have mental and physical issues resulting from chronic addiction. The theory is that if we can offer these people the support they need, we can stop them relapsing, and creating a further strain on the health service."

Susie flashed her own smile, murmured agreement. She had heard about this – it was an NHS plan to deliver more community care and take the pressure off frontline services such as A&Es by reducing the number of alcoholics, drug addicts and those who self-harmed visiting casualty by tackling their problems before they reached for the bottle, the needle or the knife. Predictably, the Tories hated it, branding the idea "just another government smokescreen to mask the true scale of the problem by reclassifying patients and depriving the NHS of the funding it desperately needed".

Looking past the spin, Susie thought it made sense, but what did she know? She was a detective, not a self-appointed health expert.

"So, what did you want to ask me, Susie?" Diane asked, glancing at a clock on the wall. Cleared calendar or not, she wanted this over with as soon as possible.

Susie took a moment to flick through her notes. No way was she going to let Pearson dictate the pace of this. Interview technique 101 – always stay in control. It was one of the things she and Doug agreed on.

"Ah, I actually wanted to ask about Danny's father, Gavin. You said yesterday that he had no contact with you or Danny, has that always been the case?"

Diane picked at the sleeve of her jumper. "Yes," she replied, voice impassive, the fake empathy disappearing. "As I said, he was jailed just before Danny was born. I took him to visit a few times at Saughton, but that just... just fell apart over time and we never saw him. Which suited me, it was no place for a baby, especially Danny."

"And you never heard from him when he was released?"

"No," Pearson snapped back. "Sorry, detective, but this isn't an easy subject, especially at the moment when... when..."

Susie leaned forward, gave her best reassuring smile. "I know, Mrs Pearson, Diane. I'm sorry. I can't imagine what you're going through. I just need to know a little more about Gavin."

"But why?" Diane asked. "You don't still think someone intentionally hurt Danny do you?" Her eyes grew wide, voice dropped to a whisper. "You don't think Gavin did this?"

Susie held up a hand, thought briefly of the nondescript figure in the hospital, the baggy jacket and the baseball cap pulled down tight. Could have been Gavin.

Could have been anyone.

"We're investigating every possibility, Diane," she said. "And, as Danny's father, Gavin is a gap in our knowledge. We just want to speak to him, so anything you could tell me could be vital."

Diane dropped her head, shook it. When she looked up, the mask had gone, replaced by a haggard old woman with the scars of a hard, loveless life slashed across her face and haunted eyes that locked onto Susie's.

"Gavin was a soldier," she said. "We met when he was on leave, just down the road in the old Alcove bar, you know it?"

Susie nodded. She had heard of the place. It was gone now, destroyed years ago in a fire that ripped through the heart of Edinburgh's Old Town. A fire that smouldered for days and put Edinburgh on the map for all the wrong reasons.

"Anyway, we got married, and everything was fine to start with. But then… then he got shipped out to Iraq and it all went to shit from there."

"Why?" Susie asked.

Diane paused for a moment, cold eyes searching Susie's. Then she twitched her head, as though making a decision. "Susie, have you ever heard of Gulf War Illness?"

"Vaguely," Susie said. "Some soldiers who came home said their service in the Gulf made them ill, called it Gulf War Syndrome. Is that it?"

"It's more than reports," Diane said. "And it's not a syndrome, it's an illness. When Gavin went to Iraq, he was a strong, vital young man. Was in the gym five days a week, ran a couple of infantry marathons. Six months after he came home he was riddled with arthritis, skin lesions and acute paranoia. The Army drummed him out, gave him a medical discharge and a pension not worth a shit."

"And that's why you… ah, drifted apart?"

Diane flashed the horrible, leering smile again, as though she were talking to a child who didn't know that there was worse than fairy tales beyond the bedroom curtains.

"He came home a stranger," she said. "Couldn't do what he once could, trapped in a body that was failing him with a mental timebomb ticking in his head. He went to get his passport photographs taken one day – the flash triggered an episode and it took three security men to subdue him."

It fitted, Susie thought. The reports on the nightclub referred to the assault being "extremely violent".

"So, what happened?"

"What happened?" Diane spat, anger flashing behind her glasses. "We tried to get him help, but no-one wanted to listen. The Army turned their back on him, called him a nutter, local doctors didn't know what to do. Local politicians ran a mile from us, no matter how many times we told our story. He couldn't hold down a job, took work where he could, and then… then, that poor boy."

"Martin Everett," Susie whispered.

Diane nodded, tears threatening in her eyes. "We tried to tell them it wasn't his fault, not really, that the illness made him paranoid. Unpredictable. But they wouldn't listen. And when he was sentenced, well, he just shut us off. Said he was a monster and deserved to be locked away."

Susie took a breath. She didn't want to do this, but had no choice.

"And you've no idea where he could be now, what he might be doing?"

Diane looked away at the clock on the wall. She watched the seconds march by – one, two, three – then turned back to Susie.

"I have no idea where he could be, Susie," she said, "but I do know one thing. Wherever he is right now, he's suffering. And he won't want to keep that to himself. He always used to say 'suffering shared is suffering halved'. And I imagine he's working very hard on halving his pain right now."

40

Burns sat barricaded behind his desk, worrying at the cigarette packet he had fished from the bin like he was torturing a small animal. In front of him, the Pearson file sat open, dog-eared by the number of times he had run through the pages.

Suggestive, not conclusive, he had told Drummond. Looking at it now, it was a hell of a lot more than that.

He made a sound halfway between a cough and a growl, squeezed down on the cigarette packet as though it had insulted him. Drummond was right, it was a strong lead, but thanks to the diktat from upstairs to "make sure she stays on the straight and narrow and on a short leash", he had to make doubly sure that she was playing by the book. But did that mean he was hampering the investigation by doing so?

He leaned back, considered what he knew. The son of an ex-soldier with a criminal record had been killed after being in a freak accident. Looking at the file of Daniel Pearson, it was obvious that the poor kid had been suffocated.

Burns had seen it before – years ago when he was a young PC working in Dundee. A man had suffocated his wife at their home, snapping one night after dementia robbed her of her memory of him and their forty-six years together. Burns could still remember him, a small, neat man, with snow-white hair and an old bobbled green cardigan draped around blade-like shoulders. He had called the ambulance and police himself after he killed her, had the tea made and waiting by the time they arrived. He had taken a seat in the front room, in a battered old leather chair that seemed to be moulded to him, drank his tea with a shaking hand, tilting the cup at an odd angle so he could drink around his long, hook-like nose.

"I just couldn't stand her not remembering us," he said quietly, eyes red-rimmed and strangely peaceful. "We always said we'd know when the time was right, and when she looked at me tonight, all that confusion and loss, I knew. So I settled her the best I could, gave her her tablet, then..." He trailed off, lost in the memory of what he had done. Then he looked up, fixed Burns with a cold, hard glare that was full of pain and defiance.

"Forty-six years and I never raised a hand to her once," he said. "And by Christ, that woman could give me cause. But not once. Never. Not until tonight. And I did it because I loved her, you understand? Because I loved her."

While the confession had been enough, cause of death was also quickly confirmed. The pathologist at the scene, a small, squat man with a taste for Paisley ties and hideous waistcoats, had shown Burns when he was sent to see the body.

"You see," he said, lifting the lids of the eyes gently and nodding towards the small blotches of red flecked through the whites of the pupil. "Petechial haemorrhaging. Classic sign."

Classic, Burns thought. And just like Daniel Pearson.

So there was a possibility that Pearson had killed his son. If so, that was three murders in the city within the space of twenty-four hours. But was he the common cause?

And if so, why? He had been released about two years ago, led a quiet, anonymous life off the radar, with no-one sure where he was or if he was still alive. So if Gavin Pearson had suddenly decided to go on a one-man killing spree, why? Why start with his son, then move on to two people who were, from everything Burns had seen, total strangers to him?

There was nothing in any of the files that indicated a link between him, Jonathan Greig or Charming Charlie. Burns had briefly toyed with the idea that Charlie had been part of Pearson's trial, but there was no record of that. Same for Greig. Nothing to show why Pearson would assassinate him in such a brutal, public manner.

Burns pushed the Pearson file aside, glanced briefly at the report on Charlie's death, shuddering at the image from the scene of the knife jutting from his ruined temple.

Steeled himself and opened the Greig file. It was like turning the page to a nightmare. Blood and terror seeping from every page, violence described in minute detail in all the reports.

Just three shots – one, ballistics said, to calibrate for wind and range, and two dead centre on Greig.

Burns grunted. From the report, McGregor had been a lucky wee cunt not to have been hit by the first shot, which had burrowed into the wall less than a foot from him.

Pity. It would have made for one less problem. McGregor was at the top of the Chief's most-hated list. Which was, Burns had been told, the reason for Susie being kept out in the cold.

"We need to contain this McGregor," the Chief had told Burns after summoning him to his office not long after the Buchan shitstorm had subsided. "It's obvious Drummond fed information to him. While we can't act against her, especially in light of the way she dealt with Charlie Morris and Derek McGinty, we'll have to watch her closely. Understood?"

Burns said he understood completely. What he didn't say was that he could smell shit when he was near it, and that was what this was. Bullshit. Cops talked to reporters and the media all the time, it was part of the game, especially these days, when careers could be made or broken by a tweet or a cameraphone snap. And Susie had done nothing but work every angle she had to solve a very messy case.

No, this was something else. If they were pissed about McGregor getting information, they would have hauled her in on a disciplinary and made an example of her. Whatever they wanted her sidelined for, it was a hell of a lot more than her relationship or otherwise with Doug McGregor. And she deserved better than that. Despite her temper, and a way with insults and soap-boxing that reminded Burns of his daughter Maria, Drummond was a good copper. Hardworking, diligent, intuitive.

He smiled, remembering her words from yesterday: *By keeping me on the sidelines of this case, you are depriving this investigation of a valuable asset, sir.*

Cheeky bitch. But she was right. And, looking at the carnage spread before him, he needed all the assets he could get.

He reached for the mangled cigarette packet, picked out the remnants of a broken cigarette. Laid it carefully on the table and plucked out the tobacco, making a small pile in his hand.

Fuck it.

He reached for the phone as he shoved the tobacco into his mouth and started to chew. Almost gagged on the vile, burning taste that flooded his mouth, like swallowing a bottle of Tabasco. He took a moment, blinked away the sudden tears in his eyes, then dialled the number from memory.

Drummond was right. Pearson was a strong lead, one of the few they had. He had to keep her on the sidelines, make sure she jumped through all the hoops the brass wanted her to, ensure anything she found was totally watertight.

Fine. But nothing said he couldn't give her a little help with that.

Off the record, of course.

41

Esther was in the dining room by the time Doug walked back into the hotel, clicking off the phone after phoning the *Tribune*. He had stayed away from the newsdesk, calling straight to the number of Chris Blackley. He was a graduate from Napier, taking shifts and hoovering up the shit jobs as if they were candy, working his ass off to try and get a full-time job and start a career in the business. Doug wanted to warn him, tell him not to bother, but he couldn't. After all, hadn't he started the same way? The only problem was, there wasn't likely to be a Harvey Robertson in Chris's future.

"Doug, hey! You okay? Everyone's worried about you," he said after Doug said hello.

"Yeah, Chris, I'm fine. How you doing?"

"Busy," he said. "Trying to get into the Greig death and away from the back-of-book fill. You looking for Walter? He's in conference just now."

Doug smiled. Fancy that. In conference and unavailable. Shame.

"No, I actually wanted to talk to you, Chris. Need your help with something."

"Really? What? Anything you need, Doug, just tell me."

"You know Walt's keeping me off the Greig story, but I'm going nuts here, so I thought I'd catch up on a feature I was meant to write. It's about former soldiers and what they're doing now, how they fit back into society when their duty's done. I'm nosing in on all the publicity about veterans coming home injured at the moment, and all the moves in the Middle East."

"Nice," Chris said, his voice horribly eager. "But what can I do?"

"Well, Walter doesn't want me working at the moment, but I need to do a bit of background. So I was hoping you could run a library check for me, see what comes back?"

"No problem, Doug. The classified team are logged into the library now, but I'll do it as soon as they're out. What do you want me to look for?"

Doug sighed. Fucking typical. Ten years ago, the *Tribune* had a physical library, with every copy of the paper stretching back over its 137 years neatly filed away. With the downsizing and the move, the number crunchers had decided to do away with all that – and the staff who maintained it – and transferred everything online. Problem was, the online search only allowed for ten users to be logged in at one time. And when advertising targets were looming and the sales teams wanted to look back at what had worked for previous customers, reporters were the first to suffer.

"I'm looking for stories related to a Gavin Franklin Pearson," Doug said. "Former Gulf War vet, got himself into a bit of trouble around 1993, I think."

He could hear the faint scratch of pen on paper, remembered that Chris insisted on using fountain pens. "Uh-huh. Okay. I'll have a look, send you what I find."

Doug thought of what Hal had said earlier. "Send it to my Gmail account, will you? Easier to access on my phone. And Chris, don't tell Walter, okay? He'll just give me a bollocking for working at the moment."

"No problem," Chris said. "And, Doug?"

Doug nodded. The quid pro quo. "I'll speak to Walter when I'm back, try to get you on something front-of-book, okay?"

Chris's voice was an explosion of gratitude. "Thanks, Doug! I'll get this to you as soon as I can."

"Great, thanks, Chris. Speak soon."

Esther was sitting at one of the tables with an ornate silver teapot in front of her and a rack of toast she had barely touched.

She smiled as she saw him, waved him over.

"Douglas! Good morning. I hear you slept late. Come have breakfast with me."

Food was the last thing on Doug's mind, but he crossed the room and sat opposite her. "Thanks, Esther," he said. "I'm starving."

She nodded, pleased. She looked better in the daylight, the sun restoring some warmth to her pallid skin. But Doug could still see the sickness there, lingering beneath the make-up she had caked on, plain in the lines etched around her mouth and eyes and the sallow skin around her once-tight jaw. Her hair, which she had styled, looked thin and brittle, and he noticed the spattering of liver spots and fading bruises on the backs of her hands.

"So, are you feeling better this morning?" she asked, sliding a small menu over the table towards him. "You seemed very upset yesterday when you arrived. Not surprising really, given what you've been through."

He smiled. Same old Esther. Always the worrier. He remembered when Harvey had started dragging him home after late shifts at the *Tribune*, partly as a shield against Esther's wrath for the late nights or the drinking, partly to make up for the shit wages by giving him a decent meal. She had always fussed over him like an honoured guest, made sure he had enough to eat and warned Harvey not to "drive this boy too hard. We're not all as obsessed as you."

Problem was, Doug was worse than Harvey.

"I'm fine, Esther, thank you. It was just a bit of a shock, is all. And besides, shouldn't that be my question? How are *you* feeling this morning?"

She gave him a smile that once would have made him weak at the knees, now did nothing more than twist a knife in his guts. "I'm fine, Douglas. You know, good days and bad. But I'm getting there. And Harvey is being wonderful – though he'll deny it if you ask him."

Typical Harvey. For a man who made a career of chasing

headlines, he hated the spotlight or publicity more than a Catholic priest at a child abuse inquiry.

"Speaking of Harvey, where is he? I've not seen him this morning."

"Oh, oh, he had to nip to Broadford for supplies," Esther said, busying herself with calling over a waiter. Doug looked at her for a half a second. Something about the way she had said that, the kneejerk call for the waiter...

...what...?

Oh, for fuck's sake, he thought, now you're jumping at shadows. This is Esther, not Derek McGinty. Give it a rest, Doug.

He asked for coffee, leaned back as the waiter poured a cup. He skimmed the menu, aware of Esther watching him expectantly. Went for salmon and scrambled eggs, hoping he could shovel at least some of it down.

The waiter retreated and Esther shifted forward, looking at him.

"So, Douglas, what have you got planned today? There are some beautiful places on the island, and the MacDonald castle is just up the road, you could visit that..."

"Thanks," Doug said, sipping his coffee. "But I'm heading back today, I've got work to do."

Esther's skin paled behind the make-up mask. "Oh, Douglas, is that a good idea? I read about what happened; surely after what you've been through, you'd be better up here with us than in Edinburgh?"

He took another sip of coffee, considered. It would be so easy just to stay. Lie to himself that he was doing it for Esther, stay where it was safe, where his boss wasn't killed in front of him, where people weren't beaten to death. He swallowed the thought down with the coffee. No. He had a job to do, a story to cover. And if he didn't go back now, he knew he never would.

"I'm sorry, Esther, but I have to. And I've already started the ball rolling, so there are people waiting for me. But I'll come back and visit, I promise."

Esther gave him a long, even glance. Her eyes, which had once been so clear and piercing, were yellowing with jaundice, dulled by a rheumy film that was slowly dropping over her pupil like a curtain. How sick was she?

"I hope you will, Douglas," she said. "And please, don't leave it too long. After all, Harvey… Harvey will…"

He reached over, put a hand over hers, ignored the clamminess he felt. Saw the tears welling in her eyes, felt something twist in his guts. Took a breath, asked the question he didn't want answered.

He started slowly, picking the words as though he were navigating loose stones across a stream. "Esther, what is it? I know you're getting the scan results next week, but is there something else? You said something about Harvey. Is there something wrong, something I can help with?"

She looked up at him, something like confusion dancing across her face before it settled back into the impassive mask she was hiding behind. She patted his hand. "Oh, ignore an old woman, Douglas, it's just this medication, it puts me under a black cloud sometimes, you know? Makes me see the worst. We're fine. We're both fine. We just miss you, is all, and we'd like to see more of you."

He leaned back, gave her hand a gentle squeeze, scared he was going to crush it. Gave her the reassuring, confiding smile Harvey had taught him for interviews all those years ago. "Well, I'm sure we can arrange that. Now that I know where you are, and how well the hotel is doing, I'll be back. Who knows, I may even write up a holiday piece for the *Trib*."

"Don't you dare," she replied. "Last thing we want is all you uncouth lowlanders coming up here and spoiling the peace and quiet. There's been enough of that already."

Doug laughed. "Aye, fair enough. Don't want to scare off the rich foreign tourists, after all. Though it seems like you've got your fair share."

She nodded, cup chittering gently against her saucer as she picked it up. "We've been lucky, but it's a lot of work. Especially now. But Harvey says he'll cope and he really loves it here, has since the moment we arrived."

Harvey says he'll cope?

He looked at her, letting the silence draw out between them, filled only by the tick of the grandfather clock. She smiled weakly around the cup. He could see the tears threaten in her eyes again.

"Look, Esther, if there's..."

She cut him off with a raised hand. Her voice was as brittle as the china she drank from. "Douglas, please. Enough. Here's your breakfast. Can't you just eat and talk to me? I don't care about what, just not what happened to Jonathan – I've had quite enough bloodshed for now, thank you."

Doug hesitated for a moment, saw the quiet pleading in her eyes. They were both acting now, dancing around a conversation neither of them wanted to have. The problem was, he didn't know exactly what the conversation would be about. All he knew was, he wouldn't like it.

Douglas, please, enough.

He raised his coffee in a toast. "Here's to Robertson's Retreat," he said. "And breakfast with old friends."

She smiled, relief flooding into her eyes as her shoulders relaxed. "Thank you, Douglas," she said as he shovelled the first forkful into his mouth and swallowed quickly, not giving his mouth time to register he was eating. "So, tell me, are you seeing anyone at the moment? Harvey mentioned something about a young lady you sometimes work with...?"

He felt his cheeks burn suddenly, and not just from the food. "Long story," he said meekly.

"So why don't you tell me?" she replied, a ghost of the old wry amusement dancing in her eyes. "After all, I've got time."

42

Stevie padded along the short corridor to the spare room where Paul was crashed out. He was lying exactly as he had left him, face up on the bed, the quilt pulled roughly over him, towel discarded on the floor like an afterthought.

Creeping around the bed, he watched Paul breathe gently. His skin was pale and dull, the only colour a spray of acne that reached from his chin to his forehead in a rough question mark pattern. His lips were cracked and dry, his nose crusted with dried blood, a sure sign that he spent a fair amount of his time sticking things up it.

Not a surprise, that was why he was here.

Stevie leaned forward, gently pulled back the quilt. Looked in disgust at the emaciated body in front of him, the ribs visible through paper-thin skin, which was mottled with bruises and cuts. His eyes drifted down to the withered cock that sat nestled in a thick bush of pubic hair and he smiled. The poor little shit really hadn't had a lot of luck in his life.

He took Paul's arm gently, gently, watching intently for any glimmer of consciousness in his face. There was none; he murmured a little, snored gently. Unaware of what was about to happen.

It'll just be like he went to sleep. If you do it right, he'll never know, Frankie had said. Stevie swallowed down the bile that rushed into the back of his mouth, hot and bitter, took a deep breath to steady himself. Drew the needle from his pocket and primed it, not bothering to check for air bubbles. After all, what was the worst that could happen? The little shit would have a heart attack? Different cause, same result.

With his free hand he took a firmer grip of Paul's arm, squeezed gently as before. Spotted the small red dot from the previous injection that stood out on the blue-green vein under the skin. Closed his eyes, forced his hand to stop shaking, aimed for the dot and drove forward.

The vein squirmed away as the needle plunged into Paul's arm, twisting and coiling like a worm beneath the skin.

Fuck! Missed!

Paul bucked once, wildly, throwing Stevie off and sending the needle clattering to the floor. Gave a howl that echoed off the walls and hurt Stevie's ears as he grabbed at his arm, eyes wide and filled with terror and pain.

"What the fuck!" he yelped, scrabbling out of the bed like a stunned animal and throwing himself against the wall. "Stevie? Stevie, what the fuck? My arm, my fucking arm!"

Stevie moved very slowly, hands held up, eyes darting between Paul and the floor, hunting for the needle. "Sorry, Paul, my fault," he said, keeping his voice calm and even, struggling to hear himself over the roaring in his ears. "Just trying to make sure you were comfortable. Frankie called, wanted me to check you were all right."

"Frankie?" The name seemed to penetrate the fog of confused pain surrounding Paul. "Frankie called? What's...? Ah, my arm, my fucking arm! What did you do, Stevie?"

Stevie spotted the needle at the foot of the bed, almost at his feet. One more step and a lunge and it would be his. But then what? Forget what Frankie had said and threatened. Could he do this?

Would he?

"I, ah, I was just checking where I gave you the shot earlier, Paul. Must have hit a nerve. Sorry. Listen, you lie back down, I'll go and get a joint, take the edge off a bit?"

Paul looked at his arm again, rubbing it furiously, pouted like a kid who had just been given a telling off. When he spoke, his voice was small, uncertain. The little-boy-lost, standing naked in a drug dealer's flat, no idea of the world of shit he was in.

"Well, I…"

"Ah, come on," Stevie said, smiling so widely he thought his cheeks would tear. "Lie down, I'll get the good stuff. And for fuck's sake, cover yersel' up. Last thing I want to be seeing is your scabby cock."

Paul looked down, smiled sheepishly. Took a step forward and froze dead in his tracks. Glanced up frantically at Stevie, eyes filling with terror and understanding.

Oh fuck, he's seen it, he's seen it, he's…

"You were trying to *stick* me?" he whispered, what little colour there was in his cheeks draining as tears welled in his eyes. His chest was heaving so rapidly Stevie thought for a moment that a rib would punch through the skin.

"Look, Paul, I…"

"No!" he roared, the voice surprisingly deep for such a wimpy frame. "Fuck you, Stevie. I'm out of here. And wait until I tell Frankie about this!"

Frankie's words: *Do it wrong then I'll know. And I'll be very upset.*

Everything seemed to happen at once. Stevie lurched down, scooped the needle up and lunged forward. Paul screamed, that same, horrible screech echoing off the walls as he leapt back, trying to get away from Stevie. He lashed out with a naked foot, catching Stevie on the temple as he straightened up and driving him to the floor. He landed with a grunt, the air knocked out of him.

"Fucking little cunt!" he roared.

Paul dove forward, aiming for the door. Stevie kicked out wildly, catching his leg and sending him clattering to the floor. He screamed again, scrambling pale and naked to try and get to his feet, half swearing, half crying.

Stevie fell on him, felt the frantic energy as Paul bucked and writhed beneath him, trying to force him off. They flipped over, Paul on top, Stevie trapped underneath like a flailing beetle trying to right itself.

"Let me go, let me fucking GO!" Paul screamed as he bucked wildly on top of him. Stevie got an arm around Paul's throat, tried to squeeze down. Paul lashed out hysterically, reaching back blindly and grabbing Stevie's hair. Stevie howled, swung his free hand wildly, aiming a punch at Paul's face…

The scream was deafening. Paul stiffened as though electrocuted, then spasmed ferociously, breaking Stevie's grip and rolling off him. He staggered to his feet, bouncing off furniture and walls as he bent over double and clawed at his face.

"Ah, fucking BASTARD! My eyemyeyemyeye! AHHH!"

He whipped round, and Stevie felt vomit flood into his mouth as he saw what had happened.

The syringe hung from Paul's eye, dancing up and down like an obscene conductor's baton as he weaved around the room hysterically. Fat, gelatinous tears glistened on his cheek and, for a moment, Stevie couldn't process what he was seeing. And then he understood. They weren't tears. They were the contents of his punctured eyeball, weeping down his face.

"Fucking bastard!" Paul screamed, weaving like he was punch-drunk. He lunged towards Stevie, hands like talons. "I'll fucking kill you. Kill you!"

Stevie staggered back against the onslaught. Fuelled by agony and hysteria, Paul was strong, frenzied, his hands clawing up Stevie's chest to his neck. He sunk his nails in and tore at Stevie's flesh, hot blood oozing from the wounds. Stevie roared, the world turning dull as fury and pain and adrenalin flooded through him.

He lashed out as hard as he could, catching Paul in the chin. He staggered back and Stevie drove forward, doubling him over with a kick so hard it lifted Paul off the ground. He collapsed in a heap, gasping for breath, blood and pus streaming from his ruptured eye. "Fucking cunt," he gargled through the blood in his mouth.

"Shut up, ye wee shite," Stevie growled, aiming a foot for Paul's chest, determined to stamp through it like a rotten bird's nest and crush the little shit's heart into the floor.

Paul rolled to his side, grabbed Stevie's foot and clung on with a manic strength. Overbalancing, Stevie lurched forward and toppled to the floor, pain exploding in his head as he collided with the corner of the bed.

He tried to get up, tried to move, to get to Paul and choke the little cunt to death, but the cotton wool crammed into his head was stopping the signals getting to his body. He flailed around, dimly aware of Paul lurching to his feet. He staggered to the bedroom door, almost collapsed against the frame.

Stevie shook his head. Trying to move, to think. He tried to raise a hand to wipe the blood from his eyes, couldn't. Everything was getting blurry and dark, the world filling with a harsh, insistent buzzing.

He blinked harder, forced his eyes to focus. Saw Paul collapsed in the doorway, his chest covered in blood, the syringe very still in the socket of his eye.

He felt a lazy smile twist across his lips as the world faded. *Got the li'l fucker*, he thought dreamily as the dark rushed in to get him. *Frankie will be happy... Frankie will be...*

The thought followed him into unconsciousness. The silence in the flat was heavy and oppressive, charged with the frantic energy of what had just happened, disturbed only by the gnawing door buzzer as the bell was pressed again and again by the woman on the other side of the door.

43

Doug paced around his room, making a final check to satisfy the paranoid nagging that he'd missed something as he packed, unable to get Esther out his mind. There was something about the too-quick way she had replied when he asked where Harvey was, about the maelstrom of confusion and fear in her eyes when he mentioned visiting the doctor, that he couldn't shake. But what could they be hiding from him and, more importantly, why? Harvey had invited him up here to get away from the fallout from Greig's murder. Why do that if he had something to hide?

He sat on the bed with a sigh. Was he just jumping at shadows? Harvey and Esther had been nothing but kind to him, and here he was, doubting them. Hardly surprising given the last couple of days, and the questions that were piling up like driftwood, but still…

He grabbed his phone and checked for messages from Chris or Hal, let out a frustrated sigh when he saw there was no signal for the phone. He flicked into his email app, hooked up to the hotel's WiFi and hit *Refresh*. A couple of junk emails dropped into his box, along with the holding line from Rebecca after the press conference yesterday. Doug skimmed it quickly, shaking his head. It was the type of statement he hated, all words and nothing to say. They might as well have said, *We're working on it, now leave us alone* – it would have been more accurate.

He thought back to Susie's call, and her suspicion that he had leaked the possibility of a link between the two killings. It shouldn't have surprised him, after all, no matter what happened, they were always the reporter and the cop, always warily circling each other whenever they found themselves working on the same story. Why wasn't it like that with Rebecca, he wondered. Okay, there was the same mutual scepticism, but there was none of the nervous paranoia that seemed to rear its head whenever he and Susie were discussing a case.

Why?

He pushed the thought aside, focused on the job in hand. He had told Susie he would look into where the rumour of the link had come from, who had ambushed the press conference. But to do that, he needed details. Who had thrown the question first, were the other reporters expecting it or hadn't they known it was coming? Did they have more detail or only a general theory?

For that, he needed to speak to someone who had been there. He could speak to some of the reporters, but he knew their recollections would be coloured by ego. It was the way of high-profile pressers, they became like competitions. The jostling to have your question heard, the race to get that elusive soundbite that everyone would pick up and use, the clamour to be the reporter that asked the question that put the interviewee on the back foot. It could be uncivilised, rowdy, boorish. And Doug loved that part of the job a little more than he should.

No, if he wanted to know how it had happened, he needed to speak to the circus master. He needed to speak to Rebecca. At least, that was what he was telling himself.

He stood up and grabbed his bag, eager to be outside and back in signal range. He was almost at the door when there was a knock on it, and he swung it open to find Harvey standing there.

"Harvey! Sorry, I missed you at breakfast, but Esther made sure I was suitably stuffed. You get what you needed in Broadford?"

"Wha'? Hum. Yes, yes. Thanks, Douglas," he said, his tone distracted, almost forced. He glanced down at the bag in Doug's hand, jutted his chin to it. "So, you were serious about heading back, then?"

"Yeah. I know what you said, Harvey, but I need to get back and see this through. It's my job. And I've got a hot tip on a possible suspect. Guy called Gavin Pearson. Was done for murder back in the 1990s. Ring a bell with you?"

Harvey shifted his weight, leaned more heavily on his cane. Ran his hand across his beard, the sound a whisper in the silence. Shook his head. "No, no. Nothing comes to mind." He forced a small, uncertain smile. "Sorry, Douglas. But sounds like you're right, Edinburgh might be the best place for you, not wasting your time up here with an old man who can't tell you anything."

Doug took a moment, looked at Harvey properly for the first time. His eyes glittered with an almost febrile energy from sockets that were puffy and dark due to a lack of sleep. His beard looked crusted with something dark and congealing, and Doug saw a fleck of red in one of his "Tipp-Ex stains", wondered if Harvey had switched from whisky to red wine last night. He watched as Harvey rocked gently from foot to foot as he tensed and released his grip on his cane as though it was a bone he was worrying on.

Bad night with Esther? Or something else?

"That's some change of mind, Harvey," Doug said, trying to keep his tone light. "Last night you were almost threatening me with violence if I even thought about leaving."

Harvey flashed a smile as empty as his eyes. "Sorry, Douglas. I was just worried about you, is all. Didn't want you getting caught up in anything after what happened to Greig. But I know what it's like to want the story – and the only place you're going to get it is back home."

"Thanks, Harvey. And I'm sorry if I've wasted your time, but I really have to get back."

Harvey waved Doug's words away. "Don't worry about it, Douglas, I understand. Edinburgh's the best place for you, son, certainly better there than here. Come on, I'll walk you to your car. Esther's gone for a rest, says goodbye, so you'll just have to settle for me."

They walked in silence, Doug casting sideways glances at Harvey as they moved. When they got to the front door, Doug leaned forward to grab for the handle, only for Harvey to grab his arm.

"Harv...What?"

Harvey seemed to be trying to look everywhere at once. Hectic colour peppered his cheeks, a thin sheen of sweat glistening on his forehead. His mouth moved silently, as though he were practising and dismissing what he was trying to say. Doug felt a cold stab of panic in his guts. Whatever it was, Harvey was terrified.

He placed a hand over Harvey's, gave a reassuring squeeze. "Harvey, whatever it is, it's okay. Just tell me. Maybe I can help. Is it Esther? Is it worse than you're telling me?"

Harvey nodded, swiping away an angry tear from his face. When he spoke, his voice was a whisper. "Douglas, I... I'm so sorry. I thought I was doing the right thing. I really did. I didn't know. Couldn't. The last thing I wanted was to lie to you, let you down. I thought you coming here was for the best, but now... now..."

He got lost in his thoughts. Doug looked at him, Esther's words in his mind. The look of confusion when he mentioned going back to the doctor. The plastered on make-up. The pallid skin.

Harvey says he'll cope.

Understanding slithered into Doug's mind; cold, uncaring, clinical. He understood, cursed himself for not seeing it sooner. All the hints had been there. He'd just been so wrapped up in his own trauma he hadn't seen it. Or hadn't wanted to.

"She's already been for the scan, hasn't she, Harvey?" he said.

Harvey nodded again, anger fighting with sorrow in his eyes. "Last week," he whispered.

"How bad?"

"Bad enough. The cancer's spread to her liver and pancreas. They're giving her chemo now, though it's only holding the tumours back, not killing them."

Doug took a hitching breath as a huge weight seemed to press down on his chest. He felt his own tears threatening as he thought of the woman Esther had been. His own Mrs Robinson. He shook himself, bit back the sorrow. There was one question. He didn't want to ask it, but he had to, he owed them that much.

"How long?"

"Six months, tops," Harvey said, his voice cold and remote.

"Oh, Jesus, Harvey. I'm so, so sorry. Look, forget going back, I'll stay. Help out. See if I can."

"You will not!" Harvey hissed, an almost feral panic in his voice. "You have to get away from here, Douglas. Back to Edinburgh. Now. Do you understand me?"

"But Harvey, why? If you need…"

"Esther would never forgive me," he said, shrugging off Doug's hand and starting to bustle past him through the door. "We said we'd keep it from you while you were here, what with everything you've been through. We thought that was for the best. But now, you need to go. Please, Douglas, please."

Doug looked at him for a long moment. It made sense to him now. Typical Harvey and Esther. They protected him from the truth so they could look after him, offer him a retreat after the Greig killing. But Harvey hadn't been able to hold it in, and now that he knew, the last thing he would want was for Doug to be around, the three of them exchanging glances and not talking about the one subject that mattered.

He took another shuddering breath, felt the tears threaten again. He wanted to stay. To look after his friend. But he knew all he could do for him was go.

"Okay, show me off the premises, will you?"

Harvey gave him an impenetrable look, then they walked out to the front of the hotel. Doug's car was still tucked up by the side of the hotel. He blipped the key fob and the boot sprung upon, tossed his bag in and slammed the boot. Turned back to Harvey, saw that same, panic-stricken glance, watched as his head darted around the trees and driveway, as though looking for someone.

Doug took a step forward, held out his hand. Harvey took it, his grip clammy.

"Douglas, I... I..."

"It's okay," Doug said. "I get it, Harvey. And I'm sorry, I'm so sorry. If there's anything I can do, just call me, okay? And I'll be back soon."

Harvey leaned forward, grabbed him in a hug that caught Doug off guard. His body was like a piece of iron wrapped in dough, every muscle tensed, as though waiting for a blow to fall. In a way, Doug guessed it already had.

"I'm sorry, Douglas," he whispered. "Sorry I lied to you, sorry I dragged you into this. Truly, I am."

"You didn't drag me into anything," Doug said. "I wanted to come. Would have been here sooner if I'd known how bad things were. And I'll be back. Promise."

Harvey nodded, glancing around again as he released Doug. "Good, good," he muttered. "You better get going, Douglas, it's going to be a long drive back."

Doug walked to the car and dropped into the driver's seat, buzzed it forward as he settled in. Odd, he didn't remember racking the seat back. He turned the car over, enjoying the slightly high-pitched rumble from the rotary engine. It wasn't a Merc or a Ferrari, but it was his. He slammed the door and slid the window down, poked his head out.

"Thanks again, Harvey, and I mean it, you need anything, just call, okay? And I'll be back before..."

Harvey seemed to swallow something painful, the chords on his neck standing out suddenly as he gave a swift grimace. He waved his cane in a goodbye. "Drive safely, Douglas," he said. "And take care back home."

Doug gave a wave, buzzed the window back up and reversed out of the space. Drove slowly down the drive and clattered over the cattle grid, watching Harvey in the rear-view mirror all the way.

"Danny DeVito's grumpy Scottish uncle", they had called him. All Doug saw now was a broken old man facing a painful future of nursing his wife to her grave in the dream home that had become a prison.

He focused ahead, blinking away the tears and heat behind his eyes. Cleared the gates, slid into second and hammered his foot to the floor. The back end kicked out and he fought the wheel for control angrily. Slid round the corner and racked up the gears, the howl of the engine echoing in his chest.

• • •

I watch him drive off, hope and terror churning in my chest as I watch the car fishtail wildly as he accelerates away. Whatever Robertson told him, it wasn't easy for him to hear.

Pity.

I wonder for a minute if Roberston cracked and told him, warned him perhaps, then swiftly dismiss the idea. He got the message last night, no doubt. He wouldn't dare defy me. Cowards never do.

I track the sights back up the drive, see Robertson standing there, lost, alone. His head is dropped to his chest, his breathing ragged. While I can't see his face, I think he's crying.

I hope he is.

I adjust the sights, sharpen the image. Feel my finger tighten slowly, slowly, on the trigger. So easy, so, so easy. Slay the monster, complete the mission. Rest. Justice at last.

But no. No. He's the last link, the final piece of the puzzle. Before he dies, he has to suffer.

And he will.

I feel a shiver of anticipation, spoiled only by the fact that McGregor didn't find the present I left him when he first opened the car. But he will soon enough. After all, it's a long road from Skye to Edinburgh.

I swing the sights from Robertson, make a quick count of the car park. Mostly empty, only staff cars and Robertson's old Land Rover left, the guests have headed out for the day.

I smile, ignoring the pain that's settled in my shoulders and back like an old friend and straighten up.

Time for my check-in.

44

It was one of those dimly lit, overpriced bars that was aiming for style over substance. The booths were filled with a variety of people in the standard uniform for Edinburgh's West End – business suits and expensive bags. The thrum of conversation that floated through the place was quiet and reserved, punctuated occasionally by the clink of glasses, or a stab of laugher at a joke that didn't deserve it.

The finance sector – tackling the recession one lunch hour at a time.

Kevin Drainey toyed with a glass of wine that cost the same as a bottle in a normal pub, a small, amused smile twitching at the corner of his lips. As usual, his eyes were dancing between her face and her chest, and Rebecca felt the growing urge to throw her own drink at the little shit and get out of here. But she couldn't. She needed him.

"So," he said, sipping at his wine just a little too noisily, "how can I help you, Rebecca?"

She grimaced internally, took a gulp of her own drink – a soda water and lime she suddenly wished was straight vodka. Even sitting across from this little shit made her feel dirty.

Kevin was a one-man-band news agency, who fancied himself as journalism's answer to the Second Coming. He'd taken redundancy from one of the broadsheets a few years ago, used the money to go freelance. He quickly found a talent for muck-raking that made him popular with the red tops and the online gossip sites, selling stories such as *Starlet's hot affair with married MSP*,

Scandal as health chiefs claim overtime for spa visit and, her own favourite, *Copper feel of this – cop caught in indecent exposure rap.* She'd heard rumours that he was also chasing the story of a certain Detective Sergeant who had a drunken one-night stand with her married boss, but had been warned off it by a crime reporter with permanently messy hair and an eye for trouble.

Normally, Rebecca blanked him at press conferences or conveniently forgot to return his calls. But now, here she was, buying him drinks on the police expenses account, tolerating his leering at her across the table. And all because she was gambling on the one quality that set Kevin apart from all the other dead ends she'd chased today.

Greed.

She flashed him a smile. "I, ah, well, I need a favour, Kevin. As you know, the press conference yesterday got a little bit… heated. There was a rumour going round that someone tipped you lot off beforehand about a link between the Greig and Montgomery murders. I'd like to know where that came from."

He snorted, leaning back in his seat, a picture of smug arrogance. "Is that a confirmation or a denial of any potential link between the cases?" he asked.

"It's neither," Rebecca replied. "It's a question. I need to know who might have been putting that rumour around. I think you might be able to help me."

"And why should I tell you that? Got to protect my sources, haven't I?"

Rebecca watched him for a moment, biting back the bitter laugh that was trembling at the back of her throat. It was the line she had been hearing all day. Every other journalist she had asked, pleaded or begged with had all come up with variations of the same two answers: "I heard it from someone else" or "I never reveal my sources". It was the journalistic answer to playground rules – *It's our game and we're not telling.*

But not Kevin.

"Look," she said, leaning forward, feeling disgust as his eyes darted below her neckline again. "Kevin, let's be honest for a minute, okay? You're a pain in the arse to me and the police. You've written a lot of shit about us in the past, but I'm willing to let it slide. And I'm willing to help you with access in the future. But if you want that, you have to help me first, okay?"

He took his time reaching for his wine and taking a long sip, enjoying the moment of power. Rebecca felt anger flash behind her eyes, the near-overwhelming urge to just tell the little shit to go fuck himself, and instead look for the answer somewhere else.

Only problem was, she couldn't think where that could be.

She was starting to think he wasn't going to say anything when he put his glass down, arranged it carefully on the table, then smiled.

"I want an interview with Burns," he said. "Exclusive. If and when there's a definite line of inquiry on this case and you confirm there is a link. Okay?"

Rebecca weighed it up. It would be a disaster. Kevin trying his smart-arse hack routine with Burns? It would last about five minutes, with Rebecca giving even money on Burns keeling over with a heart attack or Kevin getting his neck snapped.

But…

Any interview would be under her control. She'd be the chair, with a ringside seat to the carnage. And the thought of Burns using this little shit as a chew-toy for a while had a certain appeal.

"Okay," she said. "Done."

He smiled, leaned over to offer her his hand. She took it, gave his knuckles a hard sudden squeeze that caused the smile to slip and his eyes to widen. The gym sessions with Susie were working.

"Okay," he said, eyeing her warily as he took his wounded hand back. "But this is strictly off the record, okay? Last thing I want getting round is that I can't be trusted by sources."

Fuck forfend, Rebecca thought.

She nodded agreement. "Fine. So, who did you hear it from?"

The name meant nothing to her at first. But as he droned on, embellishing the story with his own great achievements, she felt something click in her mind.

She knew that name. Had heard it on the phone only yesterday. Had been talking about it last night.

But that meant…

…meant…

She stood up, made her excuses about going to the toilet. Barely felt Kevin's eyes on her ass as she walked. Turned the corner calmly, calmly, until she knew she was out of sight of the booth. Bolted for the door, adrenalin and panic searing her lungs and burning her blood as she flailed for the phone in her bag, hoping she was in time.

45

Doug's phone started to ring just as he was approaching Eilean Donan – an imposing castle fortress sitting on a small island that lies in a section of water where three lochs meet. It was a magnificent sight – the stone it was made from seemed to glow like burnished bronze in the sun, reflecting strange ripples onto the water that lapped around the rocks running up to the main bulk of the island.

It was an ancient site, its origins dating back to the sixth century, which made Doug feel vaguely embarrassed when he realised his knowledge of the place stretched as far as knowing it featured in the film *Highlander*.

He never was one for history.

He drove into the car park, gravel spraying onto the underside of the car as he turned a wide arc and parked up facing the water. Reached across for the phone sitting on the passenger seat, clicked *Answer* with a smile.

"Hal? Hope you realise I parked up especially to take this call. Safety first and all that. I know how you worry."

Hal Damon laughed down the line. "I'm honoured," he said. "Wish I had better news, though. There's nothing in any of the cuts agencies that has a story featuring Greig and Montgomery. They both pop up, of course; Greig's byline is everywhere for a few years, and then there's the shitstorm he kicked up at Leveson. Love his line about the Ministry for Truth, by the way. And Montgomery is all over the court scene in Edinburgh, and for going after the council over the trams. But as for something that ties them together... sorry."

Doug chewed his lip. He wasn't totally surprised. "Well, thanks for trying, Hal, I appreciate it."

"Not a problem. And I'm not done yet, I'm checking with a couple of clients and sources in Edinburgh, see if they know anything."

"Cheers."

"You had any luck your end, anything else I can help out with?"

Doug looked out on the water, considering. It was probably a waste of time; after all, Chris was already running Pearson through the *Tribune*'s library, which would give him the whole story on that. But he could trust Hal to keep it quiet – and not scoop him on the story.

"Actually, there is one more thing. There's a possible suspect in the Greig killing. Gavin Franklin Pearson. He was done for murder in 1993. I'm guessing there's going to be court copy on it from the time. I'm already getting the *Trib*'s version of events, but it would be useful to see other takes, see if there's something I'm missing."

There was a pause on the line, Doug could almost see Hal working the angles in his mind. "Who is this Pearson guy?" he asked. "Why did he want Greig dead – and why like that?"

Doug ran over what he knew about Pearson – the Gulf War service, the proficiency with firearms. What he knew about the nightclub murder.

"Sounds like a charming man," Hal said slowly. "Just your type, Doug. You always seem to attract the bad boys."

"You know me, hate a boring life. Besides, we can't all work with the corporate criminals you consort with."

"Cheap shot," Hal replied, the tiniest glimmer of hurt in his voice. "I'll look up Mr Pearson for you, see what I can get. In the meantime, you take care, okay?"

"Promise. Thanks, Hal," Doug said, and cut the line.

He sat for a moment, looking out at the lochs, trying to put it all together. A Gulf War veteran assassinates Greig, kills his critically injured son and a well-known lawyer, none of whom seemed to have a relationship with each other.

Greig made himself a pain in the arse to the government over the Leveson inquiry into press freedom, and pissed off more than a million Scots with his editorial stance against independence, neither of which was enough to earn him the kind of death he had endured. Meanwhile, Charming Charlie's biggest crimes seemed to be breathtaking arrogance, a lack of morality when it came to defending little neds who were obviously guilty and a hatred for the trams project. None of which explained why he was beaten to a pulp and stabbed through the brain.

And where did Gavin Pearson fit into all this? He had the skills to kill Greig, the criminal history to take out Charlie, but could he really kill his own son? And why?

Frustrated, Doug thumbed through his contacts list and found Chris's number. Glanced at the clock and realised Walter would be out of conference and back on the desk. Flicked to his mobile number and hit *Dial*.

His voice was low and secretive when he answered. Probably in the stairwell away from the newsroom, hand scooped around his phone. "Hello, Doug? You okay?"

Doug fought back a sigh. Great question. The real cutting edge of journalism there. "I'm good, thanks, Chris. Just wanted to call in, see if you'd found those cuts yet?"

"Ah, well, no," Chris replied, embarrassment heavy in his voice.

"Oh, don't tell me advertising are still in the fucking library?"

"Actually, no, it's not that, Doug. I managed to get in five minutes after you called."

Doug felt irritation prickle at the back of his neck. He reached back to scratch, absently thinking of Susie and her stress rash. "Then what? Don't tell me the fucking server has crashed again? How long's it going to take to get back online?"

"No, Doug. It's not that, either. I ran the check. We've got nothing in the library that refers to a murder case involving a Gavin Pearson."

Doug felt his entire face fold into a question. "What? How the hell is that possible? He shoved a bottle into a kid's neck in a city centre nightclub. That's a splash right there. Plus, all the copy from the trial, family interviews, veterans' comments, etc. There's got to be something there." A thought occurred to him. "You sure you got his name right, Chris?"

Chris grunted annoyance down the phone, the hushed whisper giving way to wounded impatience. "I'm not a complete moron, Doug. I tried the search with every variation and spelling I could. Gavin Pearson. Gavin Franklin Pearson. Franklin Pearson. Frank Pearson. Frankie Pearson. There's nothing there."

Doug shook his head. "But that's not possible," he said. "There has to be something. It would have been a massive Edinburgh story at the time. The *Trib* would have had to have covered it."

"Well, not according to the library," Chris replied bluntly.

Doug sighed again. Outside, the tranquility of the loch seemed to mock him. On the line, there was a discreet beep to tell him he had a call waiting. Pulled the phone from his ear, checked the caller ID. Ignored it.

"Look, Chris. Do me a favour, run it again, will you? Maybe there's a problem in the system, maybe it'll hit lucky this time. And check the picture library, too. Surely we've got images of him in the system somewhere."

"Okay," Chris said, the tone of a boy given extra homework. "I'll get back to you in a couple of hours. When you going to be back in the city, anyway?"

Doug glanced at the dashboard clock again. Calculated. Toyed with the idea of turning around and going back to Harvey, asking him about Pearson, then thought of Esther and rejected the idea. "Should be about three hours. But if you find anything at all, give me a call as soon as you can, will you?"

"Aye, will do. And remember what you said, Doug. You owe me for this."

"No problem, Chris. I'll speak to Walt as soon as I get back. See you."

He clicked off the phone, absently glancing at the display. Noticed that the battery was down to thirty-one per cent. He leaned over for the glove compartment and the charger inside, not wanting the phone to die halfway through his call back to Rebecca. He wasn't sure why she was calling, but it was a lucky reminder that she had. He needed to talk to her about the press conference.

He clicked the glove compartment open, surprised when a file fell out and sprayed into the passenger footwell. Curious, he reached across to scoop it up, froze when he saw the first page.

The impossible stared back at him. He sat pinned in his seat, reading so fast his eyes hurt as he felt the first shudders of shock steal through his body, robbing him of all heat like the embrace of a corpse.

Funny, I didn't remember racking the seat back.

When he finished reading that first page, he held the file in shaking hands, pain lancing up his forearms from the pressure. He forced his breathing to slow as he pushed away the images and thoughts tumbling through his mind.

What was it that women at the hotel had said? *Those footprints are waiting when you're ready to see them.*

Was he ready? Was he?

Ground his teeth. Made a decision. Tossed the file aside and turned the ignition key, hitting the accelerator as soon as the engine kicked over. The car fishtailed in the gravel of the car park as Doug drove out. An instant of second thought flashed through his mind at the mouth of the car park. He crushed it with a harsh turn of the wheel to the left and bulleted onto the road, red-lining every gear as he charged back up the road he had just driven, heading back to Skye.

46

DC Eddie King was waiting for Susie when she stepped out of Diane Pearson's office, his face as bleak as the weather and as cold as the rain-soaked stones of the buildings on Cockburn Street.

"Eddie? What you doing here?"

He gave her a look that was slightly more confused than usual. "I got a call from Burns a while ago," he said. "Told me I was to put myself at your disposal for the next couple of days, help you with anything you needed. Said he'd left you a message telling you, then told me to get my arse up here."

Susie smiled. Burns. Always playing the angles. So he'd known she was coming to interview Pearson, but why send Eddie? To help? Or to keep tabs on her?

She pulled her phone from her pocket, saw the missed call and message. She flicked the phone off silent, put it to her ear. "Drummond, DI Burns. I've been thinking about what you said, thought maybe an extra pair of hands would help. So I'm attaching King to you for the next couple of days, see if he can help you with the legwork. Oh, and don't worry, this isn't a way to try and trip you up, if I want to do that, I'll do it personally."

She shook her head as she pocketed the phone. Bastard. Even made a favour sound like an insult. But at least he was helping her. Or trying.

King stood watching her like a lost puppy. He was doing a good job of keeping the petulant annoyance out of his expression, but she could see it lurking there, like a shadow waiting to fall. He'd followed most of the CID squad by keeping her at arm's length, laughed at his share of dirty jokes and gossip relating to the Christmas party. To be told he was now her gofer must have really rankled.

Shame.

"So, what are we working on?" he asked.

Susie looked around the street, spotted a café across the road, near the mouth of Haymarket Close. Jutted her chin towards it. "In a minute," she said. "First, let's get a coffee and you up to speed."

They crossed the road, took a seat at a window table. Watched a slow stream of tourists and business people pass by, heads down against the dreich weather.

A waiter brought over their drinks, giving Eddie a glance just a little too long to be casual, then quietly disappeared. Susie took her time adding sugar to her coffee, letting the silence stretch out.

Eddie slurped noisily on whatever it was he was drinking – some reddish-brown tea that smelled of old sweat to Susie. She glanced around the café – the only other customer was a tall, lanky girl ordering takeaway at the counter – then leaned forward slightly, keeping her voice low.

"What did Burns tell you?" she asked.

"Not much. Just that you had a potentially significant line of inquiry on the Montgomery and Greig cases, but it was tenuous and needed bottoming out. Something to do with a kid who was hit by a tram a few days ago?"

She nodded. "That's about it," she said. "The kid's mum, Diane Pearson, works across there." She gestured through the window to Pearson's office.

"But how does that tie in to the Greig and Montgomery murders?" Eddie asked, sounding more confused than ever.

She laid it out for him, watched as he took notes, lips moving slightly as he wrote. When she was finished talking, he took a moment and flicked back through what he had written, then laid his pen aside and gave her a surprisingly appraising glance.

"I see the problem," he said. "A lot of the facts fit, but there's no obvious link between Pearson, Montgomery and Greig to explain it. Could be him. Could be any other nutter who managed to get their hands on a rifle."

She nodded. Made a choice. "What do you think?"

"We need to find Pearson," he said. "Now. His skill-set is too close to the killer's for this to be just a coincidence. Plus, he's got form. But how do you find a man who has lived under the radar for years?"

She grimaced at the cliché – probably cribbed from one of those trashy mystery novels that littered his desk. "Good question. Any ideas?"

"No known associates. Take it the ex doesn't know anything about his whereabouts?"

Susie shook her head. "No, she says she has no idea where he might be. That he was a stranger to their son…"

She paused, thinking. Something Eddie had just said rattled around in her brain, like a pinball waiting to hit a hole and light up the board.

She was startled from her thoughts by the impatient ring of her phone.

Annoyed, she hit *Answer*. "Drummond."

"Susie, Susie, it's Rebecca." Her voice was breathless, almost panicked.

"Rebecca? Rebecca, you okay?" Unconsciously, she turned away slightly from Eddie.

He sighed. Typical. Everyone knew Summers and Drummond were close, that they spoke in a shorthand that no-one else understood. Made sense. After all, they had shared interests.

He laughed to himself, made a note to remember the joke. Gradually felt the smile fade away as he saw the tension settle into Susie's shoulders and voice.

"Wait. What? Who? Yes, yes I know the name, of course I do. But why? How?"

A pause, Drummond crushing the phone to her ear, hand

coming up to her mouth as she worried at her thumbnail. "No. I haven't, have you? Well, keep trying him. You want to meet up? Yeah. Okay, twenty minutes?"

Eddie was distracted from the call by the ping of his own phone. He took the call, sat straighter in his chair as Burns's voice filled his ear.

"You with Drummond?" he asked. His voice was thick and guttural, as though he had a mouthful of something vile. One of the canteen's bacon rolls maybe.

"Yes, sir, we're comparing case notes now."

"Good, good. But I need you to tear yourself away from the chit-chat. Seems like Stevie McInnis had a falling out with one of his customers this morning. Neighbour called it in, said it sounded like all hell was breaking loose in the flat. Uniforms forced entry, found McInnis with the shit beaten out of him and another wee scrote with a syringe where his eyeball should have been."

Eddie shuddered. "So why are we looking at it, sir? Sounds like a drug deal gone wrong. Nothing else. And Drummond and I…"

"We're looking at it because I say we're looking at it, okay *constable*," Burns spat, the venom chilling the line. "And because McInnis is known to associate with Dessie Banks. And if there's a chance of this leading back to him. I want it. Clear?"

Eddie nodded like a cheap car toy. Dessie Banks. Edinburgh's biggest gangster. You wanted it, Dessie could get it. Drugs, guns, girls, someone's legs broken.

"We'll get right on it, sir," King said.

He clicked off the phone, turned his attention back to Drummond. Felt a brief thrill of shock at her ashen appearance and confused stare.

"You okay?" he asked.

"What? Yeah." She looked at the phone as if for confirmation. "Yeah, yeah, I'm fine. I just… just…"

"Listen," he said, avoiding the awkwardness he felt by concentrating on the work. "That was Burns. He's got something else he wants us to look in to. Seems Stevie McInnis got into a bit of a scrape this morning, left him in hospital and the other guy with an eye missing."

Susie blinked at him, as though seeing him for the first time. "McInnis? You mean Stevie Leith?"

"That's the one," Eddie replied. "Come on, I'm parked on Market Street. Should only take ten minutes to get there." He stood up. Susie stayed seated.

"You go on," she said. "I've got someone I need to see."

He frowned down at her. "But the boss said."

"Eddie, please." She looked up at him, pleading. "Just deal with this one for me, please. I've got someone to see, and something I really don't want to do. So just fucking deal with it, okay?"

He stood there for a moment. The lost look in her eyes, the confusion.

"Okay," he said. "I'll call you when I'm done. We can meet up then."

"Thanks," she said. She watched him go, disappearing onto the street, everything about him screaming police despite the business suit and fashionably untidy hair.

If only everyone was as easy to spot, she thought bitterly as she followed him out of the door.

47

Doug forced himself to slow down after sliding round the turn-off to the Sleat peninsula and almost smashing into a camper van coming the other way. Horns blared as he powered away from the junction, looking in the rear-view mirror just long enough to see the passenger door of the van swing open and a small woman hop out.

Maybe she was taking his number plate. Maybe she was going to call the police. He would worry about it later.

His phone chimed again as he drove, another missed call and text. Susie and Rebecca, both trying to get him. Probably trying to see if he'd had any luck with Pearson or who leaked the information about the Greig and Montgomery murders being linked before the press conference.

None of that mattered now, not after what he'd read in the file. It was obvious that Harvey had definitely heard of Pearson – and knew a lot more about the Greig murder than he'd been letting on.

Doug felt his anger grow, cold, scalding, as he fought the urge to floor the accelerator again. He thought of Esther, of sitting with Harvey only the night before, thinking he had been with an old friend, only now realising that friend had been lying to him. And, worse, using Esther's illness as an excuse.

But still something didn't add up. Harvey could have easily lied to him over the phone, or not got in touch at all. Why go to all the trouble of inviting him to Skye in the first place? To see Esther one more time? Before Eilean Donan he would have said yes, but now...

Now…

Harvey's words in his ears now. *I saw the reports. But what actually happened, Doug?*

Was that it? Had he brought him all this way to interview him? To see how much he knew, whether he had learned the lessons Harvey had taught him and put it together?

But then, why lie in the first place? What did he have to gain?

Maybe I'm not a reliable source, after all.

Doug thought back. He'd been stupid. He should have seen it sooner. Should have known. He would have too if he wasn't so caught up in the aftermath of Greig's death and what he had…

Look at me.

…seen.

But still, there was the why. Why had he lied, pretended he knew nothing about Pearson? What was the connection to Greig? From what Doug had seen in the file, Harvey was only doing his job. And, as usual, he'd done it well. Why lie about that?

It was clear now that the trip to Broadford had been nothing more than a ruse, a cover to give him time to get out of the hotel, into the car and slip the file into the glove compartment. No wonder the seat had been racked back – it made it easier to slide across to the passenger side. Had he stolen the car key at some point or just picked the lock? Being Harvey, Doug could believe either.

He chewed at his lip angrily, hands tensing on the wheel. So many questions, so many things that still didn't make sense. He let out a roar of frustration, the sound echoing around the car and drowning out yet another phone message. He drove on, the road snaking its way through moorland as he headed for Robertson's Retreat.

He grunted. Robertson's Retreat. Maybe. But there was no way Doug was going to let him hide this time.

48

Hal Damon sat in his office – a small room just off the kitchen in the garden flat he, Colin and Jennifer called home. He had tried to keep the room as professional as he could – tidy desk, bookshelves neatly arranged, only one picture of him, Colin and Jennifer on the wall – and yet family life was starting to bleed into his little work bubble. A discarded dummy and muslin cloth sat on the small sofa to the left of his desk, the remnants of this morning's feed, a growing knot of baby toys strewn across the windowsill like plants. He smiled. He hated to admit it, but it made the room look better.

Goodbye, Mr Aesthetic. Hello, Mr Daddy.

He turned his attention back to the printouts in front of him, didn't like what he had found. It hadn't taken long for Tracey at the office to locate the articles Doug had asked for – the Pearson case had generated a lot of headlines at the time.

It seemed like an open-and-shut case. Pearson had been working at a nightclub in town, on a typical student night where the booze was too cheap and the bar was open too late. A fight had broken out, and Pearson had come face to face with Martin Everett, who apparently had a bottle and was determined to introduce Pearson to it.

In the fight that followed, the bottle ended up in Everett's neck, piercing his jugular and leaving him to bleed to death on the dance floor.

Open and shut. Guilty, yer honour. Except there was something about it that bothered Hal. He skimmed again through the reports, found one from *The Herald*, which was a page-lead on the day Pearson was found guilty and sentenced. The copy was good – it was back in the days when they had a court reporter and didn't just rely on agency staff – but it wasn't the copy Hal was interested in.

It was the pictures.

They had run two images, one of Pearson being led out of the court in cuffs, the other of Martin Everett.

Pearson was a monster. There was no other way to describe him. Hal guessed he was at least 6'4", with shoulders that seemed to start at his ears and a neck so thick that the tie he was wearing looked like a shoelace. The cuffs that were strung between his massive, shovel-like hands looked like toy jewellery. No wonder the guards that flanked him looked slightly nervous. But despite this, there was a fragility to his face, a cored-out, hollowed look around the eyes, emphasised by the sallow complexion of his skin and the deep lines that were seemingly chiselled across his face.

Fair enough, Hal thought. Getting sent to prison for murder must be a hell of a shock. But it was something more than that.

Opposite the picture of Pearson was a collect shot of Everett. Obviously provided by the family, it was a picture of him involved in some kind of sports event – track and field, Hal guessed. He was wearing a vest that exposed thin, sinewy arms and a frame that Hal would have generously called lanky. He was a relatively tall kid, but not in the same league as Pearson. His smile was open and honest, making his face glow with a mixture of happiness and endorphins from whatever he had been doing. He was good-looking too, the only thing letting him down was a slightly weak jaw and an overbite that gave him a vaguely horsey look.

Hal tried to picture it in his mind. Everett, rangy, lanky, no real muscle, going up against a wall of muscle and aggression like Pearson. Even his picture was intimidating; Hal couldn't imagine what it would be like running into him in the flesh.

And yet, the record stated that he had decided to take on

Pearson for reasons unknown and had paid for it with his life. It was possible – Hal had been in enough clubs and taken enough booze and pills himself to know that you could get caught up in the moment – but something about it didn't sit right with him.

And then there was the gap in the coverage. The hits had come back quickly, every paper at the time reporting on the story in some shape or form. And while there wasn't any significant online coverage – the story was before the days of 24/7 online news channels and breaking news apps – there were also records of TV reports and radio reports. A big trial getting the appropriate coverage.

Except in the *Tribune*. There was no record of the story ever running in the *Trib*. Not a lead, a wing, a hamper or even an obit for Martin Everett. Which, to Hal, was all wrong. The *Trib*, at the time, was the biggest newspaper in Edinburgh, if not the whole of central Scotland, and yet it had decided to ignore one of the biggest stories of the day, right on its doorstep?

Mistakes did happen – Hal remembered the infamous story of an editor who thought the fire that gutted Edinburgh's Old Town years ago was worth nothing more than a picture and three paragraphs of copy – but this? This was something else.

He reached for the coffee Colin had brought in for him a while ago, smiled at the *World's Greatest Daddy* slogan. It was cold now, but he drank it anyway.

Something about this was wrong. He knew it. It was like pitching to a new client who was only telling you half the story. They were showing you their best, hoping you could help them deal with the unspoken worst. There was something more there, just under the surface. Something no-one wanted to talk about.

He glanced again at *The Herald* copy, at the pictures of Pearson and Everett. Considered for a minute, then reached for the phone. He knew one person who might be able to help.

He had met Ronnie Selkirk years ago, when they worked together to launch a new online bank for an insurance company in

Edinburgh. Hal handled the PR, Ronnie handled the legal head-aches of launching the bank. Despite Ronnie driving Hal insane with his almost paranoid suspicion of the press and anyone who worked with them, they'd struck up an unlikely friendship. And Hal quickly realised two things about Ronnie – he was as gener-ous as he was ruthless, and he knew the location of more rattling closets in Edinburgh's legal profession that anyone really should.

Hal dialled the number. With any luck, Ronnie could help him shed a little light on this one. After what he'd been through over the last few days, Doug could use a little helping hand.

Hal hoped he could offer it to him.

49

Eddie King hated hospitals. The smell; the squeak of rubber soles on hard, over-polished floors; the hushed, almost breathless conversations punctuated by a moan or a barking cough.

It was, he supposed, an after-effect of what had happened to his granddad. When Eddie was eleven, John "Jock" White had walked down the front path of the house he shared with Elizabeth, Eddie's mum, and collapsed halfway to the gate with a massive stroke. Eddie could still remember seeing him in the hospital not long afterwards, the strong man he had known replaced by a twisted, empty husk that could do no more than flail and grunt as Eddie walked into the room. The prognosis hadn't been good – the doctors had said that Jock wouldn't walk or talk again – but somehow, he defied the odds. He got confused easily, slurred his words and walked with the aid of a Zimmer frame, but he got there. His recovery, though, was agonisingly slow, and Eddie remembered months of evenings and weekends that were arranged around visits to the hospital and, later, the specialist unit where his granddad was sent for rehab.

Eddie hated those visits. The tension slowly filling the car like an inflating balloon as his dad drove them to the hospital, the crushing boredom of sitting around the bed, the unspoken despair and frustration festering in the car as they drove home.

Jock had lived for another eight years after his stroke, eventually succumbing to a heart attack while sitting watching the football. Eddie wasn't sure if they were happy years for him. He hoped they were.

Now, walking through the corridors of the ERI at Little France, he remembered those visits, felt the old tension and unease settling into his chest.

He had called ahead, been told that Stevie Leith was still out of it – he had suffered a severe concussion when he cracked his head off a bed frame in the fight. Scans had shown no brain damage, but he was still babbling nonsense and the doctors advised that a visit at this time would be pointless.

Which left Eddie with Paul Welsh. He found him in a private room in the east wing of the hospital, lying small and pale in a bed that seemed three sizes too big for him. The roller shutter had been pulled down, leaving the room gloomy and making the eyepatch that was over one of Paul's eyes almost glow in the half-light. Eddie had read the report before getting out of the car – paramedics had found him with a syringe sticking out of his eye socket. The syringe had punctured the eyeball and caused it to leak, what the medical report called a "globe rupture". The doctors didn't know if they could save the eye yet.

Paul tensed as he heard Eddie come into the room, head twisting on the pillow.

"Who… Who's there? Can't see, too dark… Who?"

Eddie took a step forward, offered his warrant card, made sure it was in front of Paul's good eye. "Paul, I'm DC Eddie King. I wanted to talk to you about what happened earlier today."

Paul shook his head, tried to set his jaw. "Got nothing to say," he said, false bravado trembling in his voice. "Private, between me and Stevie."

Eddie shook his head. Typical. "Well, I'm afraid not, Paul," he said, hoping his tone sounded patient and understanding. He didn't feel it. "You see, when our officers arrived, they discovered a significant quantity of Class A, B and C drugs, including the heroin in the needle Mr McInnis, ah, attacked you with."

Paul's head jerked towards Eddie. "Heroin?" he whispered. "He was giving me heroin? But why would…?"

"Are you telling me you didn't go to Mr McInnis to purchase heroin?" Eddie asked.

"Wha'? No, no, I went because I... well, I..."

Eddie looked at him. Counted to ten. "What? If you weren't going for drugs for yourself, who were you going there for, Paul? You know distribution is a more severe crime than personal use, don't you? Especially with something like heroin. If you were collecting it with the intention of distributing, that's a world of shit for you."

Paul looked at him, panicked. "No, I wasn't, I went there because I was told to, because I..."

Eddie had a sudden image of a rat running around a maze, bumping off the walls. Poor bastard didn't know which way to turn. He decided on a change of tack, add to Paul's confusion.

"Okay, okay," he said soothingly. "We'll get back to that. Paul, can you tell me why Stevie would attack you like that?"

Paul's Adam's apple bobbed up and down in his throat as he swallowed, the memory flashing through him. "I... I dunno," he said, more to himself than Eddie. "He said Frankie told him to... to... but I don't understand why." He turned to Eddie, eye pleading from behind a cloud of pain and fear.

Frankie? Eddie thought. Bingo.

"Paul, who's Frankie?"

Paul went as white as his bandage. "No-one," he snapped. "No-one at all. Just a friend, okay? Got nothing to do with this."

Eddie shook his head. "Paul, you're not helping yourself with this. I know you're in a bad place right now, and I can only imagine what you're going through, but lying to the police is a serious offence. And the last thing you want to do is rack up any more problems."

Paul shook his head in the bed, the mock bravado settling on his face like modelling clay. He clenched his jaw and gave Eddie what he guessed was a defiant stare. To Eddie, he looked vaguely constipated.

"I'm no' saying anything," he said. "So piss off."

Eddie sighed, shook his head. Fuck it, he had other things to do today. "Fine," he said. "We'll get Stevie's side of the story. I get the feeling he'll be interested to hear that you brought Frankie up in our chat. See you."

He headed for the door, nodded to the PC who was sitting outside the room. There was another outside Stevie's room.

"Stupid little shit," Eddie said.

"Aye," the PC replied wearily, as if he'd seen this kind of thing a million times before. Given his age, maybe he had. "You gonna check in on the other one?"

Eddie shook his head. "Maybe later. Listen, they have anything interesting on them when they were brought in?"

The PC shrugged. "If there was, it'll be in the office on the second floor, unless it's already been sent back to Fettes."

Eddie nodded. Helpful.

He made his way down to the second floor, to a small office that had been set aside for police use. Given how often they were at the hospital, bringing in injuries or calming the A&E down at weekends, it made sense to have a satellite office they could work from if needed.

He buzzed in, asked another uniform for the details of the personal effects from Stevie and Paul. She smiled at him, rummaged through a drawer and brought out two lists detailing what was found on McInnis, S, and Welsh, P.

It didn't surprise Eddie that Paul travelled light. All that was on his list was a smattering of change, a cheap mobile phone, a lighter and a condom. There was also a wallet listed, no cash or cards present, holding a picture of a woman, thought to be in her late-twenties, red hair, blue eyes.

Stevie's list was more or less the same. A wallet that contained three bank cards, £23.72 in cash, a small pocketknife, a pack of cigarette skins. And a business card.

Eddie read the details of the card on the itinerary. Stopped, read them again. Felt his mouth go dry and his eyes widen. What the fuck?

He looked at the PC. "Have you still got this here?" he asked, pointing to the itinerary. "Item 1863241-a?"

She looked, went back into the filing cabinet. "You're in luck," she said. "They've not been sent back to HQ yet. This what you're looking for?"

She held out a small, clear plastic bag. Eddie took it carefully, as though it was precious china. Held it close, smeared the plastic tight against its surface so the strip lights overhead didn't distort what he was reading.

It was a standard business card. Just a name, a contact number, office address, email address and a logo in the right-hand corner.

Eddie knew the address. He'd been there an hour ago.

The logo was for Edinburgh City Council. The details were for Diane Pearson, Case Worker, Department of Social Care and Community Support.

50

Doug barely slowed down over the cattle grid, suspension thudding dully in protest as shock juddered up his back. He pulled into the first space he found, car skidding to a halt in the gravel. He jumped out, grabbing the file and marching for the door.

When he found it locked, he felt more confused than ever. Started to hammer at the door, ignoring the dull pain that shuddered up his arm into his shoulder with every blow. Why was the door locked anyway? Made no sense for a hotel to lock its doors in the middle of the day. Unless…

Esther, he thought, tendrils of cold, oily panic slithering around his guts.

"Harvey!" he roared. "Open the door. Is something wrong? Is Esther okay? I got your little present, think we need to talk, don't you? Why did you lie to me, Harvey? Why the fuck after all this time did you…?"

He heard the soft clatter of the bolt sliding clear on the other side of the door, took a step back, breathing rapidly, forcing his hands to unclench, ready to give Harvey both barrels.

The door opened a sliver, Esther's face appearing in the crack like an apparition. Doug felt the panic bleed out of him as though he were a balloon that had been pricked, the relief at seeing her face quickly washed away by the roaring terror that suddenly clamoured in on his thoughts.

She looked like death. It was the only way he could describe it. The make-up that she had used to disguise her condition seemed to mock her – patches of lurid colour covering skin that was grey and slack. Her hair was tousled and unkempt, as though she'd been raking her hand through it. Hands which, curled around the door, looked like rotted stumps. The knuckles a feverish red, the fingers and skin leprously white.

"Jesus," he whispered. "Esther, are you okay? I'm sorry for the noise, it's just…"

"Shh," she hissed, desperation flashing in her eyes. "Please, Douglas. Don't say anything else. I don't want to hear it. Just leave. Please. Now."

"I can't do that, Esther, I'm sorry. Is Harvey here? Why was the door locked? Can I…?"

"No, Douglas," she said, her voice sharp with rising panic. "Please, you need to leave. Now. I'll have Harvey get in touch with you…"

She flinched suddenly, pain folding her face into a mask of agony. Doug took and instinctive step forward, pushed against the door, reached out for her.

"Esther? What's wrong? Come on, let's get inside, call the doctor for you…"

"No," she moaned, body shaking with hitching sobs as she leaned into Doug. "Douglas, please. You don't understand, you have to…"

The side of his head exploded in pain and Doug was pushed sideways by the force of the blow. He twisted awkwardly, hitting the side of the double door and then falling back, stumbling on the step and tumbling to the gravel, the wind knocked out of him.

He rolled over, trying to understand what had just happened, tried to think over the roar of black agony in his temple.

What the…?

He blinked rapidly, forcing his eyes to focus as he saw the double doors of the hotel swing open. Started kicking at the gravel frantically, desperately trying to back away from the figure emerging from the shadows.

He let out a sound that was half moan, half shout of anger.

Ignored the daggers of pain in his hands and his back as the gravel dug into them, tearing, shredding.

Above him, a man with gigantic hands and shoulders smiled. It was a soft, almost gentle smile and Doug felt his bladder weaken when he saw it.

Gavin Pearson. Thick, bull-like neck, dark suspicious scowl and thin bloodless lips that said violence was his first language, pain his second. The years had taken their toll, but he was still the same man Doug had read about in the car park in Eilean Donan. At the top of the impossible file was a page from the *Tribune* that wasn't meant to exist. It was the report on Pearson's sentencing for the Everett murder. The byline on the piece was Harvey Robertson.

Pearson grabbed a handful of Doug's shirt, exhaling sourly as he hauled Doug to his feet. "Hi, Doug," he said. "Been looking forward to meeting you face to face. You look like a man with a few questions. How 'bout we go inside and have a chat? I bet Harvey's just dying to see us."

Doug flailed out in panic, fists thumping onto Pearson's outstretched arm. Pain twisted his face into a grimace and, for an instant, Doug thought he might have a chance of getting away.

The thought died as Pearson twisted away and, with his free hand, pushed a knife into Doug's face.

"Quit it, you little fuck," he hissed, dark grey eyes wild, a sheen of sweat on his forehead, the same, fetid smell on his breath. "Quit it now, or I swear tae fuck I'll start on you and finish on his bitch of a wife, clear?"

Doug moaned. He nodded meekly, offered no resistance as Pearson dragged him into the hotel. At the door he barked at Esther to "get fucking moving" and she gathered herself up and hobbled into the hotel, Pearson dragging Doug behind her.

51

Susie met Rebecca at a small café on Leith Walk, got her to go over what Drainey had told her.

"Harvey Robertson," Rebecca said, shaking her head in disbelief. "Said he got a call from Harvey saying that there was strong evidence that the Greig and Montgomery cases were linked."

"He telling the truth?" Susie asked, not wanting to hear the answer. "Or you think he was just playing you to get what he wanted?"

Rebecca stared into her cup as if the answer was there. "I thought about that, but then I phoned around. No-one wanted to tell me who had leaked the story when I didn't have a name, but they were happy enough to confirm it was Robertson when I mentioned the name to them, so yeah, it's legit."

Susie took a swallow of her coffee. It was as bitter as her mood. "Fuck," she whispered. "So Doug caught your hint, got his pal Harvey to phone it around so he could keep his name out of it and watch us squirm." She shook her head. She had wanted to believe him when they talked on the phone earlier. What was it he said? *The last thing I'm going to do is lie to you – or Rebecca.*

So much for that.

Rebecca swirled the tea in her cup. It had been her first reaction, too. Yet there was something that just didn't feel right about it. Oh, Doug could be a bastard if he thought there was a story in it, but to see both of them out?

"I'm not sure," she said finally. "There's something that still doesn't sit right with this. Why would he do it? He told both of us where he was going, who he was going to see. So why get him to phone around the story if he knows we'd link him straight to Harvey anyway?"

Susie shrugged. She had a point. What did Doug get out of it? He had said it himself, it was a big story, no way he was going to give away a good line on it. And he hadn't known for a fact that the killings were linked – as he admitted himself, it was only when Susie confronted him that he knew for certain.

"So what's the alternative?" Susie asked. "That this guy Robertson found out about the link on his own, decided to phone it around? Why? He's been retired for years, from what Doug said. Why get back into the game now? And why leak it to rivals when he could just run the story himself?"

"I don't know," Rebecca admitted. "But something just doesn't add up about this." She paused. "You had any luck getting in touch with him?"

Susie shook her head, frustrated. "No. Phone just keeps ringing out or going to voicemail. You?"

"Same," Rebecca replied. "I've sent a couple of texts, no reply to them, either."

"He must be driving," Susie said. "He said he was coming back today. We can ask him what the hell is going on when he gets here."

Rebecca stuck her hand in the air, Susie following her gaze. Grimaced slightly when she saw King at the door of the café, waving enthusiastically. He'd called twenty minutes ago, asking where she was. She'd agreed to meet him, but had hoped he would take a little longer to get here.

He bustled over to the table, nodded a greeting to Rebecca, who flashed him her best press officer smile in return. He sat down beside Susie, intentionally turning his shoulder to Rebecca. *You're not part of this conversation*, the move said.

Susie rolled her eyes. "Eddie, whatever you've got to say, you've got my permission to say it in front of Rebecca. If it breaks any regulations, it's on my head, okay?"

Eddie gave Rebecca an uncertain glance, then fixed his attention back on Susie.

"Okay," he said. "You know that incident with Stevie Leith the boss asked us to look into?"

She nodded. She'd heard the radio chatter while on her way here, skimmed the initial incident report. The gruesome ones were always talking points and this one, with a kid ending up with a syringe buried in his eye, certainly qualified.

"Well," Eddie said, settling into his role as head storyteller, "I went down to the ERI and interviewed the suspects. Took an inventory of items found at the scene as well."

Susie made a murmur of approval. Good, solid work. "Anything interesting?" she asked.

Eddie broke into a smile so wide it could almost be genuine. It made him look like a kid again. A spoiled kid used to getting his own way, but a kid nonetheless.

"Oh yes," he said, producing his phone and flicking on the camera. "Thought this in particular might interest you."

She took the phone, peered at the image of Diane Pearson's business card. Looked up at Eddie, her face full of questions.

"I don't know," he said. "I asked the one who was conscious about it but he refused to say anything. Guess he could have been a client of hers, but we'll have to check with her or the office to find out."

Susie thought quickly. Phone and make sure she was there or try and surprise her?

She gulped down the last of her coffee, looked across to Rebecca.

"We've got to follow this up," she said. "Keep trying to get him. If you do, give me a call?"

"Definitely," Rebecca said. "And in the meantime, I'm going to do a little asking around about Mr Robertson."

"Good," Susie said. She stepped away from the table and paused, an idea threatening at the edges of her mind. Something Eddie had said earlier.

"What?" Rebecca asked.

Susie shook her head. "Nothing, just a thought. Come on, Eddie. Let's go and have a chat with Mrs Pearson. I want to know how she knows Stevie Leith and Paulie One Eye."

King laughed too loudly at the joke, made his way for the door. Rebecca looked up at Susie, rolled her eyes.

Men, the look said. Susie found it hard to disagree.

52

Harvey was slouched in one of the deep leather couches that bracketed the fireplace in the lounge area. His face was a bloodied mess, lips swollen and split, eyes already swelling with bruises, a long gash on his cheek. He was leaning back, making a lisping, spluttering sound with every hitching breath. Doug had heard the sound before. It meant his nose was broken.

Pearson barked at Esther to take a seat beside her husband, then threw Doug into the couch opposite. He stood at the end of the two couches, like the head of the table, breathing deeply, wiping sweat from his face. Doug noticed blood on his knuckles, most likely Harvey's, but there was something else about his hands: they were twisted and knotted, warped by arthritis. Doug concentrated, remembered the age he read in the copy, added the intervening years. Pearson wasn't looking good for a man of fifty-six.

"Well, well, well, isn't this nice?" he said, his voice a harsh rasp as he opened his arms out in an encompassing gesture. The knife glinted in the overhead lights. "All of us together like this. Though I'm a little surprised to see you, Doug, I thought from the way you tore out of here this morning, you wouldn't let off the accelerator until you hit Edinburgh."

Doug swallowed down the panic that chilled his throat with an icy caress. *Watching,* he thought, *he was watching. Just like…*

…like…

Just like he was before he shot Greig.

Doug forced back the images dancing in front of his eyes, of the blood and destruction and terror, forced himself to breathe, to focus.

"Why?" he heard himself say. "Just tell me why?"

Pearson laughed, the sound of glass being dragged across stone. "Why? Don't you know, Doug, haven't you worked it out? Hasn't Harvey here ever told you the story of how we met? Of how he helped destroy my life?"

"Leave him alone," Harvey murmured. "Please, he's not a part of this, neither is Esther. Please, just let them go, it's me who did this. Please…"

Pearson strode forward, slapped Harvey with a hard backhand. Esther let out a sobbing moan.

"Shut the fuck up," he snarled. "You made them a part of this with your lies. Besides, hurting the innocent never seemed to bother you before."

Hurting the innocent? Destroyed my life? Doug's mind was racing, like he was trying pieces of a jigsaw puzzle and discarding them. Nothing fit, nothing made sense. He didn't have enough of the picture. Harvey had covered Pearson's trial, then lied about it to Doug's face when asked if he recognised Pearson's name, taking the coward's option of cramming his cuts into his glove compartment to find later. Why? How had he ruined Pearson's life? Why was the story missing from the *Tribune* archives? And where did Greig fit into all this?

A thought flashed across Doug's mind. The archives. The switch from the physical copies of the *Tribune* to the online version that they used now. It was organised by the editor, administrated by senior reporters.

Like the crime reporter at the time.

"What else is missing?" he asked, turning to Harvey. "What don't you want me to know, Harvey?"

Pearson clapped his hands slowly, the sound like gunshot in the silence of the lounge. "Very good, Doug, maybe Harvey did teach you a thing or two after all."

He bent down, grimacing as he did, came back up with the file from the car.

"Here you go," he said, throwing it at Doug. "I'm guessing from how quickly you got back here that you didn't get a chance to read beyond the first article. Well, knock yourself out, it's all there."

Doug glanced between Pearson and Harvey. Harvey turned his head away.

"What? No, I'm not going to… Look," – he glanced towards Esther – "she needs to see a doctor. Let me call one and we can talk this over, I can…"

Pearson strode over to him, grabbed his hair and yanked his head back. Doug yelped, thrashed around in the sofa. "Fuck off! Let me go, you cunt, let me…"

His words died in his throat when he felt the scalding thrill of the knife blade against his skin. Then Pearson, whispering in his ear, the sound and smell of death.

"Read, cunt," he whispered. "Believe me, it's a great story. You'll love it. And if you don't, I'll paint this place with your blood. Just like I did with Greig. I promise."

Doug's head snapped forward as Pearson let him go. Fighting back tears, he glanced between Esther and Harvey. No help at all. With shaking hands, he flipped open the file, turned past Harvey's first report and started to read.

And, for the second time in three days, Doug McGregor's life fell apart.

53

Susie and Eddie found a space in the car park at Waverley Station and made their way to Fleshmarket Close. It was early afternoon, and Susie was worried they would miss Diane if she'd already left the office for her afternoon meetings.

They were halfway up the stairs when her phone beeped. She reached for it, hoping it was Doug, disappointed when a number she didn't recognise flashed up on the call ID display.

"Hello, DS Susie Drummond," she said warily. Probably just a junk call.

"Hello, Detective Drummond? Sorry for calling you out of the blue like this, but I didn't really see any other choice. My name's Hal Damon, a friend of Doug McGregor's."

Susie cursed silently. Damon. This was the last thing she needed, a PR expert trying to smooth-talk her.

"Yes, Mr Damon. Doug's mentioned you. How can I help?"

There was an edge of anxiety in the reassuring, measured tone that filled her ear. "Well, Ms Drummond, I'm afraid I'm only calling you because I couldn't get a hold of Doug. You see, I think might have found something about the case you're working on, and it seems too important to wait."

Susie felt a stab of anger. Shit. What had Doug told this guy? He had promised her he would be discreet, check things out quietly and now, here she was, taking a call from Mr PR, who would no doubt demand a fee or something else for the help.

Sometimes, she thought, Doug McGregor was more trouble than he was worth.

"And what might that be, Mr Damon?" she said, noticing Eddie's puzzled glance.

"It's Hal, please. And, Susie, don't be angry at Doug. Anything that I've found out is strictly confidential, okay? He asked for my help, but now I can't contact him. Doug speaks very highly of you, and I think he'd want you to know."

Her jaw ached gently as she ground her teeth together. So not only had Doug shared details of the case with this guy, he's been talking to him about her – about them – as well. Perfect.

"I'm listening, Hal," she said.

"Okay. Doug asked me to do a cuts check on Gavin Pearson, look into the coverage of his murder trial. I think he was trying to figure out the link between him and Greig and Charles Montgomery."

Susie took a deep breath. So Doug had told this guy about the link between the cases as well. Fucking little shit.

"Anyway, I did some digging. There were a couple of things about the court copy that didn't make sense to me. And while I couldn't find a link to Greig in any of it, I may have found a link to Mr Montgomery."

Susie jerked to attention as if electrified. "What?" she whispered, Eddie taking a subconscious step closer as she did. "What did you just say?"

"I said I think I've found your link between Gavin Pearson and Charles Montgomery," Hal repeated. "I had some contacts check out the legal teams at the trial. Mr Pearson was, as you'd expect, prosecuted by the Crown. He was defended by a…" – a soft rustle of notes on the other end of the line – "James McDermott QC."

Susie thought for a minute. The name meant nothing to her. "So?" she said.

"At the time of the trial, Mr McDermott worked for Wallace and Dean. They're a fairly big firm in the city."

Susie nodded. She knew the name, Wallace and Dean. Then it clicked.

"Oh, shit," she whispered before she could stop herself.

"Indeed," Hal said, amusement warming his tone. "Wallace and Dean, the same firm that Mr Montgomery worked for. Oh, and I checked. He was senior advising counsel on the Pearson case. Unfortunately, Mr McDermott died a couple of years ago, heart attack, but it's an interesting link, don't you think?"

Susie felt her mouth move soundlessly as she tried to fit that with what she knew.

"Yes," she said dumbly, "yes, it is. Look, Mr Damon, I…"

"It's Hal," he said again. "And don't worry, as I said, this is all confidential. My sources wouldn't want to be involved in this, and my only concern is helping Doug out. And you, if I can."

Susie had lost interest in the call, her mind too full of possibilities and theories. It was like turbocharging a car in a dead-end alley – all that power and nowhere to go. She was dimly aware that Damon was still speaking.

"Excuse me, what?"

"I was just saying to pass my regards on to Doug. And it was good to speak to you at last, Susie, he talks about you all the time."

He clicked off, leaving Susie standing stunned and confused.

Interesting link, don't you think?

Montgomery was senior advising counsel…

He talks about you all the time…

King spoke, breaking her from her thoughts. "What the hell was that all about? Who was that?"

Susie thought quickly. Risk missing Diane and call Burns now? Or try to get her before she left the office and take this to Burns later?

She glanced up the stairs. Decided.

"Just a friend," she said. "With some very interesting news. Come on, let's go and see what Pearson knows about Paul Welsh and Stevie Leith. Then we've got some lawyers to talk to."

54

Doug skimmed the pages as fast as he could, feeling Pearson's gaze boring into him as he did. He snuck glances at him as often as he dared, noticing the way he dropped his shoulders when he thought no-one was looking, wiped away sweat from his brow and rocked from foot to foot as if he couldn't get comfortable.

Given what Doug was reading, he thought it was a fair bet that's exactly what the problem was.

The file contained a series of articles from the *Tribune*, dated 1992. The subject? The trials of a brave war veteran who had come home from war, only to find his health ruined and his body failing him. The articles featured extensive interviews with Gavin and Diane Pearson talking about his failing health, the battle to get Gulf War Illness recognised, the fact that no-one, from doctors to MPs to the Army itself, was listening. They were well-written, in-depth pieces, factual, engaging, relaying the human cost of what was happening to Gavin and Diane without going for the cheap emotional gutshot or the "I fought for our country and now I'm dying" sensationalism of the red tops.

Flicking through, Doug could see there were eight articles in total, spread over a period of about three months. Speaking "from their small neat home in a new-build housing development in Fife", the Pearsons described Gavin's return from war, the first signs of health problems – "It was a lung problem, I couldn't stop coughing, couldn't get my breath" – to his battle to hold down a job and the strain on their marriage.

"Of course it's tough," Diane was quoted as saying. "He was

a strong, fit man when we first met. Now he's a shadow of that, almost holding his breath to see what goes wrong with him next. We jump at every shadow, every cough, every wheeze, every mark on his skin. We still love each other, of course we do, but it puts an enormous strain on us."

The articles stopped with a report that, following a trip to the doctor, Gavin had a "severe flashback incident" and had to be restrained and hospitalised.

Every one of the articles was written by Jonathan Greig.

Doug scanned them again, searching for a reference to Harvey. As far as he could see, there was no connection other than the court copy, which had run more than a year after the initial features on Gavin's plight.

So what…?

Doug shucked the folder pack into order, looked up at Pearson, who was now leaning on the back of a chair. At least he'd sheathed the knife again.

"Look, Mr Pearson, Gavin. I'm sorry for what you've been through, really I am, but I don't see how this…"

Pearson sneered, barked something halfway between a cough and a laugh that made Esther flinch in her seat. "Of course you don't," he said. "That's the way these fuckers wanted it. Your old boss is a clever man, Doug. Knows just how to tell a story; just what to tell, just what not to."

Doug glanced at Harvey, confused. "I don't know what you're… Still don't see…"

"Fucking tell him!" Pearson roared, in a voice that sounded like it was dipped in tar.

Harvey jerked in his seat, turned to Doug, couldn't bear to look him in the eyes.

"Douglas, I'm sorry, I only did what I thought was right, only…"

"Stop fucking snivelling and tell him!" Pearson shouted again, his voice diminished. Doug looked at him, wondered how strong he really was. All this standing and talking was taking it out of him, and if half of what he had read was true…

"Why don't you tell me," he said, standing up before he could talk himself out of it. "There's obviously something I'm missing here. I don't see…" He paused, took a breath.

Fuck it.

"I just don't see how any of this justifies you blowing Greig away, beating Charlie Montgomery to death and killing your own son. That is what happened, isn't it, Gavin?"

Pearson exploded forward, catching Doug with a vicious uppercut that made his teeth clatter together and snapped his head back. He weaved back, trying to get his footing, trying to concentrate over the roaring in his ears and the blurring in his eyes.

Pearson lunged again, huge hands clawing for Doug's throat. Doug managed to side-step then, in desperation, threw his arms around Pearson in a bear hug. He clung on as hard as he could, using his momentum to swing him to the left and try to throw him over.

Pearson staggered away, crashed into a coffee table, but managed to keep his feet. Swayed as he came to a stop. His eyes bottomless pits, teeth bared, nose flaring as he heaved for breath.

"You fucking little shite," he whispered. He bent over double and, for an instant, Doug felt a thrill of hope. He had been right, he was too exhausted and ill to go on. He took a half step forward. Stopped dead when he saw Pearson straighten up with a small gun, taken from an ankle holster, held in his massive hand as though it were a toy.

"Fucking shite," he repeated, taking a step forward. Doug shuffled back on numb legs, arms outstretched. He couldn't take his eyes off the gun. The dead, empty eye of the barrel, the way it was trained on his chest. The dull glint in the light.

Susie, his mind blurted, *this is what Susie would have seen.*

Pearson advanced on him, blinking away the sweat that was streaming into his eyes. He twitched to the right sharply, noticing

Harvey getting ready to move on the sofa. "Bit late for fucking heroics, isn't it, Harvey?" he heaved. "Sit the fuck down."

Doug was babbling, his thoughts filled with blind panic. "Look, Gavin, I'm sorry, I'm sorry. Just tell me what you want and I'll, I'll…"

The gun crashed into his jaw, a massive hammering blow that took Doug off his feet. The side of his face exploded with pain as hot, coppery blood flooded into his mouth. He turned to the side, gagging, spluttering, spat a huge wad of blood onto the floor, knew there was a tooth in there somewhere. He tried to move, tried to get his legs to work, but he was seized by shock and fear. His hands flailed uselessly as Pearson landed on him, straddling him with his massive legs.

He leered down at Doug, a horrible smile twisting his face into a death mask. His skin was ashen, his eyes bloodshot and filling with tears, blood was starting to drip slowly from his nose.

"Please, don't, please, I don't, I mean, I…" Doug mewled; hatred, anger, panic and shame churning through him as tears streamed down his cheeks. "Please, I…"

Gavin slapped him once, brought the gun up to eye level. His voice was amazingly calm.

"You're not too fucking bright, Douglas, are you? You've got it all the wrong way round. Ask your boss over there, what was happening in all those long cosy interviews with Di? If he doesn't tell you, don't worry, I've left you another little present in your boot. It's in the spare-tyre well. It should explain everything."

"Okay, I'll look, anything you want, oh please, Jesus, just don't…"

Pearson leaned back, the sound of the gun's safety clicking off was very loud. "What I want?" he whispered. "Good question. I wanted a happy life. A healthy son. A happy marriage." He laughed. "So much for that idea. Guess I'll just have to settle for telling the story your cunt of a boss never had the balls to."

He brought the gun up, pointed it straight between Doug's

eyes. Doug thought his heart might explode before the shot; the panic, the terror.

...Susie...

Suddenly, Pearson pulled the gun away. Leaned down to Doug as though he were going to kiss him. Whispered four words in his ear. Four words that cut straight through the panic and the terror and the dread.

He sat back up, looked down at Doug, the tears growing heavier. Looked over at Harvey, dropped him a wink. "He knows," he whispered.

Then he brought the gun up to his temple and blew his own brains out.

55

The receptionist at Diane's office blushed as she gave Eddie and Susie an apology. "I'm sorry, Mrs Pearson left a little while ago for a late lunch."

Eddie and Susie exchanged looks. Shit.

The receptionist glanced between them. Hesitated, then added: "But if it's urgent, she sometimes goes to the American diner around the corner on the Mile. You know, the one just down from the City Chambers?"

Susie saw the place in her head. She'd been there a few times herself. Good cocktails.

They thanked the receptionist, headed back down the stairs and on to Cockburn Street. Took the short, steep walk up to the Mile and turned right, towards the diner.

"So, you going to tell me who that call was from?" Eddie asked as they walked.

"Can't," Susie said. "Got to protect my sources."

Eddie snorted. "Sources? You've been hanging around that prick McGregor and Rebecca for too long."

Susie let the jibe go, grabbed for her phone instead. No calls or messages from Doug. Odd, it wasn't like him to be out of touch for this long. Even on the road, he normally couldn't go half an hour between phone checks.

She stopped outside the diner. She had wanted to talk to Diane first, clear up the link to Welsh and Stevie Leith, then concentrate on what Hal had told her. But there was no guarantee that she would be in there, which would mean more wasted time. And she needed something to give Burns, now.

She turned to Eddie. "Go on in and see if she's in there, will you? I'm going to brief the boss."

He pulled a face that said she got to do all the fun stuff, then pulled open the door and trudged inside. It was a large place, with a dining area at the back and a long, lounge-style bar at the front where single diners could eat and have a quick drink. She thought it would take him at least five minutes to cover the place. Plenty of time.

She dialled Burns's number, tried to ignore the growing nerves as she waited for him to answer.

"DI Burns," he snapped as he answered the phone.

"Sir, sir, it's Drummond," she said. "I might have something for you."

"What, you mean other than a fucking headache?" he snapped. Sighed, took a deep breath that echoed down the phone. "Sorry, Drummond, bad day. I take it King's caught up with you by now?"

"Yes, sir, and thank you for that. He's been very, ah, helpful."

Burns grunted. "First time for everything. Now, you said you had something for me?"

She took a breath, ran him through everything Hal had told her about Montgomery, the law firm Wallace and Dean. When she had finished, Burns murmured approval.

"Good work, Drummond," he said. "I'll get Lewis and Banks to check that out. So, we've got a potential link between Pearson and one of the deceased. But what about Greig?"

"I'm still working on that, sir, got some calls in with contacts, hopeful of a response soon."

"Don't rely too much on that little shit McGregor, Drummond," Burns said. "You remember what I said about upstairs."

Susie felt her cheeks redden. "Yes, sir."

"Good. What's your current whereabouts? This is all going to need writing up at some point. I don't want a backlog in the reports. The Chief will go fucking spare."

Susie winced. Paperwork. The backbone of modern policing.

"King and I are just about to talk to Mrs Pearson again, sir. Seems there might be some link between her and that drugs rammy you had us look into this morning."

"Really? What?"

He snorted when she told him about the business card. "Could be anything. She's a counsellor after all, speaks to drug addicts every day."

"Yes, sir, but I'd like to bottom this out, just to be sure."

"Fine, but take it easy, the last thing I want is Mrs Pearson filing a harassment complaint against you."

"Understood, sir," Susie said. "I'll let you know how it goes."

She hung up. Chewed her lip. That same nagging feeling was back again. The one she got when she was speaking to Eddie outside Pearson's office earlier. Something about what he said, and then Burns just now.

She stood, thinking. Replaying the conversation in her mind. After a moment, the answer came to her. Followed by another raft of questions.

She looked in through the window of the bar, saw Eddie's not-so-subtle attempts to attract her attention. Smiled. Time for a little chat with Mrs Pearson.

56

Doug was in a place beyond shock. He was looking at the scene as if through thick glass, with his mind screaming and wailing at one side and him on the other, calmly doing what needed to be done.

He stood up, looked at the splatter of dark blood and brain matter that was streaked across the carpet and up the wall like a bloody exclamation mark. The bullet had taken most of the left side of Pearson's skull off, leaving a gaping flap of bone hanging by a thin strand of sinewy raw flesh that glistened with fresh blood. But the path of the bullet had left most of his face intact and he still wore that same, almost calm smile.

Doug heard him whisper the words in his ear again as he looked down at him. He walked forward and picked up the gun, then moved to Esther, who had collapsed on the floor. Harvey had rushed to her, wrapping his arms around her. He was making soothing noises, the sounds muted by the ringing in Doug's ears from the gunshot. He found he was strangely glad about that. If he could hear Harvey's hypocrisy, he might not be able to resist the urge to use the gun himself.

He stood over Harvey, over the man he thought he knew, felt a flash of rage travel down his arm and bunch his free hand into a fist. Forced it to unfurl, then laid his hand on Harvey's shoulder. Hard.

"Call the police and an ambulance for Esther," he said in a voice he barely recognised. "Do it now."

Harvey looked up at him, his face a contortion of relief, pain and guilt. Doug didn't care. He just held his gaze long enough to make sure he got the message, then emptied the gun, pocketed the bullets and dropped it before turning and walking to the front door.

Outside, the world was impossibly bright, the wind in the trees a hurricane to Doug's ears. Some guests had returned and gave him alarmed, questioning looks. He ignored them, focused on his car. Walked up to it as if for the first time and plipped the remote to spring the boot. As he got closer, his phone started to beep in his pocket, message after missed message coming in now he was clear of the hotel's signal dead zone.

He ignored them. Time enough for that later.

The item was where Pearson had said it would be, in the boot well where the spare wheel should be. The well was empty apart from a small pressurised gun filled with gel that could be fired into the tyre to seal it in the event of a puncture. Before that moment, Doug had never thought about what an idiotic idea that was.

The items Pearson had left were in a large envelope, old and tattered. It contained a letter and something else, something Doug recognised immediately. A notebook. He held it in his hands, an echo of the past. He leaned against the boot of his car and read slowly. When he finished it, he stood for a moment, as though digesting, forcing himself to think everything through logically until he had an unbreakable chain of events, one leading seamlessly to another.

It was, he realised bitterly, another trick Harvey had taught him.

He read it all again, slower this time, making sure he had missed nothing. It all made sense now. Hell, he might have killed Greig that way himself in Pearson's shoes.

He stuffed the letter and the notebook back into the envelope, tossed it into the boot. Walked back to the hotel. He got halfway there when he heard the first scream from one of the returning guests. He paused, listened, heard the distant echo of a siren. Out here, it was a harsh, alien sound.

He started walking, picking up his pace. He didn't want to be here when the police arrived. Didn't have time for their questions. But before he left, he needed to have a final word with Harvey.

57

Eddie found Diane Pearson at a small booth at the back of the diner, eating a salad and reading what looked like a reference book on pharmaceutical approaches to addiction issues. He introduced himself, knowing what she looked like from Susie's description, then turned back to Susie and waved.

He offered to buy Diane another drink, which she declined, then slid onto the upholstered bench on the opposite side of the table. Susie slid in beside him a moment later.

"Ah, Detective Drummond," Diane said, voice heavy with weary sarcasm, "nice to see you again."

Susie caught the tone, and Diane's use of her title rather than her name. Good, she wanted her off balance a bit.

"Diane, sorry for troubling you again," she said. "But we had a very puzzling incident this morning, and we were hoping you could help us with it."

"Oh," she said, putting down her fork and sliding aside the salad she was picking at. "I'm not sure how, but I'll do what I can."

Susie smiled a thank-you. "Seems a drug addict fell out with his dealer this morning in Leith. Bit of a tussle ensued, and they both wound up in hospital, one of them with a particularly bad eye injury."

"I imagine that would be fairly common," Diane said. "We see a lot of drug-related violence. Not that common for a user to lash out at a dealer."

Interesting, Susie thought. "Well, we're not sure that's what happened. You see, the victim, Paul Welsh, seemed to have been staying at the flat. His clothes were in the wash and it looked like he'd recently showered."

"Interesting," Diane said, her tone growing bored. "But I'm not sure how I can help shed any light on this."

"Well, you see, that's why we're here. Among the personal effects of the dealer, we found a business card. Your business card to be exact." Susie paused, watched Diane's eyes. Nothing. It was like watching ice. "Tell me, Diane, do you know a Stevie McInnis or Paul Welsh?"

Diane leaned back, looking up at the ceiling. *I'm thinking*, the pose said.

"Paul Welsh. Paul Welsh. Wait. Runty little kid? Thinning dark hair combed forward." She mimed the action of hair being brushed forward above her head. "That him?"

Eddie nodded. "That matches the description, yes. Do you know him?"

Diane smiled. "You know I can't tell you that, detective. Client confidentiality prohibits me from discussing who may or may not be receiving treatment."

Susie twitched a smile. Clever. "Very true," she said. "But if we were to officially ask to see your client list, to identify why that business card was at a crime scene, we might find his name there?"

Diane flashed her own smile, as warm as the lettuce on her plate. "I would say it was a strong possibility," she said.

"Great, we'll get right on that." Something Eddie had told her crossed her mind, about Paul mentioning a Frankie. Maybe short for Franklin. As in Gavin Franklin Pearson. Worth a shot.

"Incidentally, these wouldn't be the sort of people your husband would associate with, would they?"

Diane paused, her throat working as the colour faded slowly from her cheeks. When she spoke, it sounded and looked as if her jaw had been wired shut. "As I told you, detective, I've had no contact with Gavin for years. I have no idea who he might associate with, or why."

Susie conceded the point with a small wave of her hand. "Of course, Diane, of course. Sorry." She paused, heard Burns in her mind, his warning from less than ten minutes ago. *The last thing we want is a harassment complaint against you from Mrs Pearson.*

Mrs Pearson.

Fuck it.

"Well, thanks for your time, Diane, sorry to interrupt your lunch. Oh, one small thing. When I asked about Gavin just now, I said 'husband', and I noticed you still use 'Mrs Pearson'. You did divorce him, didn't you?"

Diane swallowed, reached for her drink. Let it go. Eyes bored into Susie, glaring. And for a moment, Susie saw something lurking there behind the cold civility.

Hate.

"I never got round to it. I had little things like providing for my disabled son and keeping a roof over our heads to deal with," she said, her voice the model of practised calm.

"Of course, of course," Susie said. "I apologise again for the interruption. We'll be in touch about those patient lists."

They walked out of the bar, weaving through the customers. When they got to the door, Susie glanced back, saw Diane with her head back in her book. Saw the fork clenched in her hand like a weapon, hovering over her plate, ready to strike.

58

Doug ushered the guests out of the lounge where Pearson's body lay, did his best to calm and reassure those who had realised what had happened. He closed the door firmly, then went outside, looped round to the door at the rear of the hotel and back into the lounge.

He scooped Harvey up by the arm, squeezed hard enough for him to know it wasn't a request, and plucked him from Esther's side. Knelt down next to her, took her hand in his gently. She looked at him uncomprehendingly. Her face was a waxy mask, her eyes staring at something only she could see. If Doug was beyond shock, she was right in the middle of it. He wondered how long it would be before he joined her there.

"Esther? Esther, it's Doug. I just need to talk to Harvey for a minute, okay? The ambulance is on the way, they'll look after you."

She nodded, a small, birdlike motion, then went back to staring into nothing. He smiled at her the best he could, leaned forward and kissed her forehead.

Stood up and marched to Harvey, pushed him hard towards the bay window.

"Talk," he said. "Why, Harvey? Why the fuck did you do this? How could you be part of something like this?"

Harvey looked into his eyes, the facade gone. His eyes glistened with a feverish intensity, his breath was harsh and ragged. Doug vaguely wondered if he was about to have a heart attack.

"How much do you know?" he asked in a small voice.

"All of it," Doug replied. "But what I don't understand is how you could do this, Harvey. Fuck, after everything you taught me..."

Harvey jerked his gaze to Doug. "Who the fuck are you to judge me?" he hissed, a vague echo of anger in his voice. "You just said it. I taught you everything you know, got you a job. A career. Don't you fucking forget that."

"Yeah," Doug replied, gesturing to the corpse of Pearson behind them. "And look how well that turned out for us. So cut the shit, Harvey, tell me. Why? And why the fuck did you ask me up here when you knew he was here? Were you scared I'd look into Greig's death too closely, find the secret for myself? Did you hope Pearson would take care of me for you?"

"No!" Harvey hissed. "Of course not. When I heard about Greig being killed, I knew it was Pearson. I had no idea you'd be in conference, I thought I'd taught you well enough to stay the fuck off newsdesk. So when I heard you were there, I wanted to make sure you were okay. And getting you up here seemed the safest option. I thought he'd stay in Edinburgh. Had no idea he'd come all this way."

"Why?" Doug snapped. "The moment you heard about Greig and Charlie, you must have figured it was Pearson settling old scores. Surely you must have known he'd come for you?"

Harvey dropped his head. His voice was a whisper. "I just thought he'd expose me, I thought that was the deal," he said.

Doug rocked back. Fought off the urge to grab Harvey and smash him against the wall. "The *deal*? Is that all this was to you? A fucking *deal*? Harvey, these are lives you were fucking around with here!"

Harvey let out a long, weary sigh. He glanced around the room. "You know, this is all I ever wanted, Douglas. To own a place like this on this island, to have a respected hotel that people came to relax and enjoy. And now look. Just look." He shook his head, tears dribbling down his cheeks.

Doug fought the urge again. Lost. Grabbed Harvey by the

shoulders and spun him round, dragged his face into his. "Harvey. You put this all together. What were you fucking thinking?"

Harvey looked back at him, something like pity in his gaze.

"Oh Douglas," he said. "You never were good at the big picture. What was the first thing I taught you? Look for the why in every story."

"Why? What the fuck?"

"Why," Harvey repeated. "Why did Pearson choose now to take out Greig? Why after all this time?"

Doug's mind flicked through the options, like a dealer shuffling the deck. He heard Pearson's last words whisper in his mind, those four simple words.

He wasn't my son.

"The boy? Danny?" Doug said. "He started this. How? Because Pearson only found out he wasn't his after he was hurt? Something about the hospital tests? That's when he found out Danny was yours?"

Harvey gave Doug a smile that made him want to cave his teeth in. "*Mine? Mine?* Ah, so that's why you're so angry. You think I cheated on Esther?" Amazingly, he laughed, the sound chittering like insects crawling in Doug's ears. "No, no, no, Douglas. Again, you're missing the big picture. Pearson knew for years that Danny wasn't his. Danny was Greig's, but it didn't matter to him. It was only when he heard how Greig reacted to the accident, it pushed him off the deep end."

Doug stared into Harvey's face. "He didn't care," he whispered, cold understanding shivering through him. "He heard about the accident and he didn't care."

"Exactly," Harvey agreed. "Though he was a little blunter than that. As I recall, the words Greig used were, 'Good riddance to the defective little fuck. That's one less bill to worry about every month.'"

Doug felt revulsion twist in his guts. Jesus, he almost understood. It made him hate Harvey a little more. The man he once respected above all others. The man who had taught him his trade, his profession. The man who had been a dad when his real father could not be.

The stranger in front of him now.

"And of course, you just had to tell Pearson that, didn't you?"

Harvey looked at Doug, then his eyes flicked to Esther. "Why not? You know how bad Esther is Douglas, she's not going to be here in six months' time. And then what? I rattle around this old place, smiling and swapping inane chat with the over-entitled fuckers who come here? The little shits that think money buys them class?" He straightened his back. "No, Douglas. As you said, I put this whole mess in place to start with, then tried to make something good out of it. Greig made a mockery of that. So why not make him face the consequences?"

Doug shoved Harvey back, hard enough for him to lose his footing. He fought back the urge to step forward and bury his boot in his ribs. Fury raged in his chest like a breaking storm, churning up a wake of regret, betrayal, anger, pain.

He walked away from Harvey, tears stinging his eyes. Glanced over to Pearson's body. Went to check on Esther then headed for the car. Heard the sirens, closer now, ignored them and turned over the engine.

He had to get home. Everything Doug thought he knew about the man who had taught him his trade was a lie, but he still knew the truth. And telling it was more important to him now than ever. Get the story before anyone else, make it yours, tell the truth, no matter the cost. It was what he'd always believed, and he clung to it now like flotsam after a shipwreck. He could hear a small, squirming voice in the back of his mind – Harvey's voice, he realised – telling him that he was mad, that it could end his career, destroy everything he'd worked for. He ignored it.

He grunted something that was almost a laugh. The best story of his career, and he couldn't write it for the *Tribune*, wouldn't. He was too close to it now, no longer an impartial reporter but a part of the tale. But he could still tell it. He wondered if Susie would be happy with a written statement, hoped she would be. After all, it could be his last byline.

Doug didn't care. He had a duty to tell the truth, and he would, if only to prove that, unlike Harvey, he could still put what was best in front of what was published.

He slammed the car into gear and kicked down on the accelerator, the growing snarl of the engine drowning out the sirens that were rapidly closing in on him.

59

Sending Eddie back to the station to get started on the formal request for Diane Pearson's patient list, Susie arranged to meet Rebecca at the Mitre, a bar that sat just off the junction of North Bridge and the Royal Mile. She didn't want to be in the station now, just in case Burns's good mood changed and he decided she was his pet plaything again.

She broke her normal rule of never drinking during the day and ordered a vodka, soda and lime. Just a single, but she needed something. When Rebecca saw the drink she turned back to the bar and came back with another for Susie and a large wine for herself.

"That bad?" Susie asked.

"Worse," Rebecca replied, taking a long swig. "Spent most of the morning giving that shit line out to the nationals who have finally woken up to the story, then spent the rest of my time trying to find out a bit more about our leak, Mr Robertson. You?"

Susie went over the call from Hal, the link to the legal firm Montgomery worked for, the visit to Diane. The anger in her eyes when she asked about the divorce flashed across her vision. She chased it with another drink.

"Interesting," Rebecca said, fishing out her notepad. "That chimes with some of the things I've been hearing today."

"Oh," Susie said. "How so?"

"Seems Harvey Robertson was quite the reporter in his day. As you know, covered the crime beat before Doug. Surely he's spoken about him?"

Susie nodded, remembering the reaction when Harvey had phoned the night of Greig's murder. The relief. "Yeah, he's spoken about him. Seems like they're close."

Rebecca grimaced. "Not the best news. Seems Mr Robertson was tight with a lot of the legal firms in the city, had a you-scratch-my-back-I'll-scratch-yours sort of deal with a few of them, including Charlie's firm. Landed him in trouble a couple of times. Formal complaints about potentially prejudicing trials with the release of sensitive information, that sort of thing."

Susie swilled a mouthful of her drink against her tongue, enjoying the harsh bite of the vodka. "Is that the link we've been looking for?" she asked. "Robertson works at the *Tribune*, he's linked to Montgomery, Montgomery's firm is tied up in the Pearson case?"

"It's possible, but it's thin," Rebecca replied. "It's all third party. And besides, Harvey was on the crime beat before Greig was editor, so there's no direct connection there."

Susie murmured her agreement. It was sketchy, but it was the best they had. Damn, but it was frustrating. It was like feeling a familiar object blindfolded, you knew what was meant to be there but the information was scrambled, making it unfamiliar, alien.

Her phone startled her from her thoughts. She pulled it from her bag, expecting it to be Eddie. Felt a dull dread when she saw Burns's caller ID flashing on the screen.

"Sir? How can I help?"

Rebecca watched as the colour drained from Susie's face, her mouth dropping open as the stress rash started to blossom on her chest. She murmured a "Yes, sir", listened, then followed it with a "No, sir. Of course, sir. I'm on my way, sir."

She clicked off the call, looked at Rebecca, then downed her drink and moved to the second.

"Susie? Susie, what the hell...? You look like you've seen a ghost, what?"

Susie blinked, looked at her. When she spoke her voice was small, casual, as if she was reading out the weather from the newspaper and not shaking the world by its foundations.

"That was Burns," she said. "They've found Gavin Pearson. On the Isle of Skye, at Harvey Robertson's hotel. Dead. Self-inflicted gunshot wound to the head."

"Jesus Christ," Rebecca whispered, numbness settling into her like a shroud. "What about Doug? Is he...? Did he...?"

"Doug?" Susie said, an edge of surprise in her voice. "No sign of him at the scene, he must still be on the road down."

Rebecca frowned. "So where the hell is he? And why isn't he taking calls?"

"Good questions," Susie said.

60

Doug was passing Loch Cluanie when the barrier he had thrown up against what had happened started to crack. It was small things at first: he started pumping his grip on the wheel uncontrollably, felt flushes of sweat. The thought of Pearson leering over him flashed in his mind, the tickle of his fetid breath as he whispered in his ear, the laboured, rasping breathing as he charged at Doug.

The horrible, empty void of the gun's barrel as he pointed it in his face. The confetti-like spray of blood and brains as he put the gun to his head and pulled the trigger, his face horribly calm.

Doug pulled into a layby, leaned out of the car and vomited, the strain sending a bolt of agony lancing through his skull where Pearson had pistol-whipped him. He noticed there was blood in the vomit, dark, almost black, and he remembered his hand slipping into Greig's widening pool of blood after Pearson had shot him.

The tears burst through the barrier, sweeping the last of it away, and he fell out of the car, sobbing. Crouched on his knees, a sorrow too big to get past his throat, silently screaming and gagging as he rocked back and forward, everything he had seen and learned hammering through his mind, clamouring to be acknowledged and accepted.

Greig being murdered in front of him. Esther, make-up plastered across her face like war paint as she smiled and forced him to eat breakfast, focusing on not thinking about the cancer that was slowly stealing through her body, rotting her from within.

Harvey, greeting him like an old friend, lying through his teeth and making a mockery of everything he had taught him. What made it worse was he genuinely thought he was doing the right thing, getting Doug out of the way of Pearson's rampage by inviting him up to Skye, compounding one lie with another. It also gave him the added bonus of making sure Doug wasn't poking around things he shouldn't, such as the *Tribune's* library.

According to the letter Pearson had left in the boot – written by Diane Pearson – she and Greig had begun an affair around a month after he started writing articles about Gavin and her. Greig had found the couple easily enough – there was a lot of focus on homecoming troops at the time Desert Storm ended, and it was easy enough to track down a young family, especially with the aid of a few contacts in the military he'd built up during the war itself.

Doug could see how it would have happened: a stressed young wife, confronted by a husband who was now a stranger, his health failing for reasons no-one could understand or acknowledge. Enter the charming young journalist with a willing ear, a sympathetic nature and vows to use the power of the press to do whatever he could to help them.

The affair lasted as long as the articles did, Greig apparently professing his love, Diane reciprocating. They were going to be together, start a new life, a fresh beginning. *Finally free*, the letter said in the breathless prose of someone who had fallen in love with the ideal of love. *We'd be together, a relationship not built on the need to survive, the need to fight whatever comes next. Love.*

Doug looked up for a moment, wiping away his tears. Shook his head and laughed bitterly. Because that was when fate decided to twist the knife – or the beer bottle.

Before Greig and Diane had the chance to run off and start their new life together, Gavin collided with Martin Everett in the nightclub. According to what was in the boot, it happened very differently to the way it had been described in the court copy and the "missing" *Tribune* article.

The true story was contained in the battered old reporter's notepad, scrawled across the pages in shorthand. Doug didn't need to see the reporter's name in the cover to know who it belonged to. After all these years, he knew Harvey's pad and handwriting well enough.

Interview with Gavin Pearson, the heading read, the story unfolding on the page below.

He was hopped up on E or something, I could tell that the moment I saw him. He was on the dance floor, top off, bounding up and down as if the floor was a trampoline. I was heading for him, to get him to cool down, when he knocked into a girl, caught her with his elbow. She went down like a ton of shit, the bottle she was holding dropping with her, her boyfriend jumping onto Everett and laying in to him. I didn't blame him. I let it go just long enough to teach the little shit a lesson, then waded in, pulling the crowd apart. The boyfriend didn't need much persuading to back off, honour was satisfied at that point, but when I grabbed for Everett, he lashed out with the girl's broken bottle. His eyes were wide and manic, glinting in the flashing lights of the dance floor. I felt the heat of the room rise, thought of being back in the desert, wished I was. He came for me again and I dodged the bottle, felt it whistle past me. Too many people jostling for a look, no way to take it outside so I closed in on him, trying to take the bottle away. I grabbed his hand, tried to make him let go, but he twisted away, juiced up by whatever he was on. For a moment, I thought he'd got me with the bottle, the pain in my hand was so severe. But he hadn't, it was just my body letting me down again. He lunged again, and I blocked with my elbow, didn't realise I'd forced the bottle back into his neck until he hit the floor and the bleeding started.

Doug shook his head, hawked back and spat a dark wad of blood onto the gravel of the layby. Looked at it for a long moment. It was a clear example of self-defence, any jury would have seen that.

If they'd been allowed to.

Which is where Harvey came in. Doug could see it all too clearly now. Greig heard about Everett's death. Saw his chance. Went to Harvey, pleading for his help. Help to get this young, traumatised girl away from the life of pain and misery she was trapped in, with a husband who was falling apart and had already shown a history of violence. Help her start anew with the love of her life. So how about it? Of course, he wasn't asking Harvey to help him prejudice the case, that would be illegal, but surely with all his court dealings he knew someone who could ensure justice would be served?

And so, Harvey agreed. Why else would he interview the accused in a murder trial? Doug wondered for a moment how Harvey had got the interview with a man accused of murder in the first place. It was a hell of an exclusive, but it was also worthless. No way it could be run before or during the trial.

He heard Harvey's voice in his head. *You never were good at the big picture. What was the first thing I taught you? Look for the why in every story.* He closed his eyes for a moment, shook his head. Of course. He wasn't interviewing him for the *Tribune*, he was interviewing him for Greig. No doubt on the promise of a favour to Charlie Montgomery.

Why? To see how they could maximise his sentence. Pearson clearly didn't understand that rather than being helped, he was actually being used to orchestrate his own downfall. It was sickeningly easy to imagine how they did it – Greig persuading Pearson to talk to Harvey, to make sure he got the facts right at the trial. And why wouldn't Pearson believe him? After all, this was the man who had helped tell his story. As far as he was concerned, he was a friend, not the man who was fucking his wife behind his back and plotting a new life with her.

Doug bunched a fist, slammed it down on the gravel surface of the car park. Yelped at the pain, then tightened his fist on it, grabbing it, using it to focus.

According to notes in the back of his pad, Harvey made sure Greig paid for his services. Stapled to the back cover, Doug found a copy of Harvey's redundancy letter. It was glowing in its praise. Eyewatering in the details of the lump sum he would receive. It was signed by Jonathan Greig, the date left open, to be filled out and cashed in at Harvey's discretion.

Harvey evidently put Greig in touch with Charming Charlie, who arranged everything, Pearson no doubt delighted that his friends at the *Tribune* were lining up a top legal firm to help him. Charlie saw to it that witness statements were discounted or ruled out as unreliable, made sure anything relating to Gavin's medical problems was quietly forgotten or deemed classified or irrelevant, the version of events contained in Harvey's notepad quietly lost.

Doug didn't know for sure, but he guessed the military would have been quite happy to help with that. Gulf War Illness – or Syndrome as it was being called at the time – was just starting to be a big issue and they were in full denial mode.

With a defence as hostile as Gavin's, the outcome of the trial was never in doubt, and he was sentenced to twenty years. So the fairy tale was complete. The monster went to prison, Diane and Greig were free to start their new life together.

And then she found out she was pregnant.

Diane's letter, stained with tears, described Greig's reaction. He called her everything from a whore to a stupid bitch. She tried to assure him the child was his – theirs – but he refused to believe it, couldn't run the risk that he was bringing up another man's child.

Doug could smell cold feet a mile off. It was all romance and heat-of-the-moment when it was a dream, but with Pearson out of the picture and a baby on the way, romance gave way to harsh reality. And with his career on the up – he had just made deputy editor at the time – Greig wasn't for rocking the boat, especially with an angry soon-to-be ex waiting in the wings, ready to cry infidelity as grounds for divorce unless she got a juicy settlement. So Harvey stepped in – either through guilt or self-preservation, Doug couldn't tell – and brokered a second deal, with Greig promising maintenance money to take care of Diane and the kid "just in case it was his". But he cut all contact, leaving Diane Pearson to pick up the wreckage of her life.

Doug thought back to the conference room, the sound of Greig's head cracking open as he collapsed onto the table. It didn't bother him as much any more.

He leaned back against the car, knocking his head against the door panel, found it strangely comforting. Heard Harvey again: *Look for the why in every story.*

He knew the why now. It was all in the inside cover of Harvey's pad. In the note he had scrawled there for Pearson before he sent it to him. After Danny's accident, Harvey had got in touch with Greig, seeing if he was okay. After all, he was the only one who knew he had a son in the first place. Greig's brutal response – "Good riddance to the defective little fuck. That's one less bill I have to pay every month." – triggered something inside Harvey.

I'm sorry, Harvey had written, his longhand fluid, elegant, a sharp contrast to the jutting, jagged shorthand that filled the rest of the pages of the book. *I should have seen what he was sooner. I know it's of little comfort now, but this notepad gives you everything you need to expose Greig, Montgomery and, yes me, for what we've done to you. I don't care what you do to me any more, I have losses far worse to come, but if you want justice – or even revenge – then here's how. And Greig deserves it. I have no children of my own, but I think I know what it feels likes to be a father, to see a man you consider your son and be proud of him. For the way he treated your son – yours, not his, no matter what any DNA tests might say – he deserves it.*

The letter with Harvey's pad, from Diane to Gavin, showed Greig's reaction to Danny's accident when he spoke with her hadn't been much kinder:

He made me talk first. When I told him about Danny, he asked, "What do you want me to do? I provided for him, the day care isn't cheap, after all. And it sounds like this has done you a favour."

His own son, and he treated him like a problem that had been solved. I slammed the phone down, I wasn't going to let the bastard hear me cry, then I smashed it off the wall. Bastard. I hope he dies screaming.

Doug agreed. Pity Pearson's first shot had taken out most of his throat.

No, not first shot, second.

Doug straightened up. There was still something about that nagging at him. That, and something about the sight of Pearson's hands – huge, gnarled, ruined things. He shook his head, forced himself to his feet. Wiped at his face and forced himself to breathe normally.

Later, he could worry about that later. He had plenty of thinking time, he was still four hours from home. Four hours. Plenty of time for him to think about what he was going to ask Diane Pearson.

He didn't know how she was going to react when he met her. But he knew he couldn't avoid it. Gavin Pearson had taken that choice from him he moment he blew his brains out in front of him.

61

Stevie Leith's problems didn't bother Rab much; as far as he was concerned, drug dealers were nothing more than parasites feeding off others' weakness. What did bother him was the company Stevie kept – and the names he knew.

After the call from Doug, Rab had phoned round some people. As ever, Doug's instincts were right, a former soldier with firearms expertise and a criminal record attracted a certain amount of attention in some circles, especially if said former soldier was willing to use his skills to make some money and didn't mind the prospect of returning to the prison he'd just got out of.

In Rab's experience, ex-soldiers wanting to make money in that way weren't bothered by the risks – and prison was just another form of barracks to them.

However, it looked like Gavin Pearson had been a different kind of animal. According to Rab's contacts, no-one matching his description or skill set ever made themselves available for work. He seemed to have been released from prison and quietly vanished.

That was, until he stepped out of the shadows one night and beat the shit out of three guys who were looking to rip off some junkie who occasionally did some dealing for Dessie Banks. According to the story Rab had been told, the kid, who, given what he was doing must have been mentally deficient, struck a deal in a New Town nightclub. It was a gay club, known to be fairly relaxed; most of the problems happened when the customers hit the streets and were met with some homophobic little shits who were jacked up on booze and pack mentality. So maybe Dessie's dealer got careless, thought he was safe. Didn't make up for his stupidity, though. His three new friends asked for speed, insisted they wanted to make the deal outside the club in case there were security cameras nearby. The stupid twat agreed, allowed himself to be led outside and down a small alley next to the club. Predictably, he made the deal, handed over the drugs and they proceeded to pay him by trying to break every bone in his body.

He managed to get away, back onto the street, where he ran into Gavin Pearson. Apparently, Pearson didn't like the odds and took the three guys down. Forcibly. One thing interested Rab, though. He decided to check out the story and spoke to a doorman called Scott Donald who was working that night, told him what happened.

"It was fuckin' weird," he said. "Wee shit runs straight into this guy, Pearson. He's a big fucker, like, built like a brick shithoose. He tells the three guys to fuck off but they're no havin' it and give him a go, run at him, like. He fucked them up good and proper – an' just by using his legs. Kicked one guy in the chest, think he broke another's leg, booted the third in the baws so hard ah fuckin felt it. Never took his hands oot his pockets though, Rab. Weirdest fuckin' thing."

Word of the evening's festivities must have got back to Dessie, as he put the word out that, if Pearson ever needed work or a favour, all he had to do was call him. Not that Dessie cared about the safety of his employee, but Pearson had provided a very effective demonstration of what happened if you fucked with Dessie Banks' men.

The offer went ignored until a week ago, when Dessie was approached for a single favour. The use of a car and a tank of petrol. Plus a very specific firearm request.

Dessie agreed, a car was nothing for him, one could be stolen at the snap of his fingers. The gun was a calculated risk – by doing him a favour, Pearson was hardly likely to train it on Dessie. And besides, he was a man of his word. The arrangements were made through the little scrote Pearson had saved, a bottom-feeder called Paul Welsh, and the car was delivered to Pearson's digs, a small, one-bed flat across the road from the nightclub.

Rab knew Welsh vaguely – he'd been warned a couple of times about dealing in his clubs and the boys were on the lookout for him. What he hadn't known until today was that he was linked to Dessie Banks. Useful knowledge if he ever needed to get in touch with Dessie or send him a more visual message. Not so useful for Stevie Leith, who had, Rab was told, put the kid in hospital after burying a needle in his eye.

Bad news for Paul. Worse news for Stevie when Dessie found out.

Rab reached for the phone, dialled Doug's number. He wasn't sure how all this was going to help him, but a promise was a promise. And besides, it might get Janet off his back for half an hour if he could tell her how the kid was.

62

Police Scotland was meant to be an integrated national force, the end result of the merger of the eight regional forces around the country into one national entity.

As Rebecca was finding out, it was a nice theory, just not matched by the reality.

Trying to co-ordinate the press response to Gavin Pearson's death was a fucking nightmare. He had been identified by Harvey Robertson as the murderer in the Greig and Montgomery cases. Both of which were Edinburgh-based crimes. But he had taken his life on Skye, which meant the local police were involved. And while the chiefs in Edinburgh were looking to hold off on giving a press conference until the full facts were established and, given what Rebecca had found out, Robertson's full role had been ascertained, the cops on Skye were desperate to put out a media statement and hold a press conference as soon as possible.

Why? Because they were looking for a person of interest who had left the scene of the crime before officers arrived. An old friend of Mr Robertson's; one of the guests described him as tall, with tousled hair, and driving a grey sports car "like he was in the Monaco Grand Prix".

Rebecca couldn't believe it. It had to be Doug, but why the hell was he still at the hotel at the time Pearson had stormed the place? From what she knew, he was leaving that morning, heading home. He should have been crossing the Forth Road Bridge now, not still driving down the road. What the hell had happened to make him turn around?

As if in answer, her phone rang on her desk. She picked it up, almost fumbled it when she saw it was Doug calling.

"Doug? Doug, where the hell are you? Are you okay?"

The line was bad, but she could hear the urgency in his voice. "Rebecca, hi. Yeah, look, I'm fine. Take it you've heard about what happened by now?"

"Heard? Doug, it's all over the news, what the hell happened?"

"I'll explain later," he said. "But first, I need a favour."

She rolled her eyes, anger and frustration making her grab the phone tighter. Unbelievable. "Doug, you can't seriously think that…"

"Rebecca, please," he said. "I'm sorry I've fucked you around, sorry I've made such a mess of all this. I'll make it right, I promise. But right now, I just need your help. Please?"

She paused, let the static fill the line. She wanted to help him. But was he just using her – again?

"What do you need?" she asked, lips tight, only hating herself a little for caving so easily.

"You need to speak to Burns," he said. "Tell him you discovered Harvey leaked the link to the two murders. You also need to tell him you have reason to believe that Robertson deleted information relating to the murders from the archive at the *Tribune*, and withheld information fundamental to the Pearson murder trial."

Rebecca took a deep breath, trying to make sense of what he was saying. "What? Doug. What files? What information? Why would he do that?"

"I'll explain when I see you. But I need you to do this, Rebecca, please. I need the police to put pressure on the *Trib*, make sure nothing else has been deleted. They won't listen to me, I'm too close to this, but they'll have to listen to you. And…" – he paused, and she could swear she almost heard a smile in his voice – "…it might get you and Susie out of the shit with Burns a bit."

Susie again. Shit.

"Have you spoken to her?"

"Not yet, she's my next call. Thanks, Rebecca. I owe you. I'll make it up to you when we have that date."

The line clicked dead before she could reply.

63

"Doug? Doug, where the fuck are you?"

Doug flicked the wheel to the right, hammered down on the accelerator as he shot past a lorry. "I'm heading down the road now, Susie, should be there soon."

"Are you okay? Burns is going fucking mental here. He's threatening to put an arrest warrant out for you for fleeing the scene of a crime. What the fuck happened up there?"

"Long story," Doug said, speeding up for another overtake. There was a sharp turn coming, but he thought he could make it. "I promise I'll give you a full statement when I get back, okay?"

"No, not okay," Susie hissed. "You've not returned my calls, we find out that you're at the scene when a suspect wanted for three murders kills himself, that your old boss is tied up in all of this somehow, and you want me to wait? You ever think we might be worried about you, Doug? What the hell is going on?"

We? He pushed the thought aside.

"Look, Susie, you know most of it. Pearson killed Greig and Montgomery, Harvey is tied up in all of it. I'm just finishing up the background now, which is why I called you."

"Oh?" Her voice was heavy with warning. *Don't fuck with me, Doug,* the tone said.

He ignored it. "Yeah. Look, I've been digging around in Pearson's background. Seems he was vaguely connected to Stevie Leith and a small-time dealer called Paul Welsh. Rab told me about what happened with them this morning. Anything you can add?"

Susie bit down on her anger, which was battling with relief for supremacy. Little shit. He ignored calls for almost a day, then gets in touch when it suits him, looking for help with background for his story? Fuck that.

"Look, Doug, I'm not going to help you with a story at the moment," she said. "I'm up to my neck in this case, and I need you to give me a statement now. You can come to the station and see me when you get back."

"I'm not doing this for a story, Susie," he said, the emptiness in his voice giving her an icy jolt. "I can't write this one. But I've seen too much. I just need to know. Please."

She sighed. Emotional blackmail. Classic Doug. And classic Susie for falling for it.

"Well, if you've heard the story from Rab, I'm not sure how much more I can add," she snapped. "Neighbours called officers to Stevie Leith's flat this morning. They forced the door, found Stevie unconscious and this kid Welsh with a syringe full of heroin sticking out of his eye. Little shit was lucky Stevie didn't push down the plunger."

"Any indication why they got into it?" Doug asked, the engine roaring in the background as he spoke.

"Why do druggies always fall out?" Susie said, suddenly tired. "Money, product, something like that. There may be another suspect, though; Welsh kept going on about someone called Frankie."

The line fell into silence, only the dull wash of static in Susie's ear. Then, she heard Doug's voice. Flat, almost atonal. All too similar to the voice she had heard that first night after Greig's murder when he had come to her flat.

"Motherfucker," he said.

"Doug? Doug, what? This mean something to you? What?"

"Nothing, nothing," he said, distracted. It was obvious he wasn't focusing on her anymore. "Just something I should have seen a lot fucking sooner. Fucking idiot. What a fucking idiot."

"Doug, what? I really need…"

The focus snapped back into his voice. "Susie, it's fine. Sorry for bothering you. And thanks. I'll come to the station as soon as I get back. Promise. See you soon."

He clicked off before she could protest, bore down on the steering wheel and floored the accelerator, watching the speedo creep up past seventy, eighty, ninety.

He looked at his knuckles, bones glowing through the skin as he gripped the steering wheel and cursed softly. He was wrong, they all were. All the pieces were there, all the hints, even with Harvey trying to muddy the waters.

He flicked on the phone, selected a secure website. Waited for it to load, cursing the slow connection, then gave his access code and logged in. Keyed in his request, got what he needed. Mapped out the route in his head. Turned back to the road and drove faster, willing the car to its destination.

64

Doug pulled into a parking space halfway down the street, revved the engine for a moment then killed the ignition, listening as the motor spun to a slow stop. No point in playing it sneaky now, he was beyond that. Way, way beyond. As he was waiting he looked around. The voters' roll search he had run on his phone had spit the address out quickly enough. It was a small street, crowded with cars, a couple of gardens littered with kids' toys. Hardly a new-build development anymore, but it had matured well.

Mostly.

He got out of the car and walked towards the house, a mixture of relief and tension tickling his neck as he noticed a small light was on next to the front door. So she was in.

He climbed the small step to the front door, took a moment to look at the grab rail put there for Danny. Felt a rush of anger. The poor kid had never asked for any of this. At least he would never know what his father really thought of him.

He paused at the door, took just enough time to send one text message, then rang the bell. Squared his shoulders, forced his breathing to slow.

He thought again of the shots ringing through Greig's office – three shots, *three hits*, one fatality. He'd worked that out now as well. All it took was the proper perspective.

Diane Pearson swung the door open, leaned out. The years hadn't been kind. In the pictures taken to go with Greig's articles, she was young, vibrant, even with the stress of Gavin falling apart in front of her. Now she looked like a wizened husk of that woman, hollowed out and poisoned over the years by pain and suffering. Left with nothing but her strength, and an obsessive defiance that refused to let her roll over and quit.

A defiance fuelled by a lifetime of hate.

"Yes," she said, giving him an appraising glance. "Can I help you?"

"Mrs Pearson? I'm Doug McGregor. I work for the *Capital Tribune*. I was wondering if I could have a quick word?"

She stepped back, already swinging the door closed. Doug took a half step forward, placed his hand gently on the door, surprised by the force pushing against him. "I know Paul Welsh, Mrs Pearson, I know the whole story. Now, may I come in?"

She gave him another look, eyes narrowing behind her glasses then, with a grunt, swung the door open and beckoned him in.

She led him through to the living room, a small, cramped space, toys and ornaments clinging to every available inch of shelf space, the walls crammed with pictures of the most important part of her life. Danny.

Three shots, three hits…

"How can I help you, Mr McGregor?" she asked, brushing past him and heading for her seat. She didn't ask him to sit. "As I already told the police, I may know Mr Welsh, but that's a matter for them, not the press."

He looked at her, thought of Gavin's smile as he blew his brains out. Of the terror in Greig's face as his chest exploded onto the conference table. Of Harvey's pitiful justification for betraying everything he had taught Doug about telling stories as they were. *I put this whole mess in place to start with, then tried to make something good out of it.* Felt a wave of bilious fury so strong he rocked on his feet. Took a deep, shuddering breath, started talking.

"Come on, Diane, cut the shit, will you? I told you, I know the whole story. How you used Paul as a link to Dessie Banks to help sell drugs to the people you were meant to be counselling, giving him just enough to keep him on a chain of addiction. How you made sure Paul was at your beck and call to take messages

264

to Gavin whenever you needed him to, set up little visits to see Danny, and make sure he had his own personal supply of whatever he needed to treat his own pain. Why was that, anyway? Guilt, maybe? Thought you'd caused him enough pain as it was? Thought maybe getting him uppers and downers and God knows what else would somehow make up for that?"

She glared at him, eyes glittering dark pits in her glasses. "How dare you," she hissed, her voice a whisper of hate. "Paul Welsh was a client of mine. I only tried to help him, only…"

"Shut up!" Doug shouted suddenly, temper finally snapping. "I know all about it, Diane; a friend of mine spoke to Dessie Banks personally a couple of hours ago, confirmed everything for me. Wouldn't have made any sense without this, though." He pulled from his pocket the letter she had written to Gavin. Doug opened it up, found the sentence he was looking for, the one that was now burned into his mind, read it out to her.

"*You remember when you first asked me to marry you? How you said how much you hated the name Franklin and promised not to give it to any of our kids? I think I said something like 'If you don't like it, I'll have it'. I was joking at the time, it was something corny to say, but over time I've realised that, for you, I'll always be Frankie.*"

He chewed the words over for a moment, then glared at her. "Nice touch, that. Using a name only Gavin would recognise. Keeps you in the clear, doesn't it? But it let him know what you were really doing. Pretty cold though, manipulating the people you were supposed to be helping to make a few quid and help get revenge for a situation you created."

"Where… where did you get that?" she whispered, leaning forward in the chair, her hands claws on her knees.

"Gavin gave it to me," he replied, forcing down the sound of the gunshot in his ears. "Or, I should say, he left it for me. I think it was his way of trying to justify what he had done, making sure everything was out in the open at last." Harvey's note flashed across his mind. *If you want justice – or even revenge – then here's how.*

Another thought hit him then, washing away the fury as he blinked back sudden tears. The line from Harvey's note to Gavin. *I have no children of my own, but I think I know what it's like to be a father. To see a man you consider your son and be proud of him.*

"Eye for an eye," Doug whispered to himself, breath hitching in his throat. "It was Gavin's way of twisting the knife on Harvey – exposing him meant he would lose a son as well."

"My husband was a very, very ill man, Mr McGregor," she said, eyes not leaving the letter. Slowly, she reached a hand out. "May I?"

Doug glanced down at the letter again, swiped at his eyes angrily. "Actually, no, I don't think so, Frankie. I'm going to need this. Partly to prove you were selling those drugs to Paul, and partly to show you killed Charlie Montgomery. It was you, wasn't it?"

She rocked back as though she had been stabbed. "Wh… what do you mean? That's preposterous, I would never, could never…"

Doug looked at her with contempt, felt his fury build again. "Stop fucking lying, Frankie. It took me a while to get there, been kind of distracted with all the killing going on around me, but it was the letter that made it all make sense. Back on Skye, Gavin could hardly stand up for more than five minutes. His hands were lumps. God alone knows what it took him to keep them steady to take out Greig. But he managed it. But that was killing from a distance, with a weapon he was an expert with, where he only needed his grip to be steady for a few concentrated seconds. No way he could have gone to town on Charlie the way the murderer did. Beating him half to death then throwing him down a flight of stairs before shoving a knife into his head? No way. What was it he said about the night he killed that kid? Just my body failing me again? Gavin would have had a heart attack about five punches in. But you? Oh, you'd been waiting for years for the chance, hadn't you, Frankie? The chance to even the score with the man who helped Greig betray you."

She dropped her head, chest heaving. For a moment Doug thought she was crying, then felt his body go cold as he realised what she was actually doing.

Laughing.

"Oh, Mr McGregor," she said, not lifting her head. Her voice had taken on a sing-song lilt that grated in Doug's ears and made him glance at the door, figure out how fast he could get there. "You are a clever boy, a very clever boy. Charlie was a clever boy too, wasn't he? Thirty years I helped those fucking wasters, junkies and petty thieves. And what did I get for it?" She looked around the room, her face a sneer of contempt. "This. A dead-end life with a son who would never leave and a husband who could never come home. So when I saw the chance to do something for me, to right the wrongs we had suffered, I took it. And so what if a little shit like Paul Welsh got hurt in the process?"

Doug felt the air around him grow heavy, charged. *Oh shi...*

She exploded forward from her chair, hissing. Collided with Doug's chest and drove him back onto the couch. Lashed out at him with feral intensity, clawing, punching, gouging. She made no sound other than her panting breath.

"Get the fuck OFF ME!" Doug roared, bucking his hips and rolling her away. She fell awkwardly off the couch, rolled and came up to her knees. Her eyes were blazing with hate and intent and, in that instant, Doug saw the killer behind the mask she had worn.

She smiled at him, baring small teeth, then darted back towards the shelves next to her chair. Grabbed an ornament and hurled it at Doug. He flinched instinctively, bringing his arms up. Grunted as something small and sharp bounced off his head, felt blood start to ooze from the wound.

He lunged to his left, for the door, screamed at a bolt of agony that lanced up his leg. Looked down to see the jagged stump of a glass ornament jutting out from his thigh.

Diane pounced on him again, raining blows down on his back and neck. He thrashed around, trying to throw her off, felt his elbow connect with something hard, felt teeth collapse under the force.

She cried out, staggering back. Wiped the blood from her

mouth across her face like war paint, that same empty smile playing on her lips.

"I'm going to fucking kill you," she snarled. Doug made again for the door, managed to pry it open an inch. She kicked it closed, followed up with a thundering blow to his already wounded temple. He slid to his knees, the impact ringing in his ears and making it hard to think. Cried out as she stamped down on his hand, fingers making a brittle, crunching noise as they snapped under the weight. Instinctively, he pulled his hand to his chest and she drove forward with a knee to his chin. He collapsed and she danced around him, kicking, panting, laughing. He grunted as the kicks drove the air from his lungs, tried to gasp for breath.

Thought of Greig, also gasping for breath. Is this what he felt? Lungs heaving, unable to fill them and ease the agony in his chest. Blood spouting from his mouth, his body a traitor, his hand feeling only ragged and torn flesh where his throat should have been.

Look at me.

Another kick landed. Doug screamed as a rib gave way.

The sound of Greig's skull cracking open as it hammered off the conference table.

He grunted as a kick hit his shoulder, numbing his arm.

The feel of his blood between Doug's fingers, slick and hot and viscous.

With a scream, Doug straightened up. Adrenalin pounded through his body, washing away the pain, the fear, the doubt. He grabbed for her foot, caught it clumsily and pulled as hard as he could. Diane toppled to the floor, grunting with shock as the breath was driven out of her. Doug rose unsteadily to his feet, looked down, saw she was trying to get up.

Swung his leg and kicked her in the side of the head as hard as he could.

She cried out, head snapping to the side with the force of the blow. He lashed out again, tears streaming down his face, Greig and Pearson and Harvey filling his mind. Betrayal. From all of them.

She whimpered, tried to pull herself away.

He kicked her again.

Her arms flailed and then fell to the floor as blood dribbled from her mouth and her glasses slid from her face.

He kicked her again. And again. And again. This bitch who had led to two people dying in front of him, who had forced him to look at everything he had believed in and shown it to be a lie.

I think I know what it's like to be a father.

He looked up at the walls. Danny smiled down at him from everywhere. He vaguely noticed he even looked like Greig. Something about the nose and the eyes.

Doug backed away, slid down the far wall next to the door. Watched the bloodied lump of Diane Pearson on the floor in front of him very closely.

When he saw her chest rise and fall, he dropped his head between his knees, crying harder, everything he had been denying bleeding out of him with his tears. He had come here to confront Diane with the truth, to show her that there was a price to pay for what she had done. Instead, he had beaten her half to death, fuelled by rage and sorrow and loss. And what did that make him? Was he another of Harvey's pawns, manipulated into exacting one last dose of revenge for someone who had lied to him for years, collateral damage in his grand plan to try and justify his actions to himself? Or was he a man driven beyond his limits and lashing out against the horrors he had seen?

He didn't have an answer, and that terrified him. He had known who he wanted to be and what he wanted to do his whole life. And now what? Susie had once called him a story-hungry idealist, and look where that idealism had led him.

He took a deep hitching breath, forced his lungs to fill and his mind to quiet as he focused on Diane's ragged, guttural breathing, and dimly wondered how long it would take Susie to make sense of the message he had sent her.

65

Burns sat across his desk from Susie, red hair glowing in the desk lamp he had trained over his head. His lips moved soundlessly as he read her reports, absently gutting a cigarette and flicking tobacco off the pages. When he reached the last page, he closed the folder slowly, placed his hand over it and looked up at Susie, eyes bloodshot from a lack of sleep and too much coffee.

"I thought I told you to stay the fuck away from that wee shite McGregor?" he said finally.

Susie felt her cheeks begin to burn. "Yes, sir, you did. But it just didn't work out that way. McGregor contacted me when he was en route to Mrs Pearson's house. Given the cryptic nature of his message, I felt I had no option but to investigate further."

Burns snorted, rubbed his fingers together as he added to the growing pile of tobacco on his desk. "And it never occurred to you to contact the local station and get them to send an officer to Mrs Pearson's address?"

"Well, I, ah…"

Burns took his hand off the folder, held it up. "Forget it, Susie, I'm too tired for bullshit. You should have reported it as soon as he got in touch. He left a fucking crime scene, for fuck's sake, you knew he was a person of interest. You're just lucky Pearson was so willing to spill her guts when she woke up."

Susie nodded, remembering the scene that had confronted her when she arrived at Pearson's home. The living room looked as if an earthquake had hit it, shattered ornaments twinkling on the floor, furniture upturned and jostled out of position. Doug sitting propped against one wall, his face puffy with tears and bruises, blood oozing and pooling around the jagged stump of an ornament sticking out of his leg. Opposite him, Diane "Frankie" Pearson lay crumpled on the floor, murmuring and cackling between quiet sobs of pain.

Susie had arranged ambulances for them both, called the local station and had them cordon off the whole street as a crime scene. By the time the ambulances arrived, every house had a light on, the blue strobes from the emergency vehicles bouncing off the opening curtains and freezing curious faces in their glare. They were taken to the Victoria in Kirkcaldy, which had the closest A&E, put in private rooms with officers on the doors.

After checking on Doug, and making sure he kept his mouth shut so he didn't say something to land himself in any more shit, she went to check on Diane Pearson.

She was lying propped up in bed, white-blonde hair fanned out on the pillow behind her. The dark, angry bruises creeping across her face seemed to merge with the gloom of the room, leaving only her eyes glittering from the shadows. The doctors said she had three broken ribs, a hairline fracture of her left leg and had lost at least four teeth. Thinking about Doug's mangled hand – three fingers broken, the thumb dislocated and the bones in his palm fractured – she wished it was more serious.

Pearson looked up, smiled through bloodied lips when she saw Susie slip into the room. When she spoke, her voice sounded amused, almost mischievous, and it made Susie's skin crawl.

"Ah, Susie, good to see you again. How's your friend? I didn't hurt him too badly, did I? I hope not. He seems like such a nice boy."

Susie saw her watching her, the cold amusement and calcula-tion. She was trying to get a reaction. Fine. Fuck her. She wasn't going to get one.

"He's fine," she said quietly, slipping into a chair beside the bed, making sure it was just out of arm's reach, even with the cuffs chaining her to the side rail. "However, he did make a troubling accusation about you. That you were somehow involved in the death of Charlie Montgomery and linked to a known drug dealer in the city?"

Diane threw back her head and laughed, the sound of bottles crashing into a recycling bin. Susie could see bruises trailing across her neck like wine stains, made a mental note to make sure Doug's statement had a line in it that he felt he was in "mortal danger". Which wasn't much of a lie.

"Oh, Susie, Susie," Diane said, the manic laugh giving way to the occasional amused snort. "Mr McGregor really is a clever, clever boy."

She looked off out the window, the glow from the street lights making her bruises look gangrenous. "There's no point in denying it now, I suppose. After all, I've got what I wanted."

Slowly, she told Susie everything, as if it was a secret she had been holding on to for years and was dying to tell. About how she had found Paul and got to Dessie Banks through him, sold drugs to the patients she was supposed to be helping. How she had got in touch with Gavin not long after he had been released from prison, using Paul and Dessie as go-betweens so they weren't seen together. "After all," she told Susie, her eyes dead and calm, "it wouldn't have done for a respected counsellor to be seen with a convicted murderer, would it?" So they met in a flat Banks had arranged, with Danny getting the first real chance to meet his dad. "They spent hours together reading comics," Diane told her, as though she was sharing gossip.

When Danny was hurt, and Greig had reacted in the way he had, she had snapped. Contacted Gavin, set him on a killing spree for them all. "It wasn't hard, Susie – he loved Danny more than life. He never asked for a DNA test, you know, even after I told him about Greig. He didn't care. Danny was what he wanted him to be. Our child. His son."

So she had cashed in her favours with Dessie and got Gavin

what he needed. But Charlie was all hers. After all, Gavin was capable of shooting a coward and dealing with an old man, but taking out a relatively fit man? "No, that was woman's work. Gavin was there with me in spirit, though. He gave me a spare bullet to give to Charlie as a memento."

Burns coughed pointedly, bringing Susie back to the present. She sneered in disgust as she saw him shovel a handful of the raw tobacco into his mouth. He smiled and nodded towards her.

"Better than smoking," he said. "You know you'll have to get her statement verified, don't you? And will that little scrote who was dealing for her corroborate all this?"

"Yes, sir," she nodded. "We got the records from Diane's office, which shows he was a client of hers. We've also got her business card in the belongings taken from Stevie Leith's flat. Stevie never met her face to face, he only ever dealt with 'Frankie' on the phone. But with Dessie Banks backing her up, he wasn't going to say no to her."

Burns nodded slowly, chewing on his tobacco like it was a succulent steak. "Dessie Banks," he murmured. "I've been waiting for years to have a shot at him."

Susie said nothing, waited as Burns enjoyed a private fantasy. Finally, he refocused on her, almost surprised she was there. "Okay, get the paperwork done on this ASAP. I don't want any slips, especially with the Chief watching."

Susie shifted in her seat slightly. "Sir, ah, about that..."

Burns looked at her coolly, seemed to read her thoughts. Sighed. "I don't know, Susie, I really don't. The Chief has a thing for you for some reason, though I'll be fucked if I know what it is. He's still pressing me to keep you on the sidelines. This," – he tapped the folder – "will help, but that little shit McGregor being involved is going to create a world of problems."

A world of problems, Susie thought. That summed Doug up perfectly. The contact who was also a friend. Sometimes. The friend she had set up with another friend. So why did she feel so… jealous? Did she want more with Doug? Maybe, but was it a price worth paying? Lose a friend, and, given what Burns had said, her career. And for what? And, anyway, what feelings had Doug shown for her – or Rebecca, for that matter? She knew his type: all charm and easy smiles, more focused on his career than even she was. So what was she playing at?

"…I said you're dismissed, Drummond."

Susie started in her chair. "Sorry, sir, just thinking. Thank you, sir."

He nodded, shovelled another wad of tobacco into his mouth. "Go home, Susie, get some rest. And think about what I said. McGregor might be handy, but he's not worth it. And cutting corners like this is only going to get you in the shit."

Susie murmured agreement, closed the door gently behind her. Walked through the almost empty corridors of the station, Burns's words echoing in her ears in time with the click-clack of her heels.

He's not worth it. This is only going to get you in the shit.

She pushed the thought away, changed course for the locker room and the trainers and running gear she kept there. She could run home in less than an hour, sweat out thoughts of Doug and Rebecca and Diane Pearson's dead, leering smile long before she reached the front door.

Everything else, she could worry about tomorrow.

66

Hal sat in the living room of Doug's flat, sipping on coffee he insisted making himself and studying the page Doug had called up on his iPad.

"So," Doug asked, limping into the room carrying a plate of biscuits in his right hand, his left in a cast, "what do you think?"

Hal looked up at him. It had been a week since Doug's confrontation with Diane Pearson, and the damage was starting to heal. The bruises crept across his face like a sunset, and Hal could see him wince every time he took a breath. Not surprising, two broken ribs would do that to you. But the morose silence that marked the first days was passing, thawing like ice in the sun, the old Doug peeking through slowly.

"What do I think?" Hal asked as Doug put down the biscuits and eased himself into his seat. "Fix the PR for the hotel where a killer ex-soldier blew his own brains out in the lounge? Make it a destination resort for the rich staycation and foreign tourist markets? Yeah, I can do it. Question is, why?"

I think I know what it feels like to be a father. To see a man you consider your son and be proud of him.

Doug glanced at him from across the lip of his mug. "It's not for him," he said softly. "It isn't. It's for Esther. I want her to see the place doing well before she... you know."

Hal nodded. Harvey had some tough questions to answer, but despite Diane's letter and the recovered articles in the *Tribune*, there was no real evidence that he had done anything wrong. He had arranged for Charlie to oversee Gavin's case, but it was Charlie who had ensured Pearson got the maximum sentence. Then Harvey had made sure Greig had honoured his word to look after Diane and Danny. Yes, he'd received an overly-generous retirement package, which might go some way to explaining the cuts and financial problems the *Trib* was now facing, but there was no evidence of criminality in his actions. Telling Kevin Drainey that the Greig and Montgomery murders were linked? Nothing more than an old reporter sharing a theory. Definitely not an attempt to lure Doug away from Skye and Pearson, and back to the story – and absolutely not a way of pinning both murders on Gavin in a desperate, misguided attempt to protect Diane when he worked out what was going on.

The shorthand interview, and his notepad being in Pearson's possession was more difficult to explain, but not impossible. There was nothing in it to confirm if it was genuine or Harvey had made the whole thing up – after all, it wouldn't be the first time a reporter fabricated a source or tried to make up a story. As for the note at the front of the book, any good lawyer could argue that it was the deluded rantings of an old man pushed to the brink by nursing a terminally ill wife, trying to play himself back into the industry he loved and be part of the story again.

And if Doug had learned one thing, it was that Harvey knew a lot of lawyers.

"You're doing it again," Hal said.

"What? Oh, sorry." Doug hauled himself from his thoughts, forced himself to focus on the present. "So, will you do it, Hal?"

Hal let out a long breath. He'd flown up last week, the moment he'd heard what had happened between Doug and Diane Pearson. He told Colin he was going to spend the time working with clients north of the Border, but they both knew it was a lie. Colin sent him on his way, promised to join him with Jennifer as soon as he could. They were arriving tonight.

"Okay," he said. "But you promise Robertson won't benefit from any uptick in business we generate for him? That all additional cash will go towards Esther's care and any charity she chooses?"

Doug nodded. "And when – if – she... you know, then you're free to gut the bastard any way you want."

Hal smiled. He'd already thought of a few creative ways for Robertson's Retreat to take a sudden veer into negative publicity. After all, food hygiene standards were exacting, all it took was one bad meal. Or a well-known name to complain about the "abysmal service and poor management". He had a couple of willing candidates selected for the job.

"Fine, I'll start tomorrow. Take Colin and Jen up to Skye, leave them somewhere fun while I go give the place the once over."

"Thanks, Hal, I appreciate it," Doug said.

"No problem. But tell me, what are you going to do?"

Good question. Doug had spoken to Walter, who ordered him to take a holiday until the dust settled. The police asking about the *Trib*'s archive had stirred up a hornet's nest with the company directors, and Walter didn't want Doug anywhere near it. Not that they could fire him – his profile was way too high at the moment and to do so would be as good as an admission of guilt.

He shrugged. "I dunno. I'll probably go back to the *Trib* when this all clears up. No more newsdesk, though, I'm strictly reporting from now on."

The thought of Greig's office reared up in his mind, and he knew he could never step into that room again. Never stand in front of those windows, waiting for that sharp echoing crack, the cries as the window shattered. The splintering *thwump* as the first bullet dug into the wall beside him, shattering the framed front page that was there – Greig's first splash on the launch of Operation Desert Storm.

Four sounds. Three shots. Three hits. It took Doug a little while to figure it out, mostly because he was always sitting with his back to the page when he was in conference. But a call to Walter had confirmed it. The first shot hadn't been a calibration shot. It had been a signal of intent. Doug wondered if Greig had enough time to get the message before the second bullet tore his throat out.

"You know, you could always come and work with me," Hal said, his gaze cool and even.

Doug coughed in surprise, making his ribs ache. He couldn't believe what he was hearing. "What me? In PR?" He laughed, slightly disturbed to find he was actually considering it. Better pay. Better hours. Never seeing Greig's office again, never being threatened with a gun. A simpler life. A safer one. "No way. I'm a reporter, Hal, that's what I do. Find the stories, tell the stories."

Hal shrugged. "That's what I do. Find the lines, sell the lines. Tell the good news tales, minimise the bad news ones. You might find you like it, and I promise it's a lot more lucrative than journalism. Safer, too."

"Hal, thank you. But I couldn't. I'm just not that guy. I'm a reporter, plain and simple." He flashed back to sitting in the wreckage of Diane Pearson's living room, willing her to keep breathing as he waited for Susie to arrive. Gave Hal a small smile. "Besides, Harvey's had enough victims. My byline isn't going to be another one. There are stories to write – and someone's got to keep you slick PR types in line."

Hal laughed, held up a hand in surrender. "Fair enough. Just a thought. And the door's always open if you change your mind. Now…" He folded away the iPad, stood up. "I have to get going. Colin's arriving with Jen in a couple of hours, I want to get out to the airport to meet them. You still up for drinks tonight?"

"Oh yes," Doug replied. Drinks at the Balmoral Hotel on Princes Street, where Hal was staying. Definitely more lucrative than journalism.

"Good," Hal said. "You going to bring Susie along? After all, you owe her after she covered your ass with Diane Pearson."

"Haallll," Doug said. But he was right. He did owe Susie. He'd sent her a simple text as he arrived at Diane Pearson's house: *Diane also uses the name Frankie. Linked to Dessie Banks and Gavin through Paul. I'm at the house now. Be good to see you.*

When she arrived, he had been sitting with the bloodied remains of Diane, praying he hadn't killed her. Susie told the police she had a verbal statement from him that it was self-defence.

She wrote that statement for him that night, after Diane Pearson had told her everything. Got him to sign it the next morning.

But then there was Rebecca to consider. Rebecca who was good to her word and made sure Burns asked the *Trib* some hard questions; Rebecca who broke the rules and gave him the press statements from Burns and the Chief before they went public. Who had believed him when he said he wasn't the leak who linked the murders.

Rebecca, who he was keeping at arm's length.

He shook himself from his thoughts, smiled at Hal. "Look, I'll see you tonight. Maybe I'll invite someone, maybe I'll come on my own, okay? Whatever happens, I'll still be the most fashionably bruised guy in the room."

"Fair enough," Hal laughed. "We'll see you tonight. Take care, Doug." He gave him a gentle hug then was off, taking the stairs two at a time, loving being a husband and a dad.

Doug swung the door shut slowly, mind filling with thoughts of Greig and his attitude to parenthood. An inconvenience. An embarrassment, especially when the poor kid had learning problems. And then there was Pearson, who loved the boy as his own, knowing he wasn't biologically his, desperately hoping he was.

There were theories that he had killed the boy because he was Greig's, because he was a reminder of the man who had fucked his wife and help ruin his life. Doug wasn't so sure. He thought it was possible Pearson had smothered Danny to death because he knew there was no future for him – the medical reports indicated that the tram accident had left him with additional brain damage. Chances were, that, if he ever woke up, he would be unresponsive for the rest of his life, unable to communicate with the outside world, locked in a body that had betrayed him. Pearson could relate to that, Doug thought. And he would have done anything to save his boy from that fate.

He hobbled into the kitchen, grabbed a bottle of Jameson's from the counter. He shouldn't be drinking with the medication he was on, but it would help the pain in his leg.

Heard Harvey's words: *Don't fall into the bottle, Douglas.* Poured a healthy shot anyway. Harvey Robertson had nothing left to teach him.

He grabbed his phone on the way back to the living room, got himself comfortable in his chair. Stared at the screen for a moment, considering. Rebecca and Susie. He was treating them both badly, but why? Because he didn't want to face the uncomfortable questions he was asking himself. Because, he realised, he didn't want to have to face the truth.

He took a swig of the whisky, decided.

"Time to man up, Doug," he whispered as he thumbed through the contacts and found the number he was looking for. Hit *Dial*, smiled when the call was answered.

"Hey," he said. "What you doing tonight?"

Acknowledgements

Thanks, as ever, to super-agent and all-round super-star Bob McDevitt for his support and wise advice, and to Sara, my infinitely patient editor Craig, Laura and everyone at Contraband for letting me fulfil a lifetime's dream for a second time. Thanks also to Joe Farquharson for remembering a childhood conversation and delivering another brilliant cover – and to Alasdair Sim for the early read-through and for keeping me on track with some of the technicalities of transport in Edinburgh.

And, lastly, to Douglas Skelton, Craig Robertson, Russel D McLean, Michael J Malone, James Oswald, Caro Ramsay and all the other crime writers who have made me feel part of the club (even with the odd threat of a food fight or a mean paper cut). Thanks for the welcome – and the reassurance that it's okay to dream up imaginative ways to kill people, and have a little fun while doing it.

About the author

Neil Broadfoot's high-octane debut, *Falling Fast*, introduced readers to the world of Edinburgh-based investigative journalist Doug McGregor and DS Susie Drummond. Widely praised by critics, crime fiction authors and readers alike, it was shortlisted for both the Dundee International Prize and the prestigious Deanston Scottish Crime Book of the Year Award, immediately establishing Neil as a fixture on the Tartan Noir scene.

Before writing fiction, Neil worked as a journalist for fifteen years at national and local newspapers, covering some of the biggest stories of the day. A poacher turned gamekeeper, Neil moved into communications, providing media relations advice for a variety of organisations, from public bodies and government to a range of private clients.

Neil is married to Fiona and has two daughters. An adopted Fifer, he lives in Dunfermline, where he started his career as a local reporter.